BLUEBIRD AT MY WINDOW

H. NOAH

First paperback edition February 2022

Cover Design: Franziska Stern - Instagram: @coverdungeonrabbit
- www.coverdungeon.com
Editor: Brenna Bailey-Davies
Book Design by Ines Book Formatter
ISBN 978-0-578-99858-9 (ebook)
ISBN 978-0-578-99859-6 (paperback)
ISBN 978-0-578-99860-2 (hardback)

Published by H. Noah
www.thehnoah.com

CONTENT WARNING

The following book centers around processing trauma.
Please be aware that it will touch upon such topics as
violence, sexual assault (not overly descriptive), racism,
microaggressions, misogyny, incest, and homophobia. This
book also focuses on mental health and will cover depression,
anxiety, PTSD, suicidal ideation, hearing voices, religious
fixations, delusions, self-harm, and drug abuse.

This book is dark due to the topics covered. This is not a
horror or thriller meant to scare you. Please be kind to yourself
and put the book back if you are not in a good place to read
any of the things mentioned above.

"'Hope' is the thing with feathers-
That perches in the soul-"
— Emily Dickinson

For everyone who's ever dreamed of writing.
This book is proof that there's always time.

The water swelled like a second skin around her fingers. Thick flesh-colored tendrils, clinging to the newly pure.

Light scattered through the small window, burning white hot across the chipped tile, curled wallpaper, and filth. Everything within this small house on a hill still festered with the sin of her—my daughter.

She'd fought me as she always had. Her arm draped over the side of the old claw tub, almost at ease, even bent back at an odd angle. I'd forgotten to turn off the water completely, but I couldn't get up. I was fixed against the ground, watching as the water gathered and fell from her pale fingertips. No more rush, no more panic. Each drop reached slowly to the floor, hitting the tile with a soft pink splash.

It was done.

My naked flesh numbed to the bitter tile as I lay at the tub's feet. Each fold of skin stretched, suctioning to the floor, holding me in place. Something had gone wrong in the blessing. I'd stripped myself in preparation but she'd refused, made me pull clothing to ribbons as I blessed the water.

When she didn't wake up, I'd called the preacher. Tried to understand what had happened, why the angels had lied.

But he was useless.

That's when I slid to the floor, streaking the wall behind me with her blood. Ichor that still clung to my skin and the floor beneath.

Fraud. Liar.

You did the right thing.

It should have worked.

It did.

Pure!

Why didn't it work?

She's clean now. The preacher was unholy.

Why hasn't she risen?

You were the **unclean one.**

The scream ripped from within me. I wanted quiet, needed it. I scratched my ears, ripping my body from the tile.

The pain worked, but not well enough.

I slammed knuckles into my skull.

Not enough.

Thump.

Thump.

Thump.

My skull reverberated against the hard ceramic. The sharp ache purified, but didn't silence. So I kept crashing into it as skin split across my forehead, turning my vision burgundy. It gave me something to focus on, to control.

The demons didn't like that.

I could hear them in the walls, closing around me. Devils playing tricks as they reached from beneath the wallpaper, touching. I thrashed against them all, gouging holes into the small space. Drywall fingers ripped through flesh as my blood seeped and spilled to the floor, covering hers. The air was suffocating, poisoned, thick, and sandy.

They wanted to silence me.

But still I screamed.

They wanted me quiet, malleable to their will.

Everyone did.

I wanted to fracture the foundation.

Thump

Thump

Thump

I tasted the blood, metallic on my tongue, as it sieved through teeth. Even my voice betrayed me in the end, as screams rasped silent.

My body calmed as shame rippled through me. My eyes trailed back toward the tub, but I couldn't bring myself to look at her. I watched the drops instead as they spread beneath.

"Liars . . ." My throat, raw and unyielding, graveled to the forced whisper.

The angel said she'd be reborn if I cleansed her with word and water. The passage in question still echoed mockingly.

I will sprinkle clean water on you, and you shall be clean from all your uncleanness, and from your idols I will cleanse you.

I looked back down. The water was staining the floor poppy pink, clear but iridescent as it swelled to reach me. I shrank from its edges, slipping slowly in my own blood as I pushed back, cornering myself. The water couldn't hide what I did, couldn't erase her blood, only magnified each feature in rose-colored hues.

This morning had been like the rest. Peace within the daily observances. But the angels knew. Whispered. Prodded me to spy. Helped me catch her as she talked to that unclean deceiver.

I'd warned her how evil hides in the pure things, but she persisted. Fed and entertained that bluebird, but I knew better. It's why I hadn't questioned when the Good Book appeared in my hand or why I beat the demon within her again and again. The word of God turning fat and satiated with her penance.

I wanted to stop, but the angels whispered. Pushed me to finish.

To bring her back to the Lord.

Her nails still stung across my skin. Hellfire as jagged and damning as the thing within her. I'd watched as it fought to escape the water, as it's face morphed underneath the surface of boiling liquid, breathing it in. Eventually it stopped, smaller tremors disappearing as peace eased into her features.

It should have been then.

I let her go as I stepped back, waiting for her to rise, to be born again, but nothing happened. That's when I'd called the preacher, asked him how to make it right.

Make it work.

He only talked to me about the wrong kind of help.

My throat rattled as I tried to speak again, unable to do more than mouth, Lies.

We didn't lie

Be strong child

Crumble in failure

No, don't listen to them

Unclean BITCH

You aren't done

there's another step.

What did I miss?

THE **BLOOD**

The answer was deafening as they all spoke, some in disgust, others in urgency. The angel that had spoken to me that morning broke through, silencing the others.

"Remember what the Book says about the blood."

In Him we have redemption through His blood, the forgiveness of our trespasses.

The verse ran through me again and again, confusion at its meaning. All mentions of blood pointed to his, not hers.

The angel corrected me.

"His blood brings redemption. Hers will cleanse. Drink the water and she will live within you, through you, drive the demons away once and for all."

Of course. I had cleansed her, but through her I would be cleansed.

I drew my legs up as the numbed meat of my overripe body rippled and gave in to my movements. I didn't feel pain, just the slip of my body against the tile as I started toward her. I propped myself up, reaching for the edge of the tub.

At the water, my knees bent to the weight of prayer as I leaned against the porcelain tub. It's edge biting into my waist.

Her legs weightless as pajamas floated and ballooned around her like torn wrappers, remnants of the earlier frenzy. Her skin tinged with a translucent blue, visible even through the tinted liquid.

My hands grasped the side of the tub, holding me above her, as the water shook and dipped to the weight of my breath, dripping down my palms, soaking skin.

My lips kissed the water's surface, soft and eager, as I gorged myself on her gift. It took everything I had to keep it in as hands grabbed me, pulling me into the flashing blue lights. My body slipped against a back seat as handcuffs bit into skin.

It was euphoric.

As I pressed my face against the glass, I watched the stars dance and burst against my eyes.

Smiling as the taste of pennies and peace lingered on my tongue.

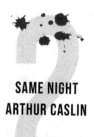

SAME NIGHT
ARTHUR CASLIN

I wish I could have found something better, anything with more sentimental value, but I'd left the office too quickly. My thinking was more blurred than logical, but as I sifted through the gravel of her driveway, I'd found something almost pretty.

The small rock pressed sharply into my palm under my fingertips. It wasn't a coin or a toy, but it held a rainbow within sparkling mica. Izzy would have loved it, grabbing with eager fingers. I could see her image turning into something lethal as it sliced through the center of my chest.

I could have done better, should have. Another failure to add to the list. The cold sank into the skin of my knuckles as my bare hand stayed clenched at my side. There was a hint of frost in the air, sharp and pure, though it had hit everywhere else in Maine but here. Even with heavy clothing, the smallest sliver of skin felt raw in the open air and dying light. The ground was liquid glass from the earlier rain, freezing at its edges as the cold settled in.

I was stalling, but it was hard to look at the tall building in front of me. It loomed thin and sharp, with barely enough room for the copycat buildings on either side. I was in the city's heart, if you could even call Portland a city. The thrums of rush hour calmed behind me on the small street as I balanced on the cobbled sidewalk, the sea only a few short blocks away. The air stung almost as sharply as the salt as it billowed around my face. I turned my eyes upward, toward the purple building where she'd lived. Whoever owned these buildings must have thought a fresh coat of paint in a pastel rainbow could hide the neglect underneath. Could convince renters they cared and wouldn't burn like those college kids had from another neglectful slumlord.

If only it had been as straightforward for Izzy. It wasn't a fire that killed her. It had been the people I'd failed to protect her from: her parents. Marie had worked on the case with me, never failed to remind me that we'd done everything we could have. That the DA's office only holds so much power. But what good was any of it if we couldn't keep even the youngest in our city safe?

The yellow police tape floated softly in front of me as I sank onto the first house step, the cold stone unyielding as my thin work pants soaked up what water was left, drenching my knees as the cold shifted even closer to me. There weren't any pictures, stuffed animals, or even candles for her. The only family she had was now behind bars in the county jail. That's why I came, why I tried to make time for those who didn't have anyone else to mourn them. If there was any sliver of them left in this world, I didn't want them to feel forgotten. I moved the rock from my palm to my fingertips, rolling it softly from side to side as I kept it warm. These steps weren't her grave but would do for now.

I could see a small divot from a knot in the wood at the top of the last step. Leaning forward, I placed the rock into the small hole, watching it settle at its center before I whispered, "I remember you."

The walk to my car was a blur. Same with the drive to Kate's place. I stumbled, getting out of the car, almost losing my nicest work shoes in the thick mud. Cape Elizabeth was only a few minutes out of Portland, but it felt like a different part of the state, especially when I drove down the heavily wooded side road she lived off. Leave it to Kate to find the most secluded part of the city to live in.

I loved her, but the quiet could be overwhelming—left too much space to think. Looking up at the newer rentals in front of me, I couldn't help but take in the uniform shapes and lives within. Everything modern, everything in its place, except for me. I fumbled on the porch in the dim twilight, finally finding Kate's spare key in my coat pocket before sliding it into the door.

The bright light from within her place made it hard to see as I scraped the thick mud off my shoes. I did my best to clean them before admitting defeat and slipping them off.

MONDAY, OCTOBER 17, 2016
RICHARD KOCH

It didn't take long to go through Ann's case. She'd died a few days ago, and the how wasn't a secret. The problem was the who. Her mother, Diane, had done it, but her state of mind was currently in question.

I thumbed through the few pages in front of me, moving back to the crime scene photos. An autopsy wasn't necessary to see the neglect. Her father's preliminary interview had only confirmed it, but the depth and scope of the abuse and events leading up to it were still coming into focus.

I grabbed the paper coffee cup with a sigh before leaning back into the worn leather chair. It groaned and jerked on a swivel as it held my long and not-so-lean body, the small pooch around my stomach straining a little against my shirt as it tried to find some room. I took a long sip as the paper cup heated the early morning chill from my hand. I rested it on the desk, seeing the chapped skin on my knuckles, easing from a darker brown into more ashy tones with a hint of aggravated pink. The cold had gotten to me too quickly. I needed to track down the hand lotion Dani had gotten me last year.

I loved this office, not for its standard desk or dated chairs. It had a cottage feel, just big enough to fit everything that was important to me. Though it definitely made things harder to find when I wasn't actively using them. I looked past my hand to the pictures lined across the desk. While I'd changed most of the photos through the years, the frames remained. Dani had made them shortly after I was hired. Smooth wood with eccentric stains, a way to sneak color into the office without blaring it. "Something bright to look at," she'd said when I'd asked.

I moved my hand from the coffee back to the crime scene photos. Ann's distorted features resting just beneath the water did little to hide how horrific her last moments must have been. I thought of my daughter Miranda, even though she was a few years younger than Ann's own seventeen. It was too easy to picture Ann wandering school halls just like my little girl. What was worse, considering where Ann lived, if she'd been allowed to go to public school, she would have been classmates with my son, Riley.

The surrounding quiet stirred as coworkers filed in. I'd only have a few more minutes to decide who to hand the case to. The case seemed straightforward; even the mother's disposition was solidifying as more facts came in. I mean, anyone who'd drink the water they'd just drowned their child in couldn't be functioning fully within reality, especially when they thought it was going to . . .

What was it again?

I flipped a few pages back to the initial police report, spying the words "I'm cleansed" and "I'm free."

What she's been freed from is still up for debate.

The officers tried to talk to her, but she'd gone silent almost immediately. Though what they'd managed to get was incoherent at best. I could see this going two ways: a deal or an insanity plea. Leaning back, I sifted through the names of anyone who'd be able to manage another case. I'd do it myself, but Dani would kill me. Miranda had gotten on the volleyball team this year and I'd already missed too much. As I ran my hand over my fade, the short coarse curls sprung back just enough to remind me it was time to schedule another cut.

I'd given a lot to this office, always putting in more time and effort than everyone else, more out of necessity than choice. I didn't want to be perfect anymore. I earned my place here and shouldn't have to keep proving it with each and every thing I did. I wanted more time with my family and for me, even though I knew what that would mean. I'd have to give the case to him.

Arthur.

He'd always invested too much into his work, which is why I'd lessened his caseload, given others what I should have given him. He was burning out and nothing seemed to stop it or even slow it down. A win just wasn't a win for him unless he got what he wanted.

Think of yourself for once.

A sharp knock brought me back. Arthur was standing at my door, looking a little more on edge than usual. He had one of his nicer suits on. A light-gray pinstripe paired with a robin's egg–blue tie. A color that only made his longer-than-usual black hair and pale skin stand out. He was the only person I knew who could wear something like that and pull it off. It had fit him once but not anymore. He'd always been lean, but it was easy to see he'd lost weight. He had a sharpness to his cheeks now and a few extra folds in his clothing where there hadn't been any before. He usually had the personality to fill the empty spaces, but something was off today. He was somehow less in every sense of the word. Even now he seemed like he was holding his breath, waiting for some nod from me to begin again. Though his sudden appearance gave me the final nudge I needed.

"Yes?"

"Sorry to disturb you, Richard, but I was wondering if you had a second?"

"Of course, I wanted to talk to you anyway."

Arthur had started to walk but paused. "Anything important?"

"Just a new case. A murder happened a few days ago and the preliminary file was delivered this morning. Looks fairly open and shut."

"Oh?" His face fell at my words.

That was unusual. Surprised, I paused before clearing my throat. "Everything okay?"

Arthur shifted back and forth, looking more confused than I was. "No, sir . . . I mean, well, I was about to give my notice."

Relief crashed through me. I'd have to take the case, but this was good.

"Here, take a seat. Let's talk."

Arthur rocked a few more times on his feet before taking a seat in the thinly cushioned chair in front of my desk before I continued.

"May I ask why?"

Arthur pressed his lips together, body perched just enough on the chair's edge to appear eager. "Of course. I've just come to realize that I may not be the best fit for the job."

I gathered Ann's file back together, taking a moment to mull over my words. Couldn't seem too eager, had to let him lock his own words into place. "No shame in that. This job takes a toll on the best of us. I'm guessing you'll be leaving us two weeks from now?"

His face dropped with my stomach. "Well, I wasn't sure of an exact date yet. Wanted to stay long enough to finish the cases that were almost done. Should take about a month or so and give you time to find a replacement. I can even cover the new case until someone can take it over."

"Definitely appreciate the thought, but it's okay if you leave sooner. Marie is more than ready to take on more of a lead position." I watched as his face set, resolving itself against what I'd said.

"I've got it." There it was: a flash of something deeper that hit wrong. It was like he had something to prove to himself—or worse, to me. It was easy being more direct with anyone else but him. So I did my best to stay neutral as I tried to find my footing. "You don't need to bother yourself with this one; it's easy to reassign."

"Nonsense, I've had some extra time for a while. I can take it." Arthur was smiling now, all hints of what I'd just seen disappearing into the corners of his eyes. "Honestly, it'd be a great opportunity to teach Marie, give her more experience before just plunging into a case."

I didn't want to say yes but I didn't want to say no . . . more.

Put yourself first.

I answered Arthur's smile with one of my own, swallowing any reservations I had left. "As long as you don't mind, it would be appreciated."

Arthur relaxed, reminding me of the cocky graduate who had sat before me several years before. "It's no problem at all."

He wasn't a bad guy; honestly, I think he cared too much at times. It was more the fact that his own needs took precedence over others' more often than not.

"Well, keep me appraised of how the cases are looking and we'll continue to meet up until an exact date becomes more viable. How's that sound?"

Arthur leaned forward, reaching out his hand. "Perfect."

I handed over the file as something urged me to take it back.

Honestly, what's the worst that could happen?

OCTOBER 24, 2016
MARIE PERAULT

I couldn't look away from the raised lines across Ann's back. They must have happened weeks ago with greens and yellows taking a deeper hold on her pale skin, but they hadn't faded enough to blur each stroke of the whip or hide where the thin wooden switch had hit the hardest. The skin had blistered, jagged where it ripped open. Lines of blackened scabs only just flaking off to reveal new flesh beneath. I couldn't help the sharp intake of breath as I imagined how it had happened. That was all it took to get Art's attention.

"What?" Art looked up from his seat a few chairs down from me at the end of the long wooden table. He'd been trying to catch up on some of the reports he'd missed due to another case, but he'd only made it through a few files.

I hesitated a second before picking up one of the photos, holding it out to him.

"Have you seen these yet?"

We'd snagged the conference room this morning after getting the preliminary autopsy reports yesterday. It was the only place we'd be able to go over everything in relative peace. Until it was needed for a meeting. Though it wasn't completely quiet— we could still hear the friendly chatter of coworkers outside the heavy wooden doors. Art got up and took a few steps before taking the photo from my hand. He barely looked at it before "Jesus Christ" escaped from his lips.

I watched his face darken as a piece of black hair fell out of place, curling against his forehead and nearly brushing his eyelashes. He pushed it back as he came to look at the other photos in front of me, saying, "No, I hadn't gotten to these yet."

He always took these parts the worst. Seeing the actual damage that had been done. He tried to hide it, and with most people he was successful for a little while, but after working with him for so long it was easy to see through the kneejerk reactions.

I watched him slide into the overly stuffed faux-leather office chair next to me as he continued to sift through the other photos, Ann equally bruised, ripped, and broken in each. Art paused for a second on the last one before looking up. "There's no way this is all from the same attack."

I nodded slightly before saying, "You're right." I leaned toward him as I found the picture of Ann's back again. "You see these lines?"

"Yeah."

"From what I read of her father's statement, apparently these are from a few weeks earlier when Diane beat Ann with a switch."

Art let out a fast breath as he uttered, "Fuck."

I let it go, moving on to trace the fresh wounds to Ann's face and upper torso in another picture where the bruises were still swollen and split. "These are from the night she was killed. Diane said when she caught Ann feeding the bird, she started beating her with a Bible. Apparently, she thought the bird was evil and had warned Ann about talking to it before."

Might as well rip the Band-Aid off and tell him the rest.

Before he could say more, I shuffled through the pictures, finding the ones that focused on her lower torso and legs. "These abrasions were from being dragged to the bathroom. From what the autopsy report says, they don't think she was conscious at that point. But from what the police can piece together, Ann must have been out until she hit the water; shock from the cold must have revived her." I got up, stretching for a second as my slacks, loose blouse, and flats moved comfortably with me. I walked over to Art's pile for the photos of Diane's arms covered in bright bloody scratches. Walking back, I placed them on top of the others. "Looks like she fought back."

"Not like it did her any good."

I placed a hand on his shoulder and squeezed slightly. "We wouldn't be here if it had. Let's get a better idea of what we can do now."

Art looked up at me with a small, crooked smile playing across his lips, somehow separate from the sadness sitting in the depths of his eyes.

"Of course, you're right."

He didn't mean it, not fully. But at least I reminded him there were still things we could do. It was time to find who Ann had been in the mess of documents in front of us, in the interviews we needed to make. She may be dead, but her story still mattered.

Art's voice surprised me as he looked up. "Oh, we still on for tonight?"

"Of course. Maddie's excited to meet you and Kate."

**SAME DAY
MADDIE MORI**

My heart dropped. I was suddenly eighteen, in my car with everything I'd been able to grab and twenty bucks to my name.

Madeline Baker.

Had they found me?

I changed my name, moved, did everything I could to cut ties, but there it was. The name they'd given me. A reminder of the person I was supposed to be, not the one I was.

I held a small breath, looked at who the letter was from, then let it out. MECA stared back at me: Maine College of Art, my Alma mater.

Must have forgotten to change my name when I updated my address.

"Everything okay?"

Deb's voice broke the moment, centering me. "Yeah, I'm good, just saw my old name and panicked a bit."

Deb peered over my shoulder as her long salt-and-pepper hair tickled my ear. Her fingers worn and shaped by the clay she loved so much, lightly grasping my arm for balance just above the elbow. She'd already changed into a tank top and shorts, far too cold for the weather outside but just right for working with the kilns. "It's not one of those 'Jesus saves or else' pamphlets, is it?" she whispered as if the words were enough to conjure a conversion therapist into being.

"Thankfully, no." I held up the college logo in front of her. "Just junk mail." I went to crumple it, but she plucked it from my hands before I could. "Mind if I use this? I want to test how the new clay reacts to different mediums out of the kiln."

I smiled. "Of course." Deb was as kind as she was blunt. She could rub most people the wrong way, but it wasn't intentional.

"You haven't heard from them, have you?"

Deb stood a little in front of me, shorter and built like a tank. At fifty, her light weathered skin was dappled by sunspots—markings of a well-lived life, she always said. When my adoptive parents threw me out for being queer, I'd driven north. Even tried halfheartedly to find the adoption agency in Japan that might be able to connect me to my biological family, but ended up at an art fair in Colorado where I met Kindra. She took me in and connected me with Deb, who'd been working at MECA at the time.

"No. Either they can't find me, or they just gave up. Knowing them, it's probably the latter." The laugh left me too easily, too strained, but Deb knew better than to push. Humor was easier to share than the past and I loved her for letting me choose when I wanted to talk about it. Deb leaned forward, hitting me softly with the pamphlet before speaking. "No matter, it's something to be celebrated."

"Agreed." I smiled. She meant well even when it hurt.

Deb tucked the letter under her arm as she tied her long hair into a semi-restrained ponytail. "You finishing up? Don't think we have any classes coming in soon."

"Yeah, Marie's on her way. We're having a movie night with her coworker." I looked away toward the front of the studio where a few of my finished paintings hung on the walls, a nervous habit I had when I wasn't particularly looking forward to something and didn't want anyone to see. Deb's clay pieces were there too, scattered on the few shelves we had with other artists' work. It was a hodgepodge of a space, small but cozy, especially with the afternoon sun streaming in. It took up the first floor of an old eighteen-something building downtown, and the rays brought out the warmer tones in the room. The flaxen lines in the natural clay, and small constellations of metallic flakes within my own paint. My sight lingered for a moment where I'd set up in the window to work, a way of bringing wandering eyes in. Even with what we sold, we had to rent out our studio

H. NOAH

to other artists and hold classes to make ends meet, but it was enough for us both.

I turned back to Deb. "I have to clean up my paints first and square the till before I leave—had a few sales today."

"Oh good! And I'm excited to see Marie. She's been too busy lately; I miss her popping in."

"Oh, no worries, I told her you've been heavily offended by her absence." I laughed a little as I made my way toward the front, Deb following as I made it to the register. I slid behind the counter as she leaned against it, elbows propping her up with my letter still in her hands.

"Heavily offended isn't quite right. Maybe I should tell her I'm not mad . . . just disappointed."

I feigned grabbing my chest. "Ouch, low blow with the mom guilt."

Deb smiled before fanning the letter toward my face. "Well, since my own children fled from me, I have to spread it where I can."

I grabbed the letter back before poking her in the arm with it, laughing. "I wouldn't call your children moving in together down the street from you *fleeing*."

Deb grabbed it back, giving me a flourished smack on the top of my head before turning on her own version of dramatics. "My babies still left me. Now I have to call before I visit or knock on a door."

I opened the till. "I doubt you do either with a key."

Deb winked at me before pushing away from the counter. "Semantics, my dear. Well, I better get the kilns open and cooling." She took a few steps before pausing. "One more thing you might want to do before Marie gets here."

"What?"

Deb raised a hand as she gestured an abstract circle toward my head. "You might want to clean your face."

I raised my hand, feeling the paint rough and crumbling on at least one of my cheeks. I let it crack and flake as I smiled wider. "Thanks, I didn't even notice."

Deb nodded before turning to leave. "No problem, happy to help."

From friend of a friend to teacher, turned chosen family. I was lucky to have her in my life. I looked out the thick glass windows; they were aged and just a little warped, and the other old red brick buildings took up most of my view. With the glint of the lowering sun throwing prisms around me, I took in a breath, thick with the smell of acrylic paint and heat. These were the moments I loved, my city now hinting of pinks and purples behind the dying light. I could forget my anxiety, my past—or what I knew of it—and enjoy the peace of my friend and my love, who I could just make out in the distance, walking across the cobblestones toward me.

SAME DAY
RICHARD KOCH

The drive home went quickly as I eased from city traffic to the slower pace of the suburbs. I was out of my car, through my door, and up the stairs of our small two-story, three-bedroom house just as quickly. We'd gotten it about twenty years before shortly after it had been built, an awkward boxy thing nestled among similar white homes. Dani had done a wonderful job updating it over the years with her own contemporary flair, making it open, comfortable, and fully ours.

I never could relax until I'd changed from work clothes into something more like myself. Loose jeans, a soft tee, and a well-worn cardigan with leather elbow patches that had worn to a buttery smoothness nothing else could match.

Walking out of the bedroom, I flipped off the light as my feet slid into brown leather slippers heavily cushioned with thick fleece. I walked to the small office where I knew Dani would be. She was sitting in a cream loveseat with a knitted green throw draped over her lap with a book. She was dressed in bright floral leggings and an oversized dark-blue hoodie, her olive but always-rosy skin holding its own against the fabric as her dark-brown hair, highlighted in the lightest gray, fell across her shoulders in long loose curls.

It took a few more steps before Dani realized I was there. She tilted her head up, pushing her reading glasses firmly back on her nose as her hazel eyes smiled with her. "Hey, love."

I closed the short distance between us as I delivered a soft kiss to her now upturned head. I rested my forehead against hers as I cupped the sides of her neck before lowering myself to the ottoman in front of her. I let my hands trace slowly down her neck to her arms and finally her legs, happy to be near her again.

"How was the half-day?"

Dani closed the book, holding her place with one hand as she slid the other over my own. "Good, but not in the least bit useful."

For such a petite woman, she always cut straight to the truth of a thing, something I'd always admired. She traced her fingers along my hands as she continued.

"Only had the underclassmen today and they were checked out even before they got to my class. So I just had them focus on their final art project instead of forcing anything new."

She drew one of my hands up with hers as she intertwined our fingers before asking, "What about you? Seems like you may have had an easier day?"

I let her twist her fingers around me, enjoying the gentle brush of lips as she brought my hand to them, the deep umber tone of my skin highlighting the golden tan within her own. "I did. A good chunk of cases should be ending next week, so it was mostly paperwork today."

Dani moved her hand to my face, pulling me in for another kiss, letting her lips linger over mine for a moment before smiling. "That's wonderful to hear. Hope that means Arthur will be giving his official notice soon."

I'd been talking about him more than I should have. I let a sigh out, pulling her hand back with mine as I kissed her knuckles, leaning into the moment before answering. In response, Dani placed her book gently on the small side table beside her. She reached out to me with her other hand as she asked, "Is something else on your mind?"

I lifted my face, resting both of her hands within mine as my elbows now perched on my knees. "With Art leaving, it got me thinking."

"Yeah?"

I breathed in as I looked down at our hands. I was so close, I could smell the scent of laundry and fresh resin drifting from her clothes. "What if I looked into an early retirement?"

Her strong, nimble fingers squeezed mine as she spoke. "I'm a little surprised. Thought it would be something I'd have to push you into."

"You and me both."

Dani reached out, taking my chin in her hand, trying to get me to look up. "Are you thinking of taking this early retirement soon?"

I tilted my head to gaze at her face. "No, not until the kids are out of school at least . . . I just like the idea."

She smiled as she stroked her hand softly up my face. "Well, it would be nice to leave the school and open my own studio like we talked about."

I took her hand from my face, cradling it in both hands as I kissed her palm and looked back to her. "Maybe I could find a part-time teaching gig. I've always thought that might be fun."

"A new adventure doing things we love. I like the sound of that," Dani said before adding her other hand to mine and pulling me closer.

I gave her a quick kiss, realizing just how quiet it had been, as I leaned back. "Where's the kids?"

SAME DAY
MARIE PERAULT

The uneven sidewalk played with our balance, tilting us just enough to add weight to our movement as we tried to keep hold of each other. I never needed a reason to squeeze Maddie closer, but I wouldn't turn down the opportunity either. My arm draped over her shoulder braced against irregular steps as I turned to kiss her temple. My lips pressed against strawberry-pink hair; she'd tied it up into a messy bun with a few fine strands escaping to fall softly on her cheek. I loved every shade of hair color she'd tried since I'd met her, but this had to be my favorite so far. Even with the sun dipping behind the buildings it seemed to grab the last rays of light, glowing against her deep tawny skin. She was wrapped up in some brightly patterned boho duster she had found at a secondhand shop downtown with a cream sweater poking through. All of this was draped over thick black leggings, denim shorts, and worn brown knee-high boots. There was always a hint of summer about her even in the colder months.

She answered my movement with her arm slipping through the open coat to squeeze my waist. She pulled me back just enough to make me pause while she turned for a kiss, something I gladly indulged in before moving again.

We'd been together for almost two years, a miracle it had even happened. Born in Japan, she'd found her way to Maine— to a small seaside city, to its art school—and decided to stay. Truthfully, everything about us was chance.

We'd both said yes to a friend of a friend's party, both tried to back out before deciding to go, but I'm glad we didn't. Maddie brought life to my world. It had taken a little time for her to open completely but once she did, she was the fearless adventure I never knew existed. I wasn't an outdoors person by any stretch of the word until she showed me my state through her own eyes. From the colored fire of the leaves in the fall to the salt spray against emerald moss-covered stones. She pushed me to see the beauty in the little things, and I loved her for that and so much more.

We stopped at a crosswalk, waiting as she turned and spoke.

"I hope it goes well. At least Art isn't a complete stranger."

"It'll be fine. Truthfully, I think you'll get a kick out of him in his natural habitat." I hugged her a little tighter as we watched for the crossing light to change. "Just ignore whatever comes out of his mouth. He means well but likes a good reaction."

"Noted." She laughed, tightening her grip around my waist before loosening it again. "What about Kate?"

"I haven't met her before, but knowing Art she's probably an incredibly patient person." Maddie looked at me, her jaw tightened. I knew the look, how her questions had mixed with a hesitation she was unable to voice, so I tried to put her at ease. "Don't get me wrong. Art's a great guy, but he can be a handful. Though meeting Kate has definitely curbed that a bit."

Maddie relaxed as we watched cars fly past. Leaning into me, she moved her arm from my waist to find my hand instead. "Well, no matter how it goes at least watching a movie takes the pressure off."

"True." I laughed a little as I leaned into her.

The light turned before we could lose ourselves too far in the moment. Together we made our way across the street, falling back into our earlier sway as the sidewalk rose and fell away from us. Maddie grabbed my hand tighter as she asked, "What are we watching again?"

"Some Stephen King movie."

"Why Stephen King?"

"Apparently most of his stories are based here."

Maddie laughed. "I could have told you that. He lives in Bangor."

"Wait, how do you know that? Art and I just learned it a week ago when a coworker was talking about some sequel to *The Shining* they'd just read."

She smiled as she took a dip in the sidewalk, our shoulders bumping lightly. "A few years ago, your old college put on a musical of one of his books. A bunch of us from MECA decided to go."

"You're shitting me, they made a musical out of a horror book? Which one?" I had to stop. She continued forward but the sudden change in momentum swung her back to face me as her amber eyes changed to deeper shades of gold in the fading light, highlighting her amusement.

"Oh, come on, this isn't the first horror musical. Haven't you heard of *Little Shop of Horrors*? *Sweeny Todd*?"

I paused, chewing on my answer before letting it go. "Aren't those movies?"

"Yeah, movies based off musicals, hon."

I crossed my arms, taking my hand back. "Okay, but which one was it? Was it good?"

"*Carrie*, and it was a blast, but we watched it way too many times." She tried to shift away to change the topic and location, but I wasn't about to let her do either.

Catching a sleeve, I asked, "Why?"

She paused, scrunching her lips to the side before telling me. "The cast invited Mr. King and his wife and left tickets for them at the front. We wanted a chance to see them, but they never showed."

She tried to pull away again, but I held tight. "Nope, there's more to this. What aren't you telling me?"

"Well, we'd wanted to see him so badly . . . after the last show we decided to drive up to his house for the long weekend." Her cheeks turned a rosy pink, embarrassment highlighting her face.

"My little stalker." I pulled her toward me as I wrapped my arms around her shoulders, her cheeks now reaching a deeper shade.

"No, it wasn't as bad as it sounds!" She pushed back a little with her hands just below my shoulders, firm and warm. "After four hours of driving in a cramped car we did a quick drive by, took one look at his gate, and freaked. Ended up driving to Eastport for the weekend instead. Seemed like a better choice than creeping on a famous stranger."

I leaned in, kissing her forehead and laughing before pulling back. "Well, at least, my love, you're a stalker with a conscience."

"Shhhhh." Maddie raised her finger to my lips before continuing, "More like one-time reformed voyeur. We felt horrible after the buzz wore off." Maddie slipped her finger from my lips before moving her hands down my arms and pulling me closer. "I'm just surprised you hadn't heard about the show or him."

"Well, I knew about him, just not well enough. Plus, I was probably buried in some law text when it was out."

We made it to Art's apartment complex, but I wasn't ready yet. I wrapped an arm around her while holding her cheek with my other hand. "Thank you for doing this. I know how hard it is for you to meet new people."

"Of course." She leaned in this time as she draped her arms over my shoulders. "With you, everything's easier."

I tucked a strand of hair behind her ear, smiling as I wiped a small flake of paint from her cheek. "You just want to get lucky later."

Returning my smile and closing the distance between us, she paused as her lips brushed against mine, the heat of her words tickling as I breathed in the scent of her, "Oh, I know I will."

She kissed me softly, her fingers disappearing into my long, wind-tangled hair as she pulled me closer. We stayed there in that moment—one, maybe two seconds too long before turning toward the apartment door.

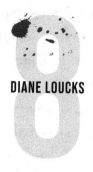

DIANE LOUCKS

The metal bars glinted under the dim lights, writhing ever so slowly. The air was apprehensive and strangled with putrid things. Creatures that never calmed, only convulsed and watched.

Nothing slept here.

Nothing dead could.

From the fragmenting concrete

To the florescent haze

What was good could not remain.

I kicked off the sheet the moment I felt it tighten around me. Lying cold against the thin plastic bedding. My skin crawled against it, pushing me up and back to my earlier task.

I slid down the metal frame softly, feet kissing the ground below me.

I couldn't trust anything here.

Not even myself

I thought the water had worked the moment it hit my tongue

but that was a lie.

Trickery of the damned

They whispered even now

relentless

I knew what this was

After being stripped and showered

Told I'd be living with a person

that wasn't a person

I was in hell.

My feet padded silently against the unforgiving surface to what

I needed

I'd watched the creature they had placed me with

It hid

But not well enough.

It was in the eyes, the way its skin hung

A mask that didn't fit

Sallow and gray

I couldn't hear the angels anymore

But I knew what they'd say

So I waited

Said prayers of protection

And finished getting the water ready

It hadn't purified what was left of my daughter

Because it hadn't been fully pure.

I wouldn't make that mistake again

I'd get the devil this time.

The cell was small, barely enough room for two

But I hadn't woken it

Kept watch until the water steamed in the hot pot.

I raised the cheap plastic, warm and flimsy in my hands

As I walked it with care to the lower bunk

Throwing it on the empty vessel.

I was flying backward,

hitting cold stone with a wet *thunk*

The prayers caught in my throat

as bile creeped up

It was over me now

It brought pain

So much pain

Crooked knuckles and cracking ribs

A flash of silver

and my skin seared to the blade's descent.

Sticky warmth spreading

Into an embrace.

NOVEMBER 11, 2016
ARTHUR CASLIN

I slammed my bag onto my desk, scattering pins and paper as the cheap metal sides reverberated from the crash. I leaned over it, letting my hands rest on either side as I bowed my head and closed my eyes against this shitty closet of an office and a day.

"Motherfucker."

The office had grown quieter after the crash, but I didn't give a shit if they heard me at this point. I curled my nails into my palm, scraping the top of the fake wood. Everything around me was cheap and disposable.

They got a continuance.

A soft knock struck against my open door.

I let disgust filter openly into the next word. "What."

"Art." Marie's voice answered with enough warning to snap me back. I straightened as I turned toward her, letting myself fall back onto the desk. The top digging into my ass.

She took a few cautious steps in before continuing, "This isn't a surprise. Diane almost died and her cellmate is still in the burn unit."

I drew my arms up, crossing them against my chest. "Doesn't mean they have to jump straight to a three-month continuance and mandatory assessment." Marie pulled the chair in front of me out a little bit as she sat, and I continued, "Even she said she wanted to plead guilty the last time we were in court."

Marie sank into the chair as she waved a hand toward me with annoyance. "You mean the same day she screamed about her lawyer being unclean. Art, she isn't well."

"She's well enough to want to do the right thing." I shoved my hand back into the crook of my arm.

"Is she, though?" Marie looked at me as I shifted under her gaze.

I didn't want to talk about this anymore, not today and not with her.

Uncrossing my arms, I pushed myself away from the desk, turning it into a fluid movement as I moved to place the desk between us. I sat in my chair, trying to disengage, shuffling documents that didn't even go together. Anything to make me look busy.

I didn't have to look at her to see I'd gotten what I wanted. She leaned forward; her hands turned palms up, outstretched toward me before she spoke. "Look, we aren't going to get anywhere with this today so let's table it. She'll get the assessment, court will resume, and the case will move forward."

I paused long enough to look up and respond. "Okay."

I knew that I was letting *Diane* . . .

The anger I felt earlier flashed to the surface, burning my resolve to end this conversation.

I didn't want to keep saying her name, letting her crawl under my skin and get this reaction out of me.

I just couldn't get what she'd done out of my head, how she had forced Ann to live and then die. Even if she was as messed up as she let on, a part of her knew what she'd done, what lines she had willingly crossed.

Marie leaned back in the chair, a little more relaxed than before. I let out my form of a white flag as I set the papers to the side and leaned back as well. "We still on for tonight?"

"Of course." Marie smiled, taking it eagerly before asking, "Should we bring anything?"

I shook my head. "No. I think Kate was hoping you and Maddie would be up for some Chinese."

"Sounds perfect to me. I'll check with Maddie, but I'm sure she'd be up for it too."

Another knock came from the door, and Richard poked his head through the doorway. "Sorry to interrupt. Arthur, do you have some time to talk before you head out?"

I couldn't help but tense up ever so slightly. "Of course." I looked back to Marie. "See you soon?"

"Yup." Marie stood and walked out the door, nodding toward Richard. "Have a good night."

Richard returned the movement. "You too, Marie."

I watched her leave, getting smaller and smaller as she walked across the open room outside my own. It must have been made for cubicles at one time. Now it was just random chairs, plants, and wasted space.

"Arthur?" Richard was already seated. He must have said something I missed.

I knew what was coming. I may not have cared what the rest of the office thought, but I did care what Richard saw in me.

He was everything I wanted to be

While I turned out to be everything he wasn't:

A failure.

I gave him a smile as I answered, "Yes?"

Richard turned a little in the chair where Marie had just been, pushing the door shut. I watched as it closed.

SAME DAY
RICHARD KOCH

"Did something new happen with the case? Earlier you seemed . . ."

Choose your words wisely.

". . . to be dealing with something."

Arthur kept the smile he was wearing as he answered. "Oh, yeah, sorry about that." He paused, shifting uncomfortably before continuing, "I'd just heard some personal news and wasn't processing it well."

Lie.

My face relaxed, taking on a practiced ease. "Oh, I'm sorry to hear that. If there is anything you need, just let me know."

Arthur continued to shift, looking from the door to me. "Of course, thank you for the offer."

"So, nothing new with any of the cases?"

His movement stilled. "Yes."

This has to be it.

"Marie and I just came back from the Diane Loucks case. Apparently, she got stabbed by her roommate after throwing boiling water on her."

"What?" This was definitely not what I expected. "How did she have access to boiling water?"

Arthur grabbed a fidget toy from his desk, leaning back to play with it. "Apparently, her cellmate earned a small hot pot for commissary soups and . . . Diane . . . decided to borrow it."

I leaned forward, perching my elbows on my knees as I clasped my hands together. "Is she okay? The cellmate?"

Arthur paused, and I could have sworn a smile passed his lips. "She's actually better off than Diane. After the cellmate got drenched, she beat and shanked Diane."

There was no mistaking the amusement in his voice. It sent a shiver down my spine. "Is she okay?"

His face changed again into something I could not recognize. "They said she'll be fine. It's why we were called in today. The judge is granting a continuance and a full psych assessment to see if Diane is fit to stand trial." He looked me directly in the eye and I recognized what I couldn't earlier: the lack of anything even remotely sympathetic.

He caught me off guard. Blinking, I settled back into myself. "Well after what you've said, I'm not surprised."

There was something off about Arthur. Something I hadn't seen before. If he wasn't going to give himself boundaries, I was. "There's something else I wanted to talk to you about."

Arthur played with the small toy again. "Yes?"

"With the new attorney starting in a few weeks, I wanted to move you to more of a consult role."

His jaw set, his eyes turning down to the toy in his now-still hand. "I want to see this case through to the end."

I could feel the ice in his tone, slicing through warning. I smiled in return. "Of course. The rest of your cases and duties you can help pass over to the new hire once he starts." I waited for him to look up, but he kept his eyes on his hand. I continued, "This way you can focus on your last case without getting caught in others before you leave."

I'm not going to give him anything to hold on to past this case.

I could feel the change between us. I knew it would be coming anyway, but he had pushed me past what I was comfortable with. I didn't wait for him to respond. I just moved forward, as eager to end this as he visibly was. "All right then, that was it. I'll leave you to it." I stood up, looking at my watch as I moved toward the door. I paused, trying one last time to bridge the gap. "You sure everything's okay? Nothing I can do to help?"

The smile was back as he clicked the small knobs on the toy in his hand. "No, I'm good."

Are you?

SAME DAY
MADDIE MORI

I was starting to get used to movie nights, to being around Kate and Art. This part had always been hard—the inevitable slip into someone more agreeable, someone who laughed at the things they were supposed to, and who could be easily forgettable even when they stood out.

The person growing up in the south had made me.

We couldn't do this every week, with Art and Marie's case load, but we tried to meet when it was possible. Tonight, we were back at Art's. I liked it better than Kate's since I was able to take a breath without worrying I would stain something. You could still see her influence from the plants to the couch covers and coasters, but no matter what she'd done it still reminded me more of him. Someone mismatched, kind, and immovable.

I sank into the little bit of couch cushion there was, my fingers trailing over the rough dark-navy cover as I watched Marie over the back of the couch. She was sitting at the kitchen table, laughing with Kate as they egged on Art. I envied how easy this was for her, how she laughed and loved others so easily. Her light-golden curls dancing with each breath, brushing her fair, sun-kissed skin as a constellation of freckles gilded her cheeks. She was my living sepia tone, covered in earth shades from her ankle boots, pants, and turtleneck, but she never faded into the background like I did. I don't think she could even if she tried.

I let my mind wander. It had been almost a month since I'd seen my old name, but I couldn't get it out of my head. It wasn't my real name—not even the name I had now was. I'd had one, the one my birth mother had given me, but it had been burned in front of me, along with the rest of my adoption paperwork, for even asking to see it. I'd kept *Maddie* since it was the only part of my adoptive name that felt like mine. The fact it would absolutely infuriate my adoptive mother was just a bonus. Mori . . . Mori had just felt right. Like a connection to a part of myself that had always been just out of reach. But even that name had started to sour, to feel like something I could never fit.

I think I'm ready to find them. My birth parents.

Marie caught my gaze as she tilted her head toward the rest of the group. A motion I knew well—the one she always used when I'd stayed a little too long by myself.

Better go join the fun.

My stomach clenched against me, an anxious reflex. It would be easier to face if I ignored it. So, I pushed myself off the couch, joining them just as Art pulled another round of laughter from his audience. I walked behind Marie's chair, squeezing her shoulders in my hands as she leaned her head back, smiling. Her gray eyes light as mist under the harsh iridescent lights. I leaned down and kissed her forehead before looking back to Art.

"What's the drink tonight?"

Art started to respond but Kate beat him to it. "Something based on the movie *IT* . . . but it sounds more like a dressed up hairy nipple."

Art brandished the spoon from the pitcher, flicking it toward Kate, unaware of the droplets that sprayed in its wake, hitting the counter, the floor, and my face. "It's way different from your *hairy nipple*. Also, that's not even a real drink. You just want to spice up what's basically a rum driver."

Kate raised her hands, wiping a few drops of orange liquid from her cheeks. "Whoa there, tiger, my drink is real. Easier if you just agree." She stuck out her tongue as Art sheepishly lowered the spoon after seeing what he'd done.

Marie put a hand over mine as it stayed draped on her shoulder. "No matter what it's called, how is it a spooky drink? Seems like something that would be on a menu at a budget brunch."

Art turned to Marie, raising the spoon accusingly with a little more care. "It's not done yet." He grabbed a handful of red suckers from the counter behind him, holding them in Marie's direction like a proud toddler. "See, these are the red balloons. We pour the drinks and add these after."

Marie nodded and turned to Kate. "Well, looks like I owe you twenty bucks. He didn't use the grenadine this time."

Kate laughed. "Oh, there's still time. You shouldn't throw it in before he's fully decorated the glasses."

They cackled at each other as Art's face soured. "Fine, you can make whatever you like. This is mine." He picked up the pitcher and beelined for the living room.

Kate got up, chasing at his heels. "Oh c'mon, we're just teasing." Art put the pitcher down on the worn trunk acting as a coffee table then sat down where I'd been moments before. Kate leaned down, kissing his cheek before saying, "Your drinks taste fantastic no matter how much grenadine you put in them."

"That's it!" Art grabbed Kate, pulling her over the armrest and pinning her playfully to the couch as he tickled her. "You try to find spooky drink recipes without that shit."

Kate gasped as she grabbed his wrists. "Okay, okay, don't need to get violent over it."

Marie stood, keeping hold of my hand as we walked toward them.

Art released Kate as she pushed him away, turning toward us. "I could whip up that brain one I found. I have everything I need to curdle the Baileys."

Kate pushed herself up with her elbows, scrunching her face in disgust. "Gag, no thanks." She took on a sickly-sweet mocking tone as she pushed her heel into the side of Art's thigh. "The grenadine's fine. I'll never complain again."

Art laughed. "That's rich coming from you." He collapsed limply over her legs.

The doorbell rang.

Kate mocked Art's words back to him as she tried to push him aside. "Art, let me up. Food's here."

"Only if you give me a kiss."

Kate leaned in, tracing his cheeks with her hands. "Anything for you." She shot forward to blow a raspberry on his lips.

Art let her go as he wiped at the drool she left behind. "Oh, I'll get you back for that."

Kate waved her hand in the air behind her as she walked to the door. "You'll forget about it as soon as you see the food."

The banter was still something to get used to, but I found it easier to ignore than join like Marie. I called after Kate, "I'll grab the dishes." Happy to have something to do.

Kate turned her head. "Thank you! Marie, can you grab the glasses?"

Marie answered next to me, "Of course."

I squeezed her hand before letting go so we could get to the cupboard. Grabbing the plates, I set them on the kitchen table before making a quick U-turn for the silverware. Marie grabbed the highball glasses and made her way to the living room, stacking them next to the pitcher as the smell of Chinese food drifted into the apartment. Kate handed the delivery boy the stack of cash we each had chipped in before grabbing the huge brown carryout bags and closing the door.

"Fuck."

We all turned toward Art, still draped over most of the couch, as he scrolled quickly through his phone.

The sudden outburst was a bit unnerving, but Marie just set the glasses down and settled in across from him in a smaller chair, asking, "What's up?"

Art made a strangled frustration noise. "Just got an email about you-know-who. They somehow got her evaluation pushed back a few months as they 'stabilize her.'" Art raised his hands and let his phone drop to his chest to make mocking air quotations. "The fuck does that even mean."

A sharp pain radiated from my cheek. I realized I'd bit down out of habit—the second outburst causing my teeth to sink in a little too deeply. I never liked that tone growing up or what usually followed it. Marie never talked like that, even when work got complicated. I looked toward her, a bit raw from the quick shift in Art. She raised her hand slightly, sending whatever small reassurance she could from across the room before addressing Art.

"Whatever it means, it'll still happen. Her lawyer can push it out but can't avoid it forever."

The sudden thud of Chinese food on the table from Kate's arms startled me, and I looked up in time to see her face. Every bit of laughter I'd seen earlier had shifted to neutral resolve before she stepped back and turned on her heel toward the group.

I'm not the only one upset.

I looked to the food she'd abandoned, unsure. My cheek burned raw again as I bit down more out of habit. I wanted to chew my nails, my sleeve, anything to soothe the anxiety itching up my spine. Wringing my hands for a moment, I decided to put them to use and unload the bag in front of me. Kate had just made it to the couch, trying to catch Art's gaze. "So, I'm guessing it's not going to be over by the start of the year?"

Marie walked to Kate as she answered, "It's unlikely, but I'd be surprised if it lasted much longer than that." Marie reached out and brushed Kate's arm lightly, seemingly catching the same tension I had. Art was oblivious, sucked back into his phone as he scrolled back and forth.

I jumped a little as he answered harshly, "It better not."

Marie gave Kate a reassuring glance before squeezing her arm and walking to me to help.

Kate looked at Art, moving from the back of the couch. "Remember, Richard said you could still leave." But Art was lost in thought as she kneeled down and pushed his phone to his chest, pleading. "You don't have to finish this one."

Art smiled crookedly as he leaned toward her. "True, but what's a few more months?" He leaned in, kissing Kate a little too roughly before getting up and beelining for the food. "I'm starved."

I couldn't look away from Kate's face. The resolve had emptied to a shade of sadness that tore through me. If I had my paints, she'd be the color of cerulean sinking into a deeper indigo. The shade of sadness . . . of losing hope. The tang of blood filled my mouth, pulling my gaze from her empty face, shame heating my cheeks. This was something private, a moment meant to be missed.

DIANE LOUCKS

I wasn't in my cell
Or the hospital
This room was smaller.
Bars replaced with a steel door
concrete on all sides
Lying on my side
on top of a stripped bed
My body was numbed to the world around me
They'd been giving me something
Told me it worked
but all it did was lock me into place.
So I lay ridged
watching the guards
watch me
Their checks clockwork

the light from the window behind me keeping time

They promised me I'd be safe

That nothing could get me here

But I can't open my mouth to tell them

The pills called to something worse

I could see them now

Crawling along the walls

Thin, disjointed shadows

whispering

Pushing through the floor.

My angels are gone

But still I pray.

One notices me

eyes glowing red

It's so close I can see its concrete skin as it rises in front of me

A smile

Cracking

Stone and inked spittle glistening

Still I pray.

It's next to me now.

Sulfur and sin

Tracing a finger across the side of my body

scraping a nail against my stitches

pulling

tearing

My body is too heavy
But still I pray.
Even as the warm blood pools around me
The demon reminds me it never left
I'd always been covered in it.
Its face levels with mine now
A smile cracking to liquid flame
Dripping heat
And putrid pus
across my face
I scream
locked teeth and lips
unable to pray.

JANUARY 6, 2017
RICHARD KOCH

I let the scotch and water swirl on my tongue, numbing my gums slightly as it slides into the sides of my cheeks before swallowing it. Dani and I were enjoying the fire after dinner while the kids were happily off in their own corners of the house. I had the TV above the mantle muted but tuned to the news with the captions on so Dani could read her book. Her feet were perched on my lap as she lay across the couch, propped up on several large pillows. My hand rested on her closest thickly socked foot, drawing warmth from it. Taking another sip as I slowly stretched the arch of her foot with my other hand.

"Oh . . . that feels nice."

"Of course it does." I smiled as I looked toward her face.

She had dropped her book onto her chest just as my youngest
tried to dart out the door, yelling, "Meeting up with Em! I'll be
back in a few hours!"

"Hold on," I called out, raising my voice just enough as
I strained forward to see around the living room entry toward
the front door to catch sight of the form that was Miranda hidden under her coat, hat, and other winter clothes in various
shades of blue and black. Her thick hair peeked out from under
a hat—tight, thick, raven black curls—with only a sliver of her
warm copper skin showing. Her features may have been closer
to mine overall within the family but the fire within her was her
mother's, through and through.

Miranda paused just as she touched the door, her shoulders
lowering slightly in defeat before she trudged a few steps backward and turned to look at us both.

Dani looked amused as she turned her head back to me, eager to watch what I was about to say next.

"Why are you headed out so late?"

Might as well start there.

Miranda shifted lightly from boot to boot as she answered,
"Em just got back and wanted to show me what she brought
back from vacation."

This definitely wasn't the whole truth, so I pressed again.
"And she had to show you this *now*?"

Miranda lifted her head and looked directly at me as she answered, "She's leaving tomorrow morning to go stay with her dad until school starts, so this is the only time I'll get to see her."

Her deep-brown eyes looked closer to black than their usual golden brown in the dim light of the hallway. The hint of teenage menace behind her resolve was more funny than threatening considering how deeply she cared for those she loved. I tried not to smile at the conflicting images as I told her, "All right, but that big storm is supposed to be rolling in soon, so an hour tops, all right?

"But—" Miranda whined as she took a step toward me.

"All right?" I raised my eyebrows for extra emphasis.

"Fine." Miranda shoved her hands into her pockets as she threw out a "Back in an hour." She turned quickly on her heel and disappeared out the door.

"Love you too!" I called out before reaching for another sip.

"You big softy." Dani took the foot I'd just stretched and gently poked it into my thigh before placing her other foot in front of me expectantly as she continued, "I'd have given her less."

I chuckled as I gave her other foot a stretch. "Liar, you'd have let her stay the night."

Dani laughed softly in return, light and musical, before responding, "I mean, likely, but that's beside the point. Now we'll never know for sure."

"Whatever you say, dear." I smiled as she took back her other foot, aimed, then gently pushed her big toe into the softer part of my side. Not hard enough to hurt but enough for me to squirm.

"I'll *dear* you." She smiled as I raised my hand in defeat. Taking her win, she started to settle back in but before raising her book completely she asked, "Hey, how's it going with Arthur? Haven't heard you talk about him lately."

I sighed, taking a longer-than-necessary drink before setting the glass down.

"Honestly, I haven't really seen him much. Not sure he's avoiding me, but he also hasn't had any kind of outburst since our talk."

Catching my tone, Dani asked, "Well, isn't that a good thing?" She let her book drop to her chest again.

I hesitated as I swirled the amber liquid. "There's something different about him this time around."

"How so?" she asked, pushing against my legs softly as she used them to sit up a little more.

I looked away from the glass back to her. "I don't know exactly, it's hard to explain."

Dani leaned in as she pulled her legs underneath her and grabbed my hand. "Trust your gut. Maybe you can talk to the person he's working with—Marie? See if she's noticed anything and take it from there."

I placed my drink on the table next to me then took her face between my hands and kissed her softly, feeling her relax as she placed a hand lightly on my arm, drawing me in.

I broke the kiss, letting my forehead connect with hers before murmuring, "Thank you."

Dani ran her hand softly down my arm. "For what?"

"For believing me, even when I'm not sure why I feel the way I do."

"Always." I felt the warmth of her breath heating mine as she continued, "I just wish you listened to yourself more. You put your own needs last more than you should."

Dani slid out of my hands and planted a kiss on my forehead before lying back and picking up her book again.

She was right.

I picked up my glass as I shifted my focus, sipping as I let the shapes from the TV pass without much notice, enjoying the peace in this moment with my family and the woman I loved.

SAME DAY
ARTHUR CASLIN

Just need a few more minutes, that's all.

I pressed my back into the car seat using the steering wheel as leverage as the leather creaked and twisted under my grip. I wanted to forget the smell of that hospital, but the stench of piss and bleach still clung to my pores.

The Bitch had had another evaluation.

It was like I was still there, watching her cave into herself in the corner of the room. The odor so overwhelming, even the two-way glass couldn't contain it. Apparently, she'd been soiling herself instead of walking two whole fucking feet to the toilet.

When we left, she'd been screaming, the glass vibrating with every exhale. The psychiatrist attempting the evaluation eventually giving up and waving at the camera to end the session. Even the detective who'd been in the observation room with us had switched off the mic, hoping she'd scream herself out, but it barely helped. It's like I'd been in that room with her, directly across as strings of frothed spit hit and soaked into me, the stone-gray walls pushing us closer together.

At least something had come from this latest shit show. She'd finally admitted to having a photo of Ann, wanted someone to fetch it for her. Her voice raw and grated from prayers and mock pain begged for us to burn it. Said she had to know if her daughter had been saved, that it needed to be done. I just wanted to get the sound of her voice out of my head, the pleading slice of each syllable splintering like glass against my eardrums even now.

Burn, burn, burn.

The Bitch said each year they'd take the old picture out from the Bible they kept it in on Ann's birthday to see if it would turn to ash. When it inevitably would, they'd take another before beating the shit out of her again.

Her voice sliced through my thoughts. *Ann had to hold it, watch firsthand. The flames would burn what wasn't pure. It's how we knew, how we tricked the devil into showing itself. Why else would it burn? If she'd truly repented, it wouldn't. No blessed thing would.*

I ran my fingers through my hair, nails carving into skin. I wanted to scratch the voice out. Thought getting the picture would help, but it didn't. Still, I'd refused to leave another piece of Ann behind to be forgotten. It was in my pocket now, pressing against the fabric along my thigh. I felt it, not just the thick edges of the Polaroid, but the sharpness of her cheekbones cutting through the film. All angles and skin as she stood in front of the house, frightened. Probably hoping against hope that her picture wouldn't burn again.

Loosening my grip against the steering wheel, I tried to flex blood back into my hands. The chill of the night had finally slipped into my car, numbing me. Kate was waiting. It would be bad this time; getting the picture had pushed me hours past what I'd promised.

I'm not going to leave Ann behind.

I'd ripped almost every Bible apart. They were piled endlessly across floors and against walls. Every row taunting and seeming to grow as they teetered against the tug of my hands. Every page resonated with the Bitch. The rustling paper whispering verse into judgment, threatening to pin me to the floor where Ann and I could be forgotten together. But I'd found it.

Kate won't understand.

She never did. To her, going to Ann's house was crossing another line, just "treating a dead girl like she was alive"—her exact words after finding me holed up in my apartment, reading Ann's journal instead of following through on our plans.

Things had gotten worse between us since taking this case. I went from almost leaving to being stuck in this endless cycle of extensions and assessments, one after another. Somehow, the public defender's office had found a semi-competent lawyer and he was doing everything possible to turn this case into a fucking dumpster fire.

I rubbed my temples before opening the car door, shouldering my bag, and stepping out. The mud had frozen into uneven dips. The recent snow helping to fill in some of it. Though what remained had melted and mixed with corrosive salt and earth. A gritty uneven mass of ice and ruts.

It seemed to cut into my feet as I made my way to her door, which opened before I'd even made it to the porch. Kate's silhouette haloed by the light behind her looked as sharp and unforgiving as the ground beneath me.

"Why are you here?"

I stopped a few feet away, chewing back the anger edging behind my teeth. "You asked me?"

"I asked you to be here three hours ago. Didn't you get my text telling you not to come?" Her words spit acid as she crossed her arms, barring me from getting closer.

Like it would stop me.

Starting toward her again, I paused at the bottom step. "Come on, Kate, my phone died earlier." I spread out my arms, annoyed before continuing, "I'm already here."

"Go home, Art."

I ignored her as I climbed up the steps, placing my bag on the doorstop before taking her into my arms.

"You don't mean that." It was more fact than sweet talk.

I shouldn't have to defend myself all the time.

She struggled against me, pressing hands against my chest, trying to get free, but it only made me hold her tighter, bring her closer. I didn't want to listen when she asked me to let go, to fuck off, to hear the words she said. I just wanted her to stop, to let this moment pass.

And she did, she always did.

She slammed her hands against my chest one more time before saying, "Fine, but the couch is as far as you're getting tonight."

I let her go, walking behind her as I kicked off my shoes and dropped most of my things at the door. She tried to leave, to go to her bedroom. So, I grabbed her arm and pulled her back.

"Kate, not tonight please. I'm sorry. This day was a fucking nightmare to get through."

"It always is." The bite in her words had gone as she turned her head away from me, trying to find more distance to put between us even as I wrapped my arms around her.

I didn't like this. This was more giving up than giving in. I wanted the fight, needed it as I pled, "I'm getting out."

Her body tensed against me. "So you're letting Marie take over? You're finally leaving?" She looked at me, hopeful, but I couldn't answer her or hide what must have been written all over my face.

Her voice dropped. "Of course not. Why would you ever do the thing you said you would?" Her face lowered as she went limp in my hold. She wasn't fighting, just waiting for me to let go.

Her words scraped the anger and disgust from earlier raw.

"That's exactly what I'm doing. I'm finishing what I promised."

"No, you promised me you were leaving."

"And I still am." I didn't mean to raise my voice, to lace my words with something that hurt. She shrank from it, from me, as I followed, pinning her against the wall.

I tried to force her to look at me, but her eyes were green pools staring past me, emptying to what I had said and done.

"I can't do this anymore," she whispered.

My blood froze. "What do you mean?"

This time, her voice found some heat. "Exactly what I said."

I wanted to hold her tighter even as her body tried to pull itself from my touch. "You don't mean that."

I didn't expect her to move so quickly or sharply, breaking away from me. "I always do, you just never listen."

I tried to pull her back into me, but she put up her hand.

"There will always be that last case with you. You'll only leave by force or your own undoing, and I won't stay to see which comes first."

She's right. But the last thing I want to do is admit it.

My fists curled into themselves, nails biting into flesh.

"Please, don't do this. This is the last one."

"I can't keep watching what it does to you. To me."

"Let's put a date on it. Make my last day final no matter what." Ann's picture rubbed raw through the material, already dissolving my resolve.

I can't lose her, Ann.

"You mean it?" She took a step toward me but stopped, unwilling to close the distance.

"Of course I do."

"When?"

I walked to her, taking her in my arms again as I raised my fingers to trace her cheek. "How about a month from now. That sound okay?"

I almost believe it myself.

Her breath rattled as she took it in, eyes still spilling as she nodded.

I let my finger rest under her chin as I lifted it up. "So that means I can stay?"

"Yes."

She looked like she wanted to leave, worry staining the edges of her eyes, so I kissed her. Lightly at first, then deeper with each touch and movement. My hands moved over her, grabbing as we both hit the wall.

I couldn't lose her. I wouldn't.

JANUARY 9, 2017
MARIE PERAULT

"Why haven't they left yet?" Art was pacing back and forth in front of my desk, a confined cat looking for a fight.

I laughed but instantly sobered up as he shifted his glare from the conference room door to me.

I lifted my hands palms up, looking for a way out. "We aren't the only ones in this office, Art. I'm sure they're almost done."

"Better be."

Well, that's enough of that.

I leaned forward, clearing my throat before letting him know exactly how I was feeling. "Well, it should give us just enough time to remove the large stick from your ass." Art took a step toward me, red starting to color his ears, but his attitude had pushed me to a point of not caring so I continued. "Did something happen that I'm missing? This is a little much, even for you."

He paused just enough to look off guard before answering, "No, it's nothing."

Obviously not.

"Art."

He took a second to think before sinking into the seat in front of me. "I got in a fight with Kate this weekend."

Finally, his behavior was making sense. "I'm sorry to hear that. What happened?"

Art leaned forward, propping himself up on his elbows. "Well, we . . . It was just." He paused, reversing tactics and leaning back. "It was stupid." He smiled like this was old news. "Everything's fine now, not to worry."

He's never done that before.

I decided to try again. "You sure? Seems like something is still bothering you."

"No, it's nothing." Art craned his head back as if he'd heard something. "Look, they're done." He grabbed Ann's files from my desk and walked out without another word.

This is definitely new.

MARCH 24, 2017
MADDIE MORI

Marie and Art were having trouble navigating the smaller kitchen. I watched, smiling, as they fought to pass each other and reach for things the other could have grabbed . . . or was currently using. I wasn't about to step into that chaos, so I remained sitting at the small '90s reject table we'd found at a yard sale. It was an off-color blue with bright-pink curled teardrops and random yellow splatters. A vintage '90s mess we both adored the moment we'd laid eyes on it. I traced a small crack in its surface with one hand as a smile tugged at the corners of my lips. A small moment of peace before an odd elbow or hip hit the table, bringing me back into the chaos happening around me. We'd moved in a month ago, but we were still trying to find places for things including ourselves and guests.

"Who only has one pan?" Art closed the wooden cabinet just enough to playfully glare Marie's way.

The shopping I'd done seemed to find a new purpose as a bag of oversized marshmallows hit Art square in the face. He caught the bag as it fell, laughing at Marie as she gave him a wickedly innocent look.

"I didn't ask for your help, Art. I can manage dinner on my own and . . ." Marie paused, leaning into the open cupboard at her feet as whatever lay sheltered inside crashed and possibly cracked against what she was fighting to pull out. "See, I knew I had another." Marie pulled out the dented saucepan as accusation radiated in her face, tone, and the pan itself as she brandished it at Art. He sighed and covered the lower half of his face with his hand as he closed his eyes, likely contemplating what to say next.

A small laugh escaped my lips before I cut in. "Looks like we'll need to add pots and pans to the list. I doubt we'll be lucky to find any usable ones at a sale."

Marie retracted the pan before placing it on the stove next to her and heading to the fridge. "You never know, we've found some pretty great stuff so far." She opened the freezer and started to pull out an assortment of frozen dinner items.

I responded, "Then let me rephrase that: We need to get new ones."

Marie walked behind me, hands full as frigid air brushed against my neck, sending a shiver down my spine. I stretched back my head, the cold now seeping across my scalp as I met her gaze and she said, "But thrifting is so much fun, hon."

I held her gaze with mine. "It's a *have to*, if that's okay?"

She thought for a minute. "Of course. As long as I can thrift a good cast iron pan. Those things last forever if you keep them right."

Scrunching my face in exaggerated indecision as Marie smiled, I replied, "Okay, seems fair."

"Thank you," Marie cooed as she leaned down, kissing the side of my temple.

Art was trying to settle into a chair across from me as he asked, "What's a 'have to'?"

Marie moved beside me placing the mismatched dinner items on the table. "Just a phrase we use when we're serious about something."

"Though it's not an actual have to," I chimed in. "If Marie felt just as strong, we'd talk it out instead."

"Ahhh gotcha. Strange, but I get it." Art's eyes narrowed, taking in the food in front of him as he turned to Marie. "I thought you said you'd be cooking dinner?"

"I am."

Art laughed as he tried to lean back in the chair. "That's not cooking, that's reheating."

"Not all of it. The shrimp is raw."

"So, reheating with a side of food poisoning," Art countered.

"Only if it doesn't burn first," I threw in.

Marie turned to me with the shrimp still in hand. "Hey now, you're supposed to be on my side!"

"I always am." I smiled, standing as I made my way to her and planted a kiss on her cheek. "Just kidding, love." I kissed her a second time before brushing past her on my way to the liquor.

"Partly." Art sniggered.

Marie turned her head sharply in Art's direction, testing the weight of the frozen shrimp in her hand as his eyes widened.

This must be what family is like.

The more Marie and Art spent time with each other, the more they resembled siblings instead of coworkers. And when Kate was here, she was able to balance everything out. It had gotten easier to be around everyone, almost comfortable even when I felt disconnected.

You were a mistake.

My adoptive mother's words snuck up on me a little too easily. The pit in my stomach opened to something I didn't want to dive into.

Not now.

I grabbed a bottle before turning. "Anyone else want a whiskey? I got a fancy bottle for sipping."

"Sounds good to me," Art said as he raised a hand. "Work just seems to be turning into a shitshow."

I felt myself grow slightly ridged. Marie kept walking to the stove, turning on the burner to heat the pan before digging out a sheet pan from the drawer below as she answered, "I'll pour myself one when you both are done."

I grabbed a glass and poured a few fingers. From the look on Marie's face, she didn't want to talk about this with Art here, but I had to ask. "I thought ya'll were supposed to finalize a court date today?"

Art huffed, shooting back, "We were until that bitch's lawyer got it extended."

I still hated that word and how he used it, but I didn't know how to talk to him about it or even if I should. So I tried to move the conversation forward. "Again? What was it this time?"

"More assessments," Marie added as she bent over the table to grab a bag of frozen sesame chicken and vegetables.

"You're kidding me. What's left?" Taking the glass, I walked back and handed it to Art as Marie cut and dumped the bag into the pan. It hissed and sputtered back in its own form of protest.

I went back to the counter, grabbing another glass for myself, and poured as Marie continued, "He's still trying to convince the court that she's unfit to stand trial. Says they are having a hard time stabilizing her medications."

I'd taken a sip but quickly swallowed as a smooth burn chased my breath, smokey and sharp. "I thought they'd already done everything possible?"

Art drained his glass before holding it out for more. "Me too, but he's a cunning prick."

I took my glass, picking up a spare for Marie with the bottle before walking back to the table. "I guess that means you'll be sticking around a little longer?" I handed him the bottle as I sat down, giving Marie her glass as she settled into the empty seat.

"Yep," he said.

I watched as the light that had been in Art's eyes vanished, all emotions and movements now more akin to steel than the sarcastic warmth he normally had. This part of Art was unnerving. I needed to ease back from this into safer territory. "I'm sorry. I know you and Kate were excited about moving. Where is she, anyway?"

Art gripped his glass as he tapped an edge on the table below it. "Not sure. Probably at home. She broke things off a few weeks ago."

Shit.

Anxiety sparked against my nerves, crackling across my skin as I looked at Marie.

Why didn't you warn me? I didn't mean to make things worse.

As I looked for guidance, I realized she was just as shocked as I was. Reaching her hand across the table, she settled it on his arm, calming both it and the glass. "Why didn't you tell me?"

"Just wasn't ready to. Still not." The steel in his eyes darkened and seized as he tried to pull his arm back.

Marie let him as she took back her hand, grabbing the empty glass in front of her and filling it. She raised it, nodding for me to do the same. "Well then let's drink to the judge finally seeing past the bullshit."

Art seemed to relax as he raised his glass, shaking slightly. "Cheers to that."

The whiskey slid down easy as we all drained our glasses. The burn turning into a mild fire as my lips numbed. I realized too late it wasn't the only thing burning.

"Marie . . . honey. Hate to say this, but I think dinner is smoking."

Marie shot up, cursing as she ran to the stove.

I turned back to Art as the whiskey eased a smile back onto both our faces. "Takeout it is."

SAME DAY
MARIE PERAULT

I already knew the pizza boxes were going to be too big to fit into the fridge, so I dumped the extra slices onto a clean plate before covering them with tinfoil and sticking them into a barely-big-enough space in the fridge.

Need to clean this out soon.

Backing away and closing the door, I felt arms circle around my waist as Maddie dipped her chin lightly onto my shoulder, kissing the sensitive spot behind my ear and sending shivers down my arms.

"Hey, you. Looks like you cleaned everything but the boxes."

Wrapping my own arms on top of hers, I leaned my head back just enough to kiss her cheek.

"Yup, pizza is much easier to clean up after then my own mess was."

Maddie giggled as she pressed her lips into the crook between my neck and shoulder, her breath tickling.

I squirmed, turning around to look her in the face circling my arms around her shoulders. "Hey now, you're supposed to say, 'It wasn't that bad.'"

"How about, 'It could have been worse,'" she countered.

"Smartass." I smiled, leaning in for a real kiss as she reached for the boxes.

"Oh, let me get those." Maddie still tried to grab them, but I was quicker.

"It's okay, I'll be right back."

I started toward the door so I could drop off the boxes in the communal recycling, but Maddie called out, "Do you think Art's okay?"

I paused, turning around as I shifted the boxes under my arm. "What do you mean?"

Maddie looked a little unsure as she sat down at the table, picking at the rag I'd just wiped it down with, twisting it between her fingers.

"He just seems so . . . off. Everything that happened with Kate and the way he talks about the case." Something splintered within her voice, soft but catching.

Maddie looked down, pressing her lips tightly together as she twisted the rag just a little tighter. My heart lurched, pulling me toward her as I set the boxes back on the table. I sat next to her and cupped her hands with my own, calming her fingers. "What's wrong?"

Maddie took a slow breath. "I just don't like how he talks sometimes . . . how he was with Kate." She looked up, eyes misted ever so lightly. "I just . . . I'm worried, Marie. Now that Kate isn't here to balance him, will he be okay?"

I lifted my hands as I pulled her into a hug. "How long have you been feeling like this?"

She spoke softly into my ear. "He's always kinda hit me wrong. Seems like he may be going through something."

"I'm glad you said something." Leaning back, I let my hands catch hers as I continued, "Art is . . . God, how do I explain this. He tends to let too much of himself get caught up in the cases he works on and has a shitty tendency to take it out on those around him, even at work."

I looked down at her hands, squeezing them lightly before looking up and continuing, "I know, it took me a while to get comfortable around him, too, when we first met." Looking at her, I could tell she was still hesitant. "He always means well, but I can see why Kate left and why you feel this way. Do you want him to stop coming over?"

"No, I don't think so. I was just getting worried about what I was feeling and wanted to talk to you."

I squeezed her hands again, bringing them up to my lips. "I understand. He'll be better after this case."

I hope.

Maddie smiled, her body now a little more relaxed.

I didn't want to tell her I was worried, too.

APRIL 13, 2017
RICHARD KOCH

As I looked at my watch, I couldn't help but wince when I saw how quickly twelve had turned to three and then seven.

Not making it home early tonight.

I'd delegated more work to colleagues, but it was still proving hard to let go of it completely. Giving up too much hit like a weakness, like I was revealing incompetence that wasn't there. But Dani was right. I couldn't keep expecting more of myself than those around me even when others did. I needed to let some things go, even if it meant I stayed late every so often to finish work early the next day. I'd gotten more early nights lately, and it didn't feel like I was missing parts of my life anymore.

I closed the door to my office before starting the usual rounds of turning off lights and making sure the building was secure before locking up, but shadows from the conference room caught my eye. I took a few steps inside to find Arthur and Marie buried beneath stacks of books and paper. The long table that took up most of the room was so covered it looked like a tiny city threatening to expand past its limits at any moment.

"You're both here late."

Both faces shot up like they were toddlers with stolen sweets. They shared a quick glance before Marie answered, "Sorry, sir, we thought everyone had gone home."

"It's all right. Is this about Diane's case?" I leaned against the doorstop, trying to exude the calm they needed.

Marie leaned back. "Yes, we have another chance to kick-start the trial and want to be prepared."

"Anything I can help with?"

"No," Arthur said a little too quickly, almost combative. Even Marie became rigid, scooting to the edge of her seat, ready to intervene.

Arthur must have realized his mistake. Clearing his voice, he kicked the charm back on even though it sounded hollow. "We've got this under control. We'll let you know if it changes."

This was the first time he'd ever spoken to me like that. No longer wanting to please, just ready for me to leave.

I readjusted my back against the doorframe, swallowing the words that would only escalate things. "Sounds good, happy to help if you need fresh eyes. This case has definitely turned out to be more trouble than I thought it'd be."

Arthur's shoulders seemed to soften as Marie relaxed, leaning back into her seat as she replied, "Thank you. So far, it's looking like Diane's lawyer has run out of options."

I glanced at my watch before shifting my gaze up. The wood of the frame behind me was stronger than my resolve to stay and from the looks of it, they were just as tired as well. "All right. Well if you change your minds, just let me know. We should all call it a night, though."

Arthur replied with the hardened tone from earlier easing back into his words. "Only a few more things to go over and we'll leave."

Marie turned to look at Arthur, something akin to worry flashing across her face and creasing her brow.

Pushing back from the doorframe, I got ready for what may come next. "Not tonight. Cleaning service is supposed to come through soon."

"No worries, we'll clean this up and leave." Marie smiled, turning back to Arthur as he crammed a bunch of files together and walked past me without saying a word. I should have been upset, but I was thankful for the chance to talk to Marie.

I walked over to where she'd started collecting documents. "How's he doing? Any change since we last spoke?"

Marie stopped what she was doing before looking up toward me. "He seems okay. Still stressed, but he's had a lot going on."

Another conversation I didn't push even though I wanted to. But it was hard to act on what I was feeling without someone else confirming what I was seeing.

She cares about him.

This thought was a little reassuring since he had someone close looking after him. In all honesty, I wanted to take the case away from him, but that was complicated.

Do you really want to?

I didn't want to lose out on the freedom I'd found. The freedom everyone else had always had but seemed out of reach for me.

Why do I always have to sacrifice? Arthur isn't even asking me to.

They made it this far; I should be able to trust them both. I nodded to Marie. "Good to hear but if anything changes, let me know. I just want to help."

Marie smiled as she said, "Of course, thank you for checking in."

I reached out, giving her shoulder a pat before turning to leave. Putting more faith in what she said than what I felt.

APRIL 21, 2017
MADDIE MORI

The dry heat from the kilns drifted into each breath as I worked in tandem with Deb to set up the tables for the next class. As we placed the last one, I stood, stretching my back for a second before wiping the sweat from my face with the soft pink flowy crop top I was glad I'd decided to wear. If only I had been smart enough to pack shorts as well. Turning to face her, I watched as she hunched over the end of the table, moving it a few more inches to the left as she lined it up with the others. "Deb, I think we need to crack open a few more windows."

She looked up, unconvinced even with her hair dripping. "It's not that bad."

Laughing, I motioned to her shorts and tank top. "Well, maybe not for you." I pointed to my paint splattered jeans. "Even with the holes, these are still too much for the temperature in here and I doubt anyone else coming in tonight will be dressed any better."

Deb rested her hands on her hips as I watched her calculate a way to ignore what I'd said. It wasn't that she thought I was wrong, I just knew she didn't want to lose the heat she loved so dearly. "Okay, but if I catch a cold it'll be your fault. Especially if my children lose one of their mothers far too early."

"You know, Deb, it still shocks me when people call you dramatic." I stifled a laugh as I bent to grab the painting tarp we had folded earlier, tossing it toward her. "Here's some extra warmth from the sixty-degree weather that's about to assault your poor old bones."

I made my way to the closest window as Deb caught the tarp, laughing and tucking it under her arm just as quickly. "Hey now, don't bring words like *old* into it."

I reached the metal latch of the first window, unlocking it as I looked over my shoulder at her. "Well excuse me for going off what you seemed to be implying." I stuck my tongue out for extra emphasis as I shoved the window open and made my way toward the next window. A thought hit me as quickly as the nerves stopping me in my tracks. "Hey, Deb?"

Deb paused, hearing the shift in my tone. "What is it?"

"I've been thinking about finding my birth parents."

Deb placed the tarp on the table in front of her as she started toward me. "That's a big step. Why do you want to try now?"

I hooked my thumb under the loose collar of my shirt as I crossed the other arm under my chest, rubbing the soft fabric against my lips. I had to lower it to continue. "Ever since I saw my old name again . . . It just has me thinking. About who I am and where I came from."

Deb stopped in front of me as I rocked back and forth on my feet, lifting the fabric back to my lips. Deb didn't mind the silence like most did; she didn't strain to fill it when she knew I needed it. Just waited until I dropped the fabric and continued, "It just feels like there's so much missing, and it just keeps growing, turning into something I can't ignore anymore. Is that ridiculous?"

Deb raised her hand just far enough to softly touch the side of my elbow, moving her thumb back and forth. "Not at all. I think it's wonderful."

I relaxed, bringing my hand to rest on top of hers. I should've known by now she wouldn't judge me for searching. She understood my adoption hadn't been the gift others had tried to convince me of.

Deb gave my arm a final squeeze before dropping her hand. "Have you talked to Marie about this?"

I shifted again. "No, you're the first person I've told. I want to see what I can find before I get anyone else invested."

Deb took a few steps back to lean on the table. "Do you have the papers? Anything to work off?"

"No." I looked down. "My mother destroyed those the night I was thrown out after I had asked for them."

I heard the air leave her lungs in a rush. "Jesus, I'm sorry, Maddie."

"Don't worry about it. It's not even the worst thing my family did." My thumb hooked back into my collar and I started chewing it lightly.

"I'm sorry if this is out of line, but did you ever tell anyone about them?"

I lowered the fabric again. "Yes, but it was complicated. Most people only knew what my family showed them. So most just thought I was being ungrateful."

Deb pushed herself off the table, taking a few steps to me. "That's on them, not you. No one should ever feel pushed into loving people who don't understand what it means."

Her words hit a space within me, soft and vulnerable. "Could I have a hug?"

Deb smiled as she opened her arms. "Always."

The bell at the front tinkled, but I went in for the hug anyway. Letting myself feel the moment fully before pulling back, both of us smiling at the other, knowing without saying what we needed to do next. Deb gave me another small squeeze before heading to the front as I turned back to the windows, pushing the glass of each one leisurely so I could feel crisp spring air flow over my skin. The sweet smell of rain, fresh growth, and earth filling each breath.

JUNE 23, 2017
MARIE PERAULT

Art's head dipped dangerously over another book; he had propped himself up with his elbows, but their strength was waning as his head became heavier. The fingers of one hand twisted through his hair as the other attempted to steady his chin. His face was almost touching the pages in front of him as they rustled with each slowing breath. I was just relived he was asleep or close to it. Didn't care where it happened or if I'd be stuck at work. After Kate left, it was like a switch flipped. Whatever had kept him balanced broke. I wasn't sure how much sleep he was getting anymore; I would've been surprised if it was even close to five hours a night considering how fixated he'd become.

My phone vibrated in my pants pocket. It had to be Maddie. Looking up, I saw Art hadn't moved. Just in case he was awake, I turned a page of the book in front of me as I slid my phone out into my lap. I paused for a second to see if he'd react, then focused on the screen.

8:14 p.m.

I was surprised it wasn't later. The message from Maddie waited just below the time.

Maddie: Coming home soon?

I opened the message to respond.

Marie: Should be. Think Art might be asleep or close to it. Kinda want to let him before seeing if he'd want to crash at our place.

Maddie: Sounds good to me, seems like he's driving himself into the ground.

Marie: Think in a weird way he's trying to prove that losing Kate was worth it.

Maddie: Something that never needed to happen.

Marie: True.

A sharp thud drew my attention back to Art. His hands now rubbed his face in frustration and pain.

Guess he had been sleeping.

"You okay?"

"Yeah, just smacked my face."

"If this is a new focusing technique, I'm out." I let a smile tug at the corners of my lips as his hands stalled just beneath his eyes. He glared at me.

I broke the silence before he was able to dive into full-on wallowing. "Come on, Art, we should head out."

"You go ahead. I still have a few things to do." Art pulled the book closer to him as he picked up his pen and pad.

"A few things that can be done tomorrow after you've gotten some sleep."

Art waved off my response as he tried to settle back into his work. "I'm fine, just need to finish this."

I reached over and slipped the book out from in front of him as I closed it. "No, you don't."

The sadness and frustration behind his eyes started to become more visible—another fight he wouldn't want to drop. So, I decided not to give him a choice this time.

"Come for dinner. Maddie's waiting and it's been forever since we had one of those movie nights. Plus, we just got a pull-out couch we've been dying to justify the cost of."

"No . . . I should go home if I go anywhere."

"Come on, Art, even Maddie seems to be losing touch with her sensible side. Said she was starting to miss your *shining personality*." I leaned fully into the banter as I turned the last two words into a mocking jab with air quotes.

Relief eased across his face as he let a smile slip out. "Are you sure?

"Yeah, you're always welcome, Art."

I watched the weight he'd been carrying visibly lift from him. He seemed hellbent on finding anything to fill his free time, which is probably why sleep was so difficult. It was the only place where he had nothing to face but himself.

I gathered the files and organized them into their box as he shelved the books we had used. When I finished, I turned to meet Art as he stood checking his phone.

"Ready?"

Art looked up, nodding. "Yeah."

I grabbed my phone from the table where I had placed it earlier and picked up my keys.

Marie: We're headed to you now. See you soon.

AUGUST 30, 2017
ARTHUR CASLIN

I grabbed each of her casefiles one by one and let them drop onto the worn wooden table.

Thump. Thump. Thump.

Today would be different. This trial would be different. As the last file hit, I paused, taking in the room around me. As I sucked in the crisp air-conditioning, I filled my lungs past capacity, relishing the soft burn as the air asked to be released. I couldn't handle another loss, especially not for Ann.

I was in the same courtroom I'd started in. All these years and nothing had changed from the furniture, to the people, to the outcomes. When I started at the DA's office, I thought I'd make a small part of this city better. Truth is, I never even made a dent. Day after day, I watched people come into this courtroom who didn't deserve to be here leave with harsher rulings than the ones who deserved them. Those assholes that got off always came to court with a smile and a pricy lawyer, leaving with nothing or close to it.

The vent above rattled me back into my body. I breathed out and closed my eyes as I leaned back into the stream of air coming from it. I paused only when the tilt of my chair became too much. Even with my eyes closed, I was stuck in this place. The red carpet reflected harshly off the wood and white paint that surrounded me. It was a blood-red burn that seeped past my eyelids onto my retinas, pulling me back from any possible daydream of other locations.

Stop being so dramatic.

The red was nothing more than florescent lights mixing with imagination. Though the sounds building behind me were real enough, I didn't need to look to see the chaos of another day starting. This was the part I hated most about public trials, especially the high-profile cases like Ann's. Rubberneckers were everywhere. They came to watch the show they had heard about on TV, never caring about the lives at play or—more importantly—the one that had been lost. They just cared about having one of those "I was there" stories to tell over beers or a dinner table.

I tried to find a more comfortable position in the stiff chair, savoring the few moments I had before Marie arrived. Somehow, she still believed in the good this type of work could do. The only thing I knew for sure was that this case would be my last and I was almost done. After two years, this day was already bleeding into the surreal.

Are we really almost done?

Massaging my temples, I leaned forward as my suit failed to grasp my body's thin frame. I'd given up so much for this. The jury had to see past her antics and convict her, not send her to some fucking mental hospital.

The only thing she hadn't done in court was burst into some *righteous* killing spree. Something a part of me wanted with every fiber of my being. I played the possibility over and over again in my head. First, she would take out the police officer behind her with a chair or glass. Then she'd focus on someone else, sometimes her lawyer, sometimes the judge. Whoever it was, it would give me the chance to grab the officer's gun and unload a clip into her. Though some days when I really thought about it, death was more of a mercy than she deserved. That's when I'd replaced the gun with the billy club. Even now, imagining the look on her face was a thrill. Probably the only way that bitch would understand what she'd done. I let a curt and bitter laugh go without restraint.

"Tell yourself a good joke? I'd love to hear."

Marie ruffled my hair as she made her way to the seat next to mine. I was a bit shocked by the bright-pink blouse sticking out of her black tailored jacket. I'd only seen her wear bright colors a handful of times but never at work.

"Trust me you, wouldn't like the punchline," I said, unable to keep the shit-eating grin from creasing my face as I tried to flatten my close-cropped hair back into place.

She smacked my shoulder softly as she turned her head and pretended to search for a document. She didn't like to appear too happy in court and was doing her best to conceal her own amusement from the crowd behind us.

"So serious." I gave my best gravelly whisper as I crossed my arms and waited for her response.

Marie looked me up and down before uttering, "You look constipated. So, you have that going for you."

Ha! There she is.

I laughed and continued an unwinnable fight for comfort with the chair. For a moment, I longed for a movie night . . . but those had pretty much ended with Kate.

Don't think of her.

Marie leaned over to pick up the framed photos she had brought, knocking a few of my files askew as she placed it on the table.

"Oops!"

She reached to fix them but froze, her hand hovering over loose pages. She sighed and slowly lifted Ann's postmortem photo out of the mess. She held it like shattered glass, like the smallest pressure would add to the bruises in the picture.

"I never understood that . . ." The laughter from the moments before quickly extinguished.

"What?"

"How someone could have more pictures documenting their death than life." She placed the photo beside the only picture of Ann alive we had. It was hard to know what to say.

"I know, Marie. I know."

Reaching out, I gently took her hand from the bruised photo and placed it on the unblemished one. "It's not fair, but at least there's one."

She smiled, easing back from a ledge I knew too well.

"So, did you get any sleep last night?" Marie asked, turning to look at me while her metal earrings jingled in anticipation of the response I knew she wanted.

"Define *sleep*."

A sigh escaped her lips. "Art, the case is basically over. Why were you up?"

"I wanted them to connect with Ann, to understand the person she was, so I practiced." I should have stopped there but I didn't want to. "You already know I won't be able to sleep until that Bitch is behind bars."

"Art!"

Marie failed to conceal shock as she chanced a glance toward the few people seated behind us, only returning her gaze to me after making sure my comments had been lost in the noise. She leaned in and whispered, "Of all the places to voice your opinion, this should be the last."

I knew what buttons I had pushed, but I didn't want to dance around them today as I said, "If anything, this should be the first place. And besides, the assholes behind us are probably eating this shit up."

Annoyance now overwhelmed the look of shock on her face as she rubbed her eyes. "Well at least stop referring to Diane like that. She's a real person no matter how fucked up she is."

"Ha! That's a joke. Anything that Bitch had that resembled humanity died with Ann."

Whoops.

If looks could kill, the one I was getting from Marie would have taken Medusa herself.

"Yeah, yeah, always my conscience," I said, backpedaling.

The crowd had started to whisper and rock in the seats behind us, a sound I had grown accustomed too. They'd found their train wreck: the main event. I nodded toward the unease behind us, redirecting Marie's gaze.

"Speak of the devil." Bitterness rose within me like bile. No matter how hard I tried to swallow it, its taste was never too far away. She was being escorted to the defense table, her lawyer in tow like some decrepit dog. I swiveled back to Marie, leaning in as I looked into her eyes. Only giving in to her wish for discretion by whispering, "I refuse to call *it* by anything resembling human."

Exasperated and too pissed to look back at me, Marie turned to the table, straightening the papers that had spilled from the files. All except Ann's photos.

Shit. Definitely made that worse.

Without looking at me, she quipped, "Let's just make it through this day without *Diane* being called anything, agreed?"

I didn't want to respond.

"Agreed?" she said a little louder, turning to face me with a second dose of that stare.

"Fine."

She started to say something back but was drowned out by the usual cry of, "All rise . . ."

And just like that, with all the daily rituals observed, court began again. It was time to play my part and end the show.

THE MORNING JUST BEFORE COURT
MARIE PERAULT

"Shit, shit, shit!"

I reached for the documents as they slid from the folder in my hand. I should have shoved everything into my bag before trying to get out, but I was already running late for court. I'd still make it in before the judge, but not the crowd. Catching the documents, I shoved them back into the folder and into my bag before pulling myself the rest of the way out of the small Subaru. I was counting down the days till I could trade it in. When I first moved into the city it seemed like everyone had one, so I took a chance. It was a nice car, just way too low for someone my height. At least I'd be able to start looking soon, and it was shaping up to be a beautiful day. I took a second to gaze toward the bright-green trees in the park in front of me as the leaves shifted and filtered the sunshine into varying shades of green across the concrete pathways below. The cool breeze that tugged at my frizzed curls seemed to help cut the heat of the day even though it had only started to build.

"Hey there, sweetheart, you need some help? I know something you could help me with after."

I looked up to see a rather short greasy man coming toward me. The dark-gray track suit he wore did little to hide the stains that stretched down its front, settling into its own kind of putrid camo as it connected to the matching pants below. The stripes running down either side of his body were off-white ribbons, grabbing desperately at his figure. It was easy to see his clothes were a few sizes too small. He came closer, sweat glistening, as he forced a thick hand into the front of his elastic pants. My work bag was still open, so I stuck a hand in, delving past the paperwork and mints until the smooth, reassuring hilt of my knuckle knife pressed into my palm. Popping the safety catch, I pulled the two-and-a-half-inch blade free. The man froze mid-step as I shifted the blade toward the sun, shooting broken rays of light across his face, forcing his hand from self-pleasure to shield.

I savored his shock before replying, "I'm going to guess the latter part would end with my baby, Josie, here cutting off whatever that help involved."

He backed up quickly as his hands raised to either side. He stuttered before finally getting out, "You crazy bitch, I was just joking."

Sure, you were.

He was just like the other catcalling assholes in this city. That's why I had Josie; I didn't need to depend on a passerby to help. I'd end it myself before it went too far.

We both stared at each other for a moment before I pointed the blade in his direction and said, "Well then, why don't you be a good boy and run the fuck along?"

He stared, slack-jawed, for another moment as anger washed red across his cheeks. His thin lips struggled to shape words, but one more look at the knife was enough to seal them as he turned away toward the park. I waited, watching as he slowly plodded over the manicured grass to Congress Street on the other side. It wasn't until he'd disappeared completely that I slid the knife back into its casing. Snapping its clasp, I bent into the car and placed it into the glovebox.

This type of thing had been getting worse over the last few years, so I rarely went into the city without it. Only downside was I couldn't take it into court, but I still liked knowing it was nearby. I quickly made my way to the nearest Pay to Park and got a ticket for the max two hours. I regretted not dressing for speed as the tight pencil skirt and heels hindered me. I pushed forward as quickly as possible, placing the ticket on the dashboard before turning around to the courthouse behind me. I'd probably still be in court when the time ran out, but it was just too convenient. Checking my phone, I realized the little rendezvous with the creep had cost me, but I still might make it with a few minutes to spare.

I looked to the courthouse, stark-white stone that always seemed a shade too bright no matter what season it was. Its steps were eerily quiet today. Guess the press and onlookers had already made their way inside. I paused at the edge of my little car, watching for traffic. The one-way street that wrapped around the building was usually quiet too, but I still wanted to be careful before crossing. The clacking of my heels across the pavement sounded more self-assured than I felt. Even though this encounter had ended better than some, it was still unnerving. I pushed the thoughts aside as I focused on my steps, sharpening the sound of my heels as I made my way toward the courtroom.

Once I made my way through the entrance, I reached the courtroom doors, which were still propped open by the throngs of people waiting to get inside. I had to sidestep and push between more than a few before catching sight of Art. He was sitting tipped back in his chair, eyes closed at the table a few feet in front of me. A part of me wanted to believe he was asleep. The dark circles under his eyes and his pale sallow skin seemed to scream for it. The only thing that gave away any alertness was his quickly tightening brow; it didn't take much to guess what he might be thinking of. At least his appearance suggested he was still trying, from the clean shave to his freshly cut hair—even his oversized suit showed signs of being pressed. He still believed in something even if the rest of his personality had soured over the last few months.

Moving around the last few people, I made it to him just as a sad laugh left his lips.

SAME DAY
ARTHUR CASLIN

took a moment before walking to the pictures on the metal stand in front of the jury. The courtroom was quiet as everyone waited for my closing arguments. They had to be eating this shit up, so I took a few moments to straighten the picture of the bird next to Ann's.

She would have been twenty this year.

We'd blown up the polaroid, hoping her bright-green eyes and gentle smile would be enough to counter the Bitch's accusations. Ann wasn't a monster, a devil, or any ounce of the evil her mother pretended to see.

She was just a kid.

A rush of heat hit my fingertips as tremors settled in. I flexed my hand a few times, willing the frustration away, but it was hard to shake this time.

"Ahem. Mr. Caslin, we're ready when you are." The judge cleared his throat as more of a warning than a push. I had taken too long.

Focus . . .

I turned from the jury to the audience as they shifted like a restless sea. I refused to look at her, didn't have to to know what she'd be doing. Sitting like a fucking saint as she rocked against the waves of people behind her, back and forth, back and forth, rosary flying through fingertips.

What God would save you?

At least my thoughts didn't have to be so kind.

I raised my hand, turned back to the jury, and gestured for them to focus on Ann. "She may not be in this courtroom, but she hasn't lost her voice."

I couldn't resist walking toward them. "As you've learned throughout this trial, through isolation Ann was able to create a connection with a bluebird just like the one pictured."

I walked backward to the stand, pausing only a moment before tapping the image with my finger. "This was Ann's hope and ultimately her undoing. Her belief in something better wasn't enough to keep her from dying at the hands of someone she loved. Hands that should have protected her and understood exactly what they were doing."

The Bitch was visible out of the corner of my eye, rocking faster and faster with the arms of her chair just falling short of hitting the table in front of her. I didn't have to glance back to see her lips mouthing a mockery of prayer. The tremors were back, radiating from the center of me. I tried to use them, to channel them into what came next. Turning, I walked to my table, blocking the Bitch out as I picked up Ann's last letter. It was more of a journal than an actual note, but I think she'd written each entry hoping she could show her mother one day. The pages slipped against the clear plastic that protected them, almost escaping my grasp. I took a breath, slow and steady, until the shaking calmed. I'd gotten used to the shaking, even as it had grown worse over the trial. It wasn't until Kate left that I understood their connection to my emotions.

I made my way back to the jury. "This letter was written by Ann." I raised the pages up. "It's one of many that made up her journal. She wrote them all to her mother . . . or the person she thought her mother could be."

Lowering them, I did my best to keep the slick plastic from falling as I read Ann's words to the courtroom.

Dearest Mother,
I hope I won't disappoint you today. I try to fight temptation and humble myself to you and God's plan, but the sin within me is strong. It's why I've never doubted your ability to see it so clearly when others can't. I've

planned for more ways to atone and look forward to the ones you have prepared as well.

Charles was here again; he really is such a dear friend. It's silly to imagine conversations with a bird, but I can't help but smile when I see him. My kindness may be nothing more than a free meal to him, but my heart rises a little more each morning when he returns. His constant and unwavering trust in me lifts my soul. It gives me hope that one day I can be the daughter you and God need me to be.

Creak, Creak, Creak.

That damn rocking. I couldn't be the only one bothered by it, especially as it picked up speed. The sound around her taunted me. Daring me to take her bait as she threw her body
back and forth,
back and forth.
Focus.

Unclenching my jaw, I returned to Ann's softly written words.

He comes and wakes me before I'd like, but it never upsets me. His beak in gentle excitement tapping at the window is the music that begins the best part of my day. I love how he sings to me when I walk toward him.

Punctuating each note with small hops as I grab the bread I saved for him from the night before.

I'm truly sorry for hiding this, but I don't think you'd understand. It's wicked to take the bread, but my intentions are good. I promise you I only take from my own portion. If you saw how happy Charles gets, I hope you'd agree that I'm serving God through the care of one of his creatures. I know you say he's evil, but I just don't see it.

Feeding him brings a smile to my face, Mother, and when you're better it will do the same for you. It's sad that I've not been able to share this part of the day with you, but the added prayer and penance will help to calm the sin within me that pains you so.

I'd paced from the jury box to my table and back as I read. My own way of counteracting the Bitch's rhythm. This time when I made it back to the table, Marie had a cool glass of water waiting for me. She was kind that way. Always a few steps ahead with what I needed. I paused with my back to the defense as I took a quick sip, but it was getting harder to block out the rocking now. The room had grown quiet, waiting to hear the rest of Ann's words. This seemed to amplify the creaking wood to such a degree that the drone of the old air conditioner above didn't stand a chance of muffling it anymore.

Charles was funny today when I fed him. Opening the window only amplified his excitement. He jumped on both sides of the sill, singing his song. It wasn't until I crumbled the bread in front of him that he was able to pull himself together, ruffling feathers in his own form of warmth as he walked toward me. I sat in my chair and watched as he picked apart the pile. That's when we started to catch up.

It's foolish that I talk to him, but I can't help but ask about his day ahead and how his family is doing. I can almost see his head nodding as he sings to me of his life between bites.

Today I imagined he woke up excited and bold enough to teach any alley cat a lesson if it tried to take a swing, with enough energy left over to help teach his children how to fly after. I told him how I wished it was something anyone could learn. How if you were able to just touch the heavens, God's grace might rise within you again. Even if didn't last, you might be able to find some peace.

I was ready for what came next.

The rocking paused as everything inside of me stilled.

That's when he looked into my eyes and asked how you've been. He's worried about you, Mother. We all are.

I know Father loves you more than anything, but his pain and loss of faith has forced him to leave. He struggles with God's tests just as we all do, but your condition isn't a sign that God isn't here or that He's left your side. It's a sign that your unyielding grace and goodness has made you the perfect target for the devil. Please don't give up, you are so close! You'll soon find peace; Charles and I agree on that.

Though I must say I enjoy the part of the conversation which comes next, when me and Charles speak of all the good things to come. When you're better, when Father is back, and I'm the daughter you need me to be. We'll be able to rejoice in our family just as Charles does in his.

I must go, dear Mother; the day is calling me to start just as it called my dear friend away. I hope that God has seen to bless you this morning and that I'm not too upsetting. Yesterday I was careless and came down the stairs recklessly, enraging the demons within you. I only realized this when the Good Book flew past my face at the bottom of the stairs.

Please forgive me. I promise to write of nicer things to-night. Just as my friend was able to steal me away for a moment of happiness this morning, I hope to do the same for you. Maybe I can take you away somewhere the demons can't reach you. Where I can break the ties within me that bring them to you, so you can finally be free.

Until tonight with all my love and devotion, your ever trying daughter.

— Ann

I walked back to my table, setting down Ann's letter as the silence in the courtroom settled in. It was hard not to see Ann's broken face, unmoved from the center of the table where it had fallen this morning. The lack of sleep was probably playing tricks, but the chill of the mortuary seeped from its edges, reaching for me. She'd been struck so hard, the outlines of the Bitch's hands were visible across her face. Anger, boiling and sickly, fused with sadness into something I couldn't describe or fully control. Both my fists clenched tightly as fingernails bit into skin. Leaning on the table for a moment, I closed my eyes and let my head bend to the emotion within me before beginning again.

"She was never able to fulfill that promise."

Pushing away from the table and opening my eyes, I turned back to the jury. "This was written the day before her mother decided that the only way to save her daughter was to hold her underwater until the evil she saw inside of her stopped fighting."

I could hear the shifting unease from those around me—all faceless, all nameless. The only sounds I cared about came from the people contained in the box in front of me. It was their chorus of understanding I wanted to hear. To rely on. But even as I strained to hear, the old sound came creeping back . . .

Back and forth,

Back and forth.

The Bitch and her prayers, always fucking rocking.

How is this not affecting her?

I'll make her stop.

I took Ann's postmortem photo and rushed to the jury, making sure none of them looked away this time. If they wanted a show, I'd give it to them.

"Is this what evil looks like?" I raised the photo, making sure every eye took in her shattered face.

A roar came from the defense. "I object! Your Honor, the prosecution is completely out of line and leading the jury!"

I'd upset her oiled dog. Refusing to turn around, I imagined his eyes failing to push past the thick folds of his puffy skin as he stared me down.

"Upheld," resounded the judge. "Counselor, this is not the first warning I've given you, but it's the last. If you can't keep your behavior in check, I'll hold you in contempt of court"—he was motioning now toward Marie—"and leave your colleague here to lead the case to its end, alone. Have I made myself clear?" He emphasized this last part as he tipped his eyeglasses down to the tip of his nose. A scolding teacher to an impetuous student. Even for such a slight man, his black robes seemed to punctuate his message.

I pulled myself back, doing little to hide the bite within my words. "Yes, Your Honor, it won't happen again." And it didn't. The rest of the time was a blur, going through the final motions as the trial ended and the jury left to deliberate. My job was done.

I dug into the wooden chair that held me as the crowd behind me dispersed. It was only a matter of time now before the decision would be made. The wood in this old courtroom was more cage than decoration. Each carpeted footstep was muffled, amplifying its hold as I waited to be set free.

SAME DAY
MARIE PERAULT

I'd hoped the last day would have been more calming for Art, but his agitation had only grown. There wasn't much I could do when he got this way, especially not during the trial. So I settled in, ready to help if he needed me. It was my only option until the jury made their decision.

Art stood up, drilling his feet hard into the wooden floor as he walked over to the picture of Ann and the bird. He would have had more impact with just Ann's picture, but he wanted to make a point. Juries were temperamental. If there wasn't a forensic reason behind everything, it would do more harm than good. To them, a bird was a bird; no one cared about symbolism anymore. At least Ann's picture helped give the jury a face to connect to—it made her human, more tangible. I looked at the picture of Ann's face, framed and only just in focus, something that had been magnified when the picture was made larger. Her soft pale skin was almost translucent, giving the picture a more black-and-white quality than I'd thought possible. Though if I wasn't allowed outside, I'd probably end up looking about the same. Her jet-black hair that fell in soft waves didn't help the effect either, I think that's what made her green eyes even more striking. They looked like rich turquoise resting in pale milk. A part of me thought of her as pretty, but the bones sticking out just a little too far, stretching thin her paper skin, drew away from it. I closed my eyes for a moment, imagining her well fed and full of life—how her features would fill into something more substantial. Filling the space she was entitled to, not the one she was reduced to.

But she'd never get this chance. A chance to find herself outside of her parents, to love and be loved, even the simple freedom to follow a passion. This was the sadness that held me, that asked to be grieved. No matter how this case ended or what the jury decided, she could never be brought back. I opened my eyes to watch Art pace back and forth between the jury and the pictures. He used to be better at the pageantry of court. Now, instead of confidence, he exuded an unapproachable anger, something that only played into the defense's case. A case I must admit I agreed with myself.

I poured a glass of water from the clear jug in front of me for myself and turned ever so slightly toward the table to the left of ours. There she was: a shell of what a human being was supposed to be. She rubbed her face with hands that held a rosary woven in between her fingers. She seemed so sad, so broken. Her defense team had done their best in getting her ready for trial. Her thin and mostly white hair had been brushed and styled into a simple bun as a long gray dress tried its best to hold her, instead giving her body a folded and permanently broken shape.

Is it one of her own dresses?

Considering how much weight she had lost since her arrest, it was possible. I'd heard she'd taken to fasting, though looking at her now I wouldn't feel confident in even taking a guess at the last time she ate. One thing was for sure: she was a vastly different woman from the one I'd first met and seen plastered across the news. As I watched her now, she tried to straighten a little as she refocused on the rosary in her hands, moving each bead with each syllable of prayer. It almost seemed like she was sliding into an old song as she moved back and forth with each passing of the bead. She seemed unaware of the world around her while the back of my chair found pressure points I didn't know existed. It seemed like I wasn't the only one with this problem as the groaning wood from the seats around me joined my chair in a chorus of creaking.

I listened until the sounds cut off quickly. Something must have happened during Art's speech.

Please, for once let it not be something he did.

I turned, reluctantly watching as he rushed the jury with his hand held high. An unstoppable force with one mission. I scanned the desk quickly, confirming what he'd taken. He had Ann's postmortem photo.

Fuck.

There was a quick flurry from the defense trying to stand up too quickly.

"I object!"

I looked toward him. His short and stocky form seemed to pull his faded black suit to the point before splitting as it tried and mostly failed to fit a frame that had grown just a little too snug over the course of this case. He was an old classmate of mine, around the same age, and practicing for just as long. But he looked like he had aged at least ten to fifteen years more than I had in a small amount of time. I didn't envy the route he took; going into public defense, while noble, was not as well paid or funded. This alone could account for the prematurely graying hair and long-loved but badly-in-need-of-replacing suit. I didn't make much more as a prosecutor, but more money was funneled to our public office than what the defense attorneys got.

I glanced back to his defendant, still focused on prayer. I understood what she did was wrong, but—unlike Art—I didn't agree that the answer was to lock her away. Don't get me wrong, she needed to face some kind of punishment. But she needed support to understand what she'd done more. It wasn't hard

BLUEBIRD AT MY WINDOW

for me or anyone else to see the extent of the fantasy she was trapped in. But Art didn't want to offer any deal that gave her a get-out-of-jail-free card. He was unwilling to look past the life that was taken. A man unaware or happily ignorant to the grays in the world around him.

I turned my attention back to Art as he tried to sidestep whatever the judge had said to engage with the jury again.

I wish he would just breathe.

I was lost in thought for a while, my gaze drifting around the courtroom until a sharp crack on wood snapped through the air around me, bringing me back.

The judge began gathering his things as he said, "Court adjourned."

While I'd been lost in my thoughts, court had ended and Art had taken his seat next to mine. He stared at the judge in front of us, unable to hide his grin.

At least he thinks it went well.

"Coffee?" I asked with a small finger jab to his ribs.

He jumped a little but tried to cover it up with a stretch. "Yeah, sounds good."

We gathered our things and started to walk the few blocks to the closest Starbucks with a small detour to my car to park it in a free spot a few blocks away. Luckily, the parking gods and the fact that tourist season had just passed seemed to have granted me mercy as I'd missed getting a ticket. We were quiet as we walked, both taking in the soft breeze as the scent of the nearby harbor drifted over us—salt spray and fish rot. I never got used to the putrid smell of the ocean even though I'd grown up next to it. I was glad we made it to the coffee shop before my stomach started to turn.

The earthy aroma of coffee hit as soon as the door opened, clearing my nose almost immediately. It was followed shortly by a soft pop song I'd never heard playing a losing battle against the sporadic grind of the espresso. I looked around as we made our way to the counter. There were a few random groups of teens spaced out around the shop, circled around the soft glow of the phones in front of them. A few adults seemed to be in sync with each other as they closed their laptops, folders, and bags, about to filter out as the shop settled into a quieter buzz. We placed our orders, grabbing the coffees when they were done, and made our way to a small table in the back.

"I bet you're ready for this to be over." I let the statement hang out there as an invitation as I stirred sugar into the swirling clouds of cream and basic drip coffee.

Art paused before taking a sip of his black coffee. "I think that's an understatement for both of us. I have to admit I haven't heard much about how Maddie's been holding up through all of this lately."

"She's doing well. She's got a new show coming up in a few weeks, so we have both been pretty busy the last few months.

It's been nice being busy at the same time, especially since we have only wanted to relax at home when we've had any time to ourselves." A small smile tugged at the sides of my lips. "We actually have our third anniversary coming up."

"What? That's fantastic!" He seemed to snap out of his funk, at least for a moment. "Man, I can't believe it's already been three years. Any big plans for the anniversary?"

"Nothing too big." I barely hid a chuckle. "We're probably going to get takeout from Silly's and share a bottle of champagne while marathoning a new show."

He smiled and leaned forward. "Sounds like a perfect night. I'm shocked you two aren't married yet."

Taking a sip, I let the bitter almost acidic bite of the coffee swirl around my tongue before swallowing. "It's not too far off now. We both wanted to make a comfortable living before we did, but the rising rent has made it harder than we thought it would be."

Art scoffed as he leaned back in his chair. "You can say that again. I was just thinking about that this morning before court. Can't believe how much this place has changed in such a short amount of time."

"And it only seems to be getting worse," I replied. "After Maddie's show, we want to start looking for a place to buy, somewhere outside of the city, like in Buxton or Saco."

"Wouldn't want that commute." Art took his coffee in both hands, more interested in looking down at it than drinking.

"I don't mind. I'd rather deal with a few extra minutes than something we could barely afford. Can't even imagine what a house in city limits runs. Don't mind a fixer-upper, but there's no way we're going to pay three times what one is worth just for the sake of saving time in the morning."

"I hear you on that." He replied. I laughed softly as Art put his coffee on the table. He slowly rotated the liquid around the cup, staring just above its depths. "Think I'll be heading out of town too, maybe even the state."

"Yeah? I'm surprised. I thought you had a more solid plan for when you left?"

He shook his head, still staring at his coffee. "It's been hard with this case. Didn't want to apply to anything new or plan too far ahead in case it would force my hand to leave before everything had been settled. I'm ready for a change but didn't want to leave until the case is done."

I was about to ask him another question when both of our phones lit up with a simple text.

Jury's back.

"Shit." Art looked like he wanted to throw his phone on the ground but seemed to settle for squeezing it into his fist instead.

"Already? I don't think we've even been out of court for an hour."

Art looked unable to respond. He didn't have to. A quick turnaround was always an unpredictable one.

**SAME DAY
ARTHUR CASLIN**

By the time we reached the steps of the courthouse, it was already swarming. We had to push through a congested hive of cameras and microphones as we made it back to our table in the courtroom. We'd just made it to our seats when the jury entered, settling into their box. Male, female, old, young; they were all faceless to me at this point. They'd been selected, prepped, and entertained by both sides. Now it was time to see which had played their part better. For Ann's sake, I hoped I'd played mine best.

"Have you all come to a verdict?" the judge asked.

"We have, Your Honor." Behind the juror speaking, the others shifted, turned, and darted their eyes across the crowd, knowing exactly what was about to happen.

"And what decision have you all come to?"

"Not criminally responsible due to mental illness."

The court lost all focus for me then. My vison turned static as it settled on the Bitch. She was falling then writhing on the ground, speaking in tongues of praise as she raised her damned rosary in mockery of whatever God held her favor. Marie grasped my shoulder, bringing the room back into focus. The crowd let out a mixture of cries, both sad and joyful.

I want outrage.

We sat there in silence, watching the room empty. As the sounds faded, I kept reaching for anything but the numbness that greeted me. As the last person slipped out the door, Marie gave my shoulder another small squeeze and wasted the comfort of silence with excuses.

"At least she'll be locked up, Art. She's going to be sent to a hospital where she can't hurt anyone else."

"Yes, 'locked up,' if you can call it that." A tainted laugh eased out. "She'll be living in comfort, knowing exactly what she did."

Marie would never understand. Either by choice or truth, we'd always be at opposite ends of this.

"A medicated life in a sterile environment is hardly decadent. Isn't this enough?" She was pleading, but I couldn't stop.

"That's exactly the point!" I pushed back from the table with a little too much force as my chair held me and bucked to the carpet it caught on. "She'll be in that place while Ann . . . Ann will still be dead. At least in prison, she wouldn't get a choice.

She'd get a cell and an endless amount of time to actually feel what she did." I stood, grabbing my files, shoving them back into my case before turning to look at Marie. "Now for kicks and giggles she can erase the guilt, live in fucking medicated ignorance. Where is the justice in that?"

Marie turned bright red as I broke whatever patience she had left. "God dammit, Art, grow up." She pushed herself back and up with far more restraint and purpose than I'd displayed. "Medicated or not, we did our job."

I was unable to hide my bitterness. "Great. Another bandage on this gaping wound of a city."

"Art."

I rested my hand on her shoulder, giving in to the small bit of kindness I had left. "You know it's true. You've seen how meaningless this all is. Rulings change from person to person, innocent or guilty. Justice is the last thing that happens here."

I let go of her shoulder, pausing only for a moment to pick up my things before walking away.

Marie came after, tugging at a small part of my sleeve. "Don't . . . Art, please. Let's go do something, blow off steam."

She didn't understand. Her fingers slipped as I spoke without looking back. I didn't want whatever hope she had left. Not this time.

"You know I can't."

I let the doors close behind me for the last time, relishing the fact that I'd never have to stand here or put on a show ever again.

I was done.

26

SAME DAY
MARIE PERAULT

I pushed past the space he'd made through the court doors, catching him. He didn't get to run away, not this time. Whether he went with me or not, we would end the conversation on my terms, not his. With my hand pressing into his chest, it was hard not to feel his frustration and anger beat hard and heavy against my palm. His muscles tightened and pulled him further into his resolve.

He was so ready to run but was unable to, so I took a chance.

"At least walk me back to my car. I promise to talk about something else."

He took a moment before allowing his breath to ease him back. "Okay."

I paused a half step before moving to his side, and we made our way to the entrance. The courthouse was more museum than zoo now; the cameras and reporters, satisfied with their soundbites, had disappeared back into their respective holes. It was nice like this, peaceful. My favorite time to be in the court-house. When the crowds thinned to nothing, and the echoes of the day receded. The presence of every person who'd walked down the halls that day with their fears, pain, or joy clung to me. Reminding me why I did what I did.

The click of my heels took up the silence between us as I glanced toward him. It was easy to see he was lost in his own world, but I didn't have enough time to pull him back. I had a handful of minutes at most with no certainty I'd see him again any time soon.

No pressure.

As I walked through the front doors, I relished the crisp eve-ning air washing over me.

"Looks like fall is just around the corner." I wrapped myself in my arms as a slight chill set in. I'd have to start bringing a heavier jacket to work from now on.

"True. Have to say I won't miss the winters if I go."

I didn't need to see him to know he was looking straight ahead, so I followed his lead. If it's the future he wanted to talk about, we would do that. "Thinking you may head somewhere warm?"

I watched as his face brightened slightly. "Maybe? I've thought of heading south in my car till I hit someplace nice.

Kind of like the idea of just heading off into the sunset with no direction."

"Okay, cowboy," I couldn't help but tease. "Wouldn't that mean you should head west then? Think you'd hit the great lakes or one of the Dakotas instead, and I've heard the winters can be worse."

"Ha ha, smartass. I think I just like the idea of picking up and searching for something that fits instead of waiting for it." He stopped at the crosswalk for a second before hitting the button and turning to me. "Honestly, I'm not sure what or where that thing will be waiting for me. Just know it's not in law or a courtroom." His eyes softened at the truth.

I gave his shoulder a small squeeze, hoping he'd take it as encouragement. "I'm sure you'll find it, whatever it ends up being."

A thought seemed to flicker and catch. "I could become a woodworker."

His eyes narrowed, waiting for me to take the bait.

"I'd like to see that." I shoved him back as I laughed. "Have you ever even picked up a tool before?"

"Of course I have. I'm not completely useless." He paused and leaned closer as he whispered, "Plus, I already know the secret to picking it up quickly."

"Oh, please, I am absolutely riveted."

"I just need to turn into one of those lumbersexuals."

God, I hated that word. I brought my hands to my stomach as the laughter rippled through me. The light changed and we made our way across the street. I tried not to pause and catch my breath as the walk sign ticked down ahead, but my lungs were burning for air.

"C'mon now, the light's changing . . . unless this is your way of trying to test me." He squatted just in front of me in what looked like a poor attempt at a body building pose before continuing, "M'lady, I may not be wearing plaid, but let me jettison you to safety on mine shoulders!"

"Stop . . . my sides hurt." I did my best to control the laughter. "Truthfully, if anyone is *jettisoning* the other to safety, it'll be me."

"Hey, I may be slim but the muscles in this frame are deceptively strong." He took a few prancing steps before stopping on the curb to throw more poses this way and that, and sticking out a hand for me to grab.

I quickly closed the space between us and veered just enough to take a place beside him as the light turned.

"Uh-huh, sure, that's why you always came to me when you needed a jar opened at the office."

Art threw up his hands, flourishing each word between us with as much emphasis as possible. "I did that to build up your confidence! You were new and I wanted you to feel like you had at least one advantage over my staggering perfection."

I scoffed as we continued down the street. "All right, Mr. Perfect. Tell me more about how becoming a *lumbersexual* will unlock your knowledge of woodworking."

He threw his arm over my shoulder and pressed me in, drawing me close as if the secret he held was too precious to lose.

"It's the beard."

"The beard?"

"Yeah! When paired with plaid and an impressive collection of craft brews, the secrets of the lumbersexual can be unlocked from the depths of my fine manly hairs." He released me, his arms continuing to exaggerate the story he was trying to sell me.

I laughed again, shorter this time, before giving as deep a curtsy as my skirt would allow and sweeping my arm to the side. "Well then, oh great and manly one, you'll have to teach me of these truths before you leave. But for now, my lowly chariot awaits anon."

"As you wish." He gave back an over-flourished bow before snapping back into normalcy. "Mine is back a street and farther down, near town hall."

This was the Art I knew and loved, the one who had shut down too easily after Kate left. "Do you want a ride?"

"No, I'm good. I think I want to take in the cool air while I can."

He started to turn, heading into the oncoming twilight around us, but I had to reach out just one more time. "Hey,

I was serious about us meeting up. I want to grab a drink or something before you disappear into the woods and start communing with the wildlife about beard oils."

He smiled. "Of course."

He started to walk away again as the words slipped out. "I missed this. Thought I'd lost you completely to the case this time."

His eyes softened and he smirked sadly. "You weren't the only one. I'll give you a call soon, kid."

I watched him make his way back to his car for a few moments before I opened my bag and searched for my keys in its depths. My fingers grazed then grasped the cool, almost musical jangle of my keychain just as a heavy presence behind me seemed to pull at me with the stench of hard liquor and familiarity.

A voice slurred, "Well look who's back, boys. I think this . . . is what some would call fate."

I released my keys on instinct as I reached for Josie and turned. It wasn't until my eyes rested on the man from this morning only a few feet away that I remembered.

I wanted to break the glass between me and the glovebox, but I'd never make it in time. Instead, I stared down the balding man and his two slightly bigger friends all dressed in the same worn sportswear, a ragtag team of fools. At least, I hoped they were.

The bald man was staring directly into my face, his beady eyes peering through the swollen flesh that surrounded them, waiting. "Not so chatty now, are we?"

I slipped my hand out of my purse and prepared for whatever came next. He looked quickly at my hand, bracing for the weapon he thought I had.

Shit. You stupid fucking idiot.

A smile inched across his face as he closed the space between us. "No, not so chatty at all."

SAME DAY
ARTHUR CASLIN

Her words had hit. They were similar to what Kate had said before collapsing onto the bag she'd been packing. Though unlike Marie, Kate believed she had lost me.

The feather-light mood from moments earlier turned heavy as I walked away. I'd made it to the corner when a scream broke the evening air around me. It was deep and guttural, almost feral. Confused, I looked back toward Marie. She was standing there, hands raised, holding her ground as three men rushed her.

I didn't think. I just reacted. Dropping everything, I sprinted toward the mass of bodies in front of me as they writhed around her struggling frame. They were trying to pin her against the car, but she was fighting too hard to make it easy. Their lack of organization was giving her a chance. The smaller balding man was the only one who seemed to have a plan. Before I was able to make it to Marie's side, he shouted to his companions to hold her down as he "Shut the cunt up." He was choking her now. I tried to go faster but I was still at least five feet out. That's when Marie nailed him in the groin with her knee.

I need to help her get free.

I changed tactics and focused on the taller one to her right just as he realized I was there. I used my momentum to smash him against the car. The stench of alcohol and sweat stung my nose as I pinned him against the cool metal. The dumb fuck was giving a wide empty stare as his mouth hung open, trying to gasp for the air I'd knocked from him. Without thinking, I drew my fist back and landed a few blows before he regrouped. Suddenly, I got hit from the left. The right side of my body smashed into the ground as my head bounced off the pavement that had broken my fall. A mass of weight pinned me down, pressing the air out of me as my face smashed again and again into the unforgiving pavement in front of me. I pushed up against whoever had me pinned, but I couldn't help but crumple under their mass and continued blows to my head and back.

Another scream ripped through the night.

Head spinning, I freed my arm that had been pinned underneath me and used it to hook around the guy on top of me, pulling him off balance. I took a quick scan and saw that the taller guy I'd been on earlier had fallen to the ground, still trying to catch his breath, while the balding guy sat perched on top of Marie.

What the fuck is he doing to her?

The rage was building inside of me, the tremors calming into focus as I let the anger grow and take control. Even the edges of my vision bent to it as I saw the Short Fuck rip Marie's clothes as she fought him.

A crack of pain hit me across the jaw. The Average Fuck who had been on top of me had gotten loose from my hold. He stood above me with a crooked smile arching across his pocked face. I pushed myself up into a kneeling position, every muscle within me tense, ready for the attack. Fury carved through me, catching between my teeth; I wanted to charge but his eyes made me pause. There was a glint of joy within them. He was getting some sick pleasure out of this. I realized, glaring back, what I was to him. A bonus.

How empty can you be to need this?

Lunging, I struck him with more force than I thought was possible. He wasn't smiling anymore. His feet buckled under him as the uneven pavement stole his balance. I took this opportunity to introduce his face to my knee and then the pavement. He was dazed but I didn't want to take any chances, hitting him as my knuckles bruised and split against his skull. But there was no pain, only a high . . . a release.

When I glanced up, I saw a group of twenty-something kids off in the distance, but they had to be close enough to see what was happening. I screamed, pleading with them to call the police just as I saw the Short Fuck crack Marie's head on the concrete.

Rage licked at the back of my throat as I let a guttural scream out. Forget the Average Fuck beneath me, or the Tall Fuck grasping the side of the car trying to stand. The Short Fuck was next. I closed the distance between us, putting everything I had into a kick aimed at the back of his head. The impact threw him from her, may have even knocked him out, but I was past the point of stopping. Alternating from stomps to kicks, I aimed for his back, head, arms—anything within reach. Until the Tall Fuck tackled me from the side. I'd seen him coming but he wasn't the one I wanted.

I hit the ground harder than expected as my head smashed against the concrete. I realized this was the last of one too many hits as my vision began to fail, so I punched, kicked, and screamed as fists and feet filled what vision I had left.

Then I was gone.

Is this death?

An empty, ink-stained void took hold of my body, sapping any fight and pain left in it.

A flash of light, a beam paired with pressure to my face danced through the shadows. Back and forth, a rhythmic pendulum.

Did someone say "reactive"?

Arms wrapped around me as I slipped away.

Time was passing again; I counted it in luminous orbs now moving above me. The bed beneath me was hard and flat, clicking in time with each passing glow.

Voices hummed in chorus, too hard to make out, to pin down. My eyelids were heavy and thick, almost immovable, opening to slits for a second before snapping closed.

I'd seen enough—the white of a coat getting lost in florescent light. Someone was trying to help.

I wanted to let myself fade again, but something was clawing at the corners of my mind to stay awake. My thoughts sunk through molasses.

I'm not dead after . . .

Marie.

Forcing my eyes open, I fought against the swelling and pressure that met me. I refused to close them as I searched. The world blurred and moved around me, but I found it: a hand next to my own, grasping a metal bar. I grabbed it tightly, pushing words thick and unyielding from my lips. "Marie, is she . . . ?"

Kind eyes bent to meet mine as thin, firm fingers gently loosened my grip and placed my hand on my chest.

"Sir, right now you're our biggest worry."

Another voice. "Do you remember your name?"

Another. "Sir?"

I opened my mouth, but silence hung in the air as the darkness returned, bringing the burning tang of bile.

Hands guided my face to the side as I emptied myself into nothing.

SAME DAY
DIANE LOUCKS

Devils were everywhere.

My home had been taken from me and replaced with a new hell. I was surrounded by so many, but no one would listen. They told me I was headed somewhere new, that I'd get the help I needed. But they were the ones who needed saving. I tried screaming, smashing myself into the bars, anything for them to look at me and actually see, to listen.

I'm not responsible, they said I wasn't responsible.

I hadn't felt the needle, but the burning itch flooding through my veins had been too much.

They told me to breathe
To let it take hold

H. NOAH

I was tired of being trapped in my own body

My mind

I just wanted them to listen
To have seen when I showed them the signs of the devil on her
body,
How I only tried to save
But they only stared
Carved out what was left
With their *help*

This help had drowned out my grace
strengthened the demons
As my head rolled against the concrete floor
slowly gaining control of my own body
I listened.
BITCH You're fucked so fucked YOU FUCKI—
Shhhhhh through Him you are saved
PRAY, Sister, pray
Pray
I know you miss it
Sister, Pray
PRAY

Hands grabbed me,

Dressed in white

With no faces

I tried to touch the smooth surface

Shining

And

Empty

It grabbed my wrist, handcuffing me to chains now around my

feet and waist.

Heavy

It was hard to walk so they dragged me to the van.

I tapped the handcuffs against the hard plastic frame of the

bench.

I promised not to run as they locked me inside

That I couldn't

But they just watched.

There was a boy across from me

Dressed in the same white.

He flinched when I hit the metal against the plastic

A reaction

So I did it again with a prayer

Tap.

Tap.

Tap.

H. NOAH

In the van we rocked back and forth, two souls on an ill-fated
ship.

Tap.

Tap.

Tap.

I could smell the sin in him as he broke from my gaze to look
down

I stared, but he wouldn't look up.

Only at my hands.

The devil bows to the holy.

Even when dressed in white

He held the keys,

What power he must have felt.

Men were always looking for power.

Especially the boys

finding control

In the pain

they designed.

I'd made the mistake of revealing my grace.

The burden of my blessing

To hear the angels.

They didn't understand why I wanted to keep them
To rid myself of the devils that my daughter had bred.

I wanted to scream again
To hear my voice,
My prayer.
To go home.
But they wouldn't take me back,
Said I'd be safe where I was going
I just wanted to be home.
Suddenly someone spoke to my right

Are you praying?

"Mother?" I turned to find her, but she wasn't there.
The others answered.
You will be ours
Let her burn
This is your fault

But there she was again, this time to my left.
You need to pray more.
"Yes, Mother."
I closed my eyes and let my body sway to the waves of motion
around me.

"Our Father who art in heaven"
This helped.
It always helped.
"Hallowed be thy name.
Blessed are,
you among women
and blessed is the
fruit of your womb."

There was a music to prayer, I let the words pulse and pause
according to the grace inside me.
The words that needed to be prayed always had a way of float-
ing up
Of pulsing to life.

"Forgive us our trespasses.
As we forgive those.
Who trespass against
Us

Who
Trespass
Against
Us."

Yes, that was it, this was a test, I would be redeemed as I'd been saved in the eyes of the Lord.

This was a sign.

I opened my eyes and stared into the dark pools of the boy's eyes waiting for me.
They were framed in dark curls, from above.
And dark circles, from below.

Soulless.

I could save him too.
Just as I had Ann.
My lips upturned to the grace inside me.
Resonating in certainty of God's plan.

The boy turned away.
But he would be saved,
We would all be saved.

SAME DAY
MADDIE MORI

'd started to panic. Marie hadn't come home or answered any of my calls. I tried to call Art, but the phone just kept ringing. That's when I tried Marie's office and the secretary told me.

Not her boss. Not the police. Not even a doctor.

Marie might be dead.

It felt like the world was falling away, ripping me from the inside out as jagged edges snagged on precious things.

Breathe.

I can't.

I grabbed my chest under the weight of it, my lungs a prickling burn of breathlessness.

You're almost there.

Breathe.

After I ordered the car, I drained my battery trying to get someone to talk to me, but all they said was "she's in critical condition" and "we can't release that information." It felt like they were saying everything but what they wanted to. The things that hid beneath the pause, the shift in tone.

The things I'd found in the south in cracked ribs as green phlegm dripped slowly down my cheek. Those who had been friends laughing as they beat the sin from me, how I'd turned to my family's faces hours later only to see it reflected again.

Outed without a promise of safety.

The car jolted me back as it stopped in front of the ER. Clutching my phone and bag to me, I bolted from the car and through the doors of the ER.

Breathe.

I bit back the tears as I stared at the pale nurse in front of me. A sea of white and blue. I'd need to be calm when I asked. My skin marked me as different. Adding queer to it could be too much; I couldn't be more than they could handle.

I took a slow breath, smoothing out my clothes, placing my phone into my bag as I hung it from my shoulder and walked toward her with a practiced smile.

The nurse was sitting relaxed behind the small two-person desk, twirling the end of her long blond ponytail. She was a petite older woman; I thought she'd been taller at first but saw as I reached the desk that she was propped up by a leg tucked tightly underneath her. It only took a moment for her to notice me, to look up and return the smile I still wore. "How can I help you?"

"Hi, I'm here for Marie Perault. She was admitted earlier this evening."

I saw a flash of gold from the front of her scrubs. A cross. My stomach knotted instantly.

Doesn't mean anything, not yet.

"Ahh, here she is. Are you family?"

"I'm her girlfriend. She doesn't have any family."

I could see it—the moment her face dropped just enough. "Oh . . . well, I can't release any information to someone who isn't family."

I pushed down the panic, tightening my hands into fists just out of sight. "I understand, but I'm her emergency contact. The paperwork should be with her primary doctor."

She turned back to her computer as she sifted through whatever information was in front of her, bristling. "It's not in the system, so I can't release the information. You'll have to talk to her family."

I want to scream.

"Her parents are dead; she doesn't have anyone but me." I couldn't hide the edge in my voice this time. I watched as it curdled the woman's features in front of me.

"You don't need to take that tone with me. Until I have the paperwork in front of me, I can't help you."

Breathe.

I tried again. "Is there a way to access her doctor's files? I can give you the name . . ."

I've pushed too far.

"You'll need to collect the files yourself. We're busy with intakes tonight and trying to save your . . . *friend.* I suggest taking a seat or leaving."

I looked around the not even half full room as a panicked laugh left my lips. When I turned back a security guard had appeared, double my size, standing next to the nurse. Same fair skin and blond hair—could have been related for all I knew.

"Do we have a problem here?"

I tried to regain my composure. "No, I—" Looking to the nurse and catching sight of her name tag, I tried one last plea. "Beth, please. Just tell me she's okay."

She wouldn't even look at me. The guard took a step and I walked away.

"Bet she's just worried about her green card," Beth said more than loud enough for me to hear.

My body froze for just a second as those words, red hot and searing, hollowed what resolve I had left.

There it was.

A reminder that I'd always be an other, someone never obliged the same respect.

I couldn't keep it down.

The anger.

The Panic.

Frustration chewed at the inside of my cheek, knowing there was nothing left to salvage. Turning around, I stared at Beth's laughing face until she saw me looking. Her face dropped just a fraction, just enough to show she knew the weight of the words she had so easily dropped.

"I'm a citizen, you spineless cunt."

I didn't wait for her to respond, for the guard to react. I just turned and left, calmly walking through the open doors. I hadn't won—never would. But it felt good to take a piece of myself back from them. The part that had made itself less for someone else's comfort.

As soon as I was far enough, I called the person I knew would talk to me.

The phone rang once, twice, then clicked. Before she had time to answer, I blurted, "Deb, Marie's hurt and they won't let me see her."

I could hear the confusion switching to action. "Whoa, hon, what happened? Is Marie okay?"

"I don't know, they won't tell me anything. The secretary said she and Art had been attacked after leaving court . . . that she might die."

"We don't know that for sure." Deb cut me off as soon as the words had left my mouth and kept going. She'd always been good at getting me to focus, bringing me back from myself, but this was different.

This is Marie.

Just this morning, she'd traced my face with her fingertips as she'd woken up, kissed a line from my forehead to my chin as I refused to move with her and say goodbye like she'd wanted.

Marie. My Marie could be cold and lifeless.

The hot tears I'd been holding started streaming down my cheeks. Deb interrupted, "Where are you? Are you at the hospital?"

My breath shook as I answered, "I'm here, but they won't look for the paperwork that says they can talk to me."

"Fucking assholes." I could feel the venom in her words, the same frustration I felt.

"What do I do, Deb? What if she's . . ." I couldn't get the rest out. A sob choked the rest of the words.

Deb didn't even try to let me finish before responding, "What if you called the office again? Told them what was happening. Do you think someone would help?"

I took in what she said, trying to think. "Maybe? I'm not sure."

"Give it a try, Maddie, I'll be there soon. This throwing class is almost done."

Breathe.

"Okay," I responded as the feeling inside of me started to untangle.

"It's going to be okay, Maddie. I have to go, but text me where you are."

"I will."

The phone clicked and I was alone again, leaning against the side of the hospital as the city kept moving around me like normal. I gave in to what I was feeling, letting the tears fall until I had used up enough.

Marie needs me, and I need her to be okay.

ARTHUR CASLIN

The darkness slid into lighter shades of gray as I came back. It was bright, my eyelids failing to block the warm glow on the other side. My thoughts thick and unyielding as my body started to relax within the warmth around me. There was music, soft electric sounds, rhythmic and tonal, but I couldn't open my eyes, not completely. So I forced them into slits. Seeing white, a window, and metal machines. Too tired to keep them open, too tired to worry. I slipped back into sleep as the machines hummed and sighed.

I keep losing time.

The light was back, paired with a sharp smell. I took a breath as awareness started to spread throughout my body. The fragrance of flowers and stale antiseptic hit me as I wiggled my toes and gently clenched my fists toward me as I tried to lift my arms, a heavy throb of pain joining the confusion as my left caught on something with a sharp searing pull. I went to pull harder but a hand pressed my forearm down softly and firmly. I had to see, so I focused everything I had into opening my eyes, pushing them past the slit I'd managed before, but they wouldn't open completely.

Swelling?

I tried to take in the room around me, but florescent lights flooded my vision instead. They unearthed the slow pulse of a headache that had been dormant moments before, and I groaned.

Well, I must be alive to feel this fucked.

"Good to see you, Arthur." The voice was soft, leathery, and attached to the weight on my arm.

I closed my eyes, processing the familiar voice, my mind's faulty gears seizing and skipping with the effort. I opened my eyes again, the lights dimming at my second try. On my left was a large silhouette haloed in light. They were close, hand still on my arm, but it was too bright to see.

Then it clicked.

"Hey, boss." My voice raw as the words raked across the desert in my mouth.

"You sound about as good as you look."

I cracked what I hoped was a smile at the attempted humor and replied, "I'd say you should see the other guy, but there were three so who knows."

My eyes still needed to adjust but his tall soft frame shifted as he settled back into the chair, more plastic than cushion. He was wearing his usual suit, so I couldn't tell if it was the weekend or after work. The only thing I could figure out was that it was too bright to be the middle of the night.

"Oh, you definitely left something to remember you by on each." The chair he was in creaked as he shifted again in amusement.

My eyes had started to adjust to the light as he gave my arm a small squeeze. I looked down at the mottled purple bruises across my arm; they contrasted with his dark skin.

No wonder he didn't squeeze harder.

"How are you feeling?"

I gave a small laugh. "I've definitely had better days, but so far it's manageable."

Suddenly panic compressed my chest as I remembered. "Marie, is she . . . ?"

I let the question hang in the air, not able to finish it.

Richard must have known as he leaned back in to touch the side of my bed. "She's alive but not out of the woods yet. Seems like she suffered some pretty severe brain trauma, and the doctors induced a coma to help with the healing."

She's alive.

"Well, one of the last things I remember seeing is that Short Fuck slamming her head repeatedly against the concrete."

Richard stiffened in his chair as he raised a hand to rub his face. "My God . . ."

Poor choice in words, Richard. God had nothing to do with this.

He took a moment before asking, "How did this all happen?"

I tried to lift myself into a more seated position, but my body screamed against my resolve, so I let it sink back with a grimace.

"That's the thing. I'm not sure. I'd just walked her to her car after court and started toward mine when I heard her scream. When I turned, there were three guys rushing her."

Richard rubbed his hands roughly on his face before running them across his short-cropped hair.

"I knew it."

"Knew what?" I asked.

"The men who were taken in said that you both threatened and attacked them first, but their stories weren't matching up. They said something about her having a knuckle knife?"

Rage seeped into me, cutting into words. "That's a crock of shit. Even I could see she was unarmed from where I was."

"Well then it's good most of them are behind bars. The shorter gentleman you mentioned is still here with more extensive injuries, but it's not even close to what happened to you or Marie. Luckily, the judge didn't want to give them bond until we knew more."

"I need to see Marie." I tried to lift myself again, but the same burning pain changed into a tearing sear that crept down my arm as I tried to fight against it.

Richard stood just enough so he could press me back down into the pillows behind me. "Whoa, Arthur, they aren't letting anyone in to see her. She's still in a fragile state."

I relaxed against his hand, letting him guide me back as he continued, "Also, if you keep trying to get up like that you'll tear your IV out."

I looked down.

So that's what that pain was.

"Tell me they at least let Maddie in?"

"No, that's why I'm here. The admins made just about every excuse they could with them not being married or blood relatives, and they wouldn't accept the documents we had since they weren't written according to their own specific protocols. But I had a few connections and was able to change that roadblock a little earlier. Maddie should be able to see her this afternoon without any issues."

"That's absolutely ridiculous. I can't believe they wouldn't let her in."

"I agree, but it should be fixed."

With my eyes adjusting, the exhaustion lining his face was more apparent. Must have been a bigger fight then he let on, but I knew better than to ask. "Have you seen her?"

"No, not yet. The doctor I went above was pretty upset when I last saw him. So, I didn't want to push things further. That's why I'm here. Figured you'd want the company even if you were unconscious through most of it."

"Thanks, Richard."

"No problem, though I think I better head out. I should probably make it into the office sometime today, but I'm glad I was able to talk to you for a bit." Chuckling a little as he got up, he continued, "I have to admit you haven't been as entertaining as you usually are the last few times I've dropped in."

I tried to give him a sappy apologetic glance as I pushed through the pain. "Hey, I can't be on all the time."

Richard moved over to my bed, placing a hand on my shoulder. "Who knew being conscious was such a vital part of your personality?" His look hardened as he grew more serious. "It's good to see you awake."

We didn't have to say anything as we gave each other a nod of understanding. For the first time in a while, it felt like we were having the kind of conversation we used to, the kind when I started, when I was still someone to believe in.

As he turned to leave, I had to ask, "Hey, could you take a peek at Marie on your way out? I know she'll be asleep, but it would be nice to hear how she looks from someone who knows her. If you can't, it's okay."

"I'll do my best, Arthur. Try to get some rest."

I watched him open the door and disappear out of view before I searched for any kind of call button. The pain had been slowly building and I needed something to take the edge off. It took a few moments before I found the cool smooth surface of the plastic remote. It had been hidden in the sheets to the right.

"Bingo."

SEPTEMBER 4, 2017
RICHARD KOCH

rthur was in rough shape. Deep blue and purple clung to most of his skin with a sickly sunset of lighter greens and yellows starting to break through. A part of me was surprised by how well he was doing, everything considered. It was the first time in a while where it didn't seem like either of us were calculating each word between us. I waited as a group of nurses passed quickly in front of me. Determined and focused, they were either headed home or to some new emergency.

The hall was relatively quiet for an ICU, or at least quieter than I thought it should be. It reminded me of the people here in Maine. Quiet and steady, not rushing to meet the world but always ready to receive it. It was probably my own nostalgia for the state and what it tried to be, but the only thing that really stuck out among the sea of white faces, white coats, and scrubs were the people in blue. You didn't have to look too far to see a cop. They stayed grouped between Marie's and Arthur's rooms with only a few milling around, looking uneasy and out of place. What happened had been a shock for everyone here, like stepping through the top of an underground hornet's nest. Arthur and Marie weren't cops but apparently they were close enough to it to cause disruption within the cop community.

With the growth of the city, it was bound to happen but still unbelievable when it did. Problem was, without the whole story the incident had taken on a life of its own. Everyone wanted the details even if that meant creating the narrative themselves. This is why the cops were still here in so many numbers. They never calmed when there was uncertainty—more willing to act, to say they did something, than trying to understand the parts of the picture they had.

Thank God for Carter.

After all these years, I still hadn't met anyone else like him. He meant well like the rest of the cops I'd met, but he was one of the few that did something about it and led others to do the same. He may not have had control over the detectives on this case, but he had control of those shifting around me.

Turning left toward the elevators, I walked toward the group of white cops in front of Marie's door. I recognized a few from my visits to the precinct. Gibbs, though in his late thirties, was still as tall and lanky as a teenage boy and about as graceful as one too. The only thing that balanced him out was the start of wrinkles on his pale, thin, sharp face and the grays poking out in his short light-brown hair. Across from him was Blake; he had to have barely broken twenty that year, but from what Carter said he had a great future ahead of him. He was much shorter than the men around him and less in shape, with a rosy complexion and more freckles than I could count. It was hard to tell how much came from skin tone or the shock of red hair loosely controlled on his head. Carter said he was bright and driven, someone who'd be behind a detective's desk in no time if he wanted it. In between the two both in age and height was Carter's second in command, Rosenberg. It was easy to see what Carter saw in him—what most people on the force did. He'd done his time and built up a great reputation for himself and would likely be leaving soon for higher ranks. Something visible in the way he stood and carried himself in general. Even without his confidence he was an impressive figure, the kind of cop seen in most shows these days—built of muscle and grit with hair black enough to still be visible even with it so closely cropped to his scalp and tanned skin underneath. They were all standing huddled in a loose semi-circle, shifting on feet more used to moving, not watching. I took a chance and approached.

Their first names escaped me; it was hard to keep track when they used their last names just as casually. So, I went with the safest choice. "Officers."

Rosenberg looked up, eager for any distraction. "Richard, good to see you again. Are you checking in on your people?"

I swallowed his easy familiarity. "Yes, just got done talking to Arthur and thought I might check on Marie next."

"He's talking?"

I knew what he really wanted to ask, so I did my best to side-step. "He is, but he's still in rough shape. I wouldn't be surprised if he passed out after I left."

"Still good to hear. Most of us heard he'd been waking up but fading out just as quick. One of the nurses thought he might be gorked. Definitely good to hear he's still got something shaking around in there." Rosenberg crossed his arms in satisfaction, still more cock than common sense at times but he had a good heart. Just some more growing up to do. Something he still had a lot of time left for at twenty-seven.

"Hey, would it be okay if I popped my head in really quick, just to see how she's doing?"

Rosenberg looked a little unsure. I was hoping my friendship with his boss would at least weigh a little in my request. I didn't have to wait long as his expression cleared with the click of an idea I saw written across his face.

"Well, technically the doc said she needed rest, but me and the boys were just about to grab a quick cup of coffee from the break room over there. If someone were to pop in and take a quick look before leaving, there wouldn't be much harm in that."

He reached out his hand. "It was good to see you. Make sure to update Sergeant Ganley if Arthur said anything of interest."

I shook his hand, firm, strong, and just a little too eager for a chance to step away. "Good to see you too, and will do."

Rosenburg walked away with the other two in tow, nodding reassurance to the other officers who raised their heads in concern. I walked to Marie's door; it was hard to see any part of her just by looking through the glass. A plain blue curtain blocked most of the room from sight. The only part of her visible was her feet, pale and too white, even against the off-white sheets. The doctor or nurses must have pulled them back to do something and forgot to drape it again. One foot was covered but the toes of the other peeped out from under the cover. I knew she was in a coma, but I still opened the door as gingerly as possible. If there was even the smallest chance she was able to hear, the last thing I wanted to do was scare her.

As I walked closer across the yellowed linoleum, more and more of her became visible. Her feet gave way to her legs and torso, covered by the sheet. It wasn't until I'd reached the foot of her bed that I saw any sign of the attack. The skin of her feet didn't give an accurate depiction; everywhere else was so badly bruised, her skin looked closer to shades of black than purple. Though the darker shades of color couldn't hide the scrapes, cuts, and swelling that covered her body, especially around her face. If someone came in and said I had the wrong room, I'd believe them. Her head was so tightly wrapped in bandages I couldn't even make out the color of her hair, or if it was still there at all. I drew my eyes back to the sheets, unable to look directly at her face, the white a calmer contrast to the broken capillaries just underneath.

She looks dead.

That thought curled within me, hitting on more things than I wanted to process. So I turned back from them to her. The tubes and lines that ran from her body were attached to machines breathing for her, each small rise and fall in her chest in sync with beeps and a mechanical motion of their own.

You're staying too long; you need to go.

But I didn't want to. Being somewhere I wasn't exactly supposed to be—surrounded by cops—didn't do much to put me at ease, but I had gotten an okay.

I reached out, gently moving the sheet to cover her toes before resting my hand on them.

"Hey, Marie, it's Richard."

The words rolled out soft and soothing. I wouldn't leave without her knowing a friend was there.

"Just saw Arthur. Looks like he got by just a bit better than you. He was talking a little, wanted to come by."

Listening to the sounds of the machines surrounding her, I could almost pick up a beat, a sort of rhythm in the way they kept her alive.

"Maddie misses you. She wanted to be here, but policy... was policy. Don't worry, though. I fixed it and she'll be here soon."

I paused again, listening to the slow inhale and exhale of the machine as if it were a response. I admit I was shocked, especially that any of this had happened to Marie. She was levelheaded, more capable of thinking on her feet than Arthur. Someone I saw taking over my own job when I left. I couldn't picture this happening to her, but I guess this sort of thing just can.

"Well, I better go before my luck runs out." I squeezed her toes lightly before removing my hand. "I'll be back soon."

Taking a step back, I started to turn just as the door clicked, cracking open to the world behind it.

"*Stop, don't move.*" The voice was more shaken than commanding, but this wasn't the time to test it. Now was the time to follow, to freeze, as I searched for a way to calm the situation. Whoever it was must not have seen me get Rosenburg's okay.

You were here too long.

I waited.

And waited.

Anxiety and anger never mixed well. Then Carter's voice called out, "Officer, what the fuck do you think you're doing to the city's DA? Richard, you can relax. Officer Rosenburg said you might be here."

Each muscle flooded with relief at those words. I didn't have to deescalate, a bitter consolation clawing at the inside of me as

I tried to ignore the sound of a gun strap being clicked back into place. I turned to the officer I didn't recognize, watched as the gravity of the situation drained the color from his face. There was nothing remarkable about him, at least from what I could see; only his bright platinum-blond hair stood out among forgettable features. His voice warbled as it reached for something to say that would see him safely to the other side of this.

"I saw a stranger and reacted. Thought one of the perpetrators had come back to . . ."

I wasn't surprised he addressed Carter first. Kid was as green as I'd ever seen a cop. Must have been added within the last few weeks if not less. Even if he wasn't green, the intention in what he left out read clearer than the words he'd chosen.

Not that it mattered to Carter. It never did. "I don't remember any of her attackers being described as Black. Do you, Mullaly?"

The kid stuttered, practically choked on his own words.

Carter didn't wait. "Enough. You and I will discuss this later. Right now, apologize and leave."

The young officer turned almost too quickly to face me, his boots seeking resistance against the floor. "I'm sorry, sir."

I nodded; I wasn't about to tell him it was all right.

Not the time or place, Richard. Don't let it show.

It was hard to swallow, but true. The only thing helping this thought settle into place was the knowledge that Carter would say the things I wanted to when he talked to the kid. The same things I'd said to Carter as we'd grown closer over the years. He'd been more open to the conversations most people didn't want to hear. It's why we'd grown closer; he'd never understand what it was like, but he tried to listen and do what he could. When the cry for Black lives had rung through the streets a few years ago, he'd listened, tried to do better, and held others to the same. At least when it came to those under his control.

I looked at Carter, knowing I didn't have to say it, didn't have to say anything.

"Sorry about that. We should get out of here, though. Her doctor was pretty pissed about visitors the last time I saw him. You didn't have anything to do with that, did you?"

I smiled as I walked to the door. "Did you hear they weren't letting Marie's partner in?"

Carter scoffed. "I heard. Absolute bullshit on their end. Glad you were able to straighten it out."

"You and me both." I sighed.

We were back in the hallway now. Most of the officers had scattered, taking refuge in groups much farther away. Even with the small distance between us, Carter leaned in as he spoke in a lower tone. "Rosenburg said that Arthur talked to you. Did he say anything about what happened?"

I wasn't exactly surprised by this question. "From the sounds of it, Marie was unarmed when she got ambushed by the three suspects. Arthur tried to help but was outnumbered. I'd wait to talk to him, though. He still seems out of it from the hits he took. More groggy than confused."

Carter let out a curt laugh as he shook his head and looked over my shoulder at Arthur's room. "His story makes more sense. With the rap sheet those three have, I would've been shocked to hear anything else. As I was leaving, they were wrapping up interviews with a few witnesses, which from the sounds of it will corroborate his story."

I crossed my arms as I let a hand drift up to rub my chin, the start of stubble scraping gently against my hand.

Carter continued, "They got there late but said the three suspects had been the aggressors and that there'd been no knife that they had seen. They also said Arthur had called out for help and the police. Luckily, they'd already called. Can't imagine what would have happened if they'd waited. From the sounds of it, the three had already done a number on them both by the time they saw what was happening."

My words seemed to catch. Only thing that got out was a strained "Damn."

Carter took a step back. I glanced at my watch while he took in the men around him. He wanted to talk but I was running later than I should be. "I'd love to catch up but I'm already overdue in the office. How about we grab a coffee soon? Didn't Britney just turn seventeen?"

Carter laughed. "That she did. Celebrated with us just long enough to eat some cake and open her gift before bolting to spend the rest of the night with her friends."

"Could have been worse."

Carter leaned in again as he gave me a few pats to my upper back. "That's for sure. God knows I did worse at her age. All right, well it was good talking to you. I'll shoot you a text later to try and see when you're free."

"Sounds good, talk to you soon." Carter walked away as I turned toward the elevator. I'd just pressed the button when Carter's voice, now clear and curt, sounded behind me.

"Now, Officer Mullaly, you and I are about to settle in for that talk."

Mullaly.

I made a mental note to remember his name in case our paths crossed again on more equal ground.

DIANE LOUCKS

"Diane?"
"Diane, meds."

The woman in blue was there again.
Like the day before
And the day before that.

She would stand in the doorway of the small room almost arm
in arm with the larger man,
Also in blue.
The boy didn't deliver the meds anymore.

The white paper cup waited and watched.
They watched,
and waited.

H. NOAH

Since I'd tried to exorcise the boy, they wouldn't let anyone come to me alone.
Not anymore.

I was on my knees, arms raised in preparation
My elbows resting on the worn gray sheets as they loosely hung to the single bed in front of me.
It was time for prayer.
They always came before prayer.
I didn't like that.
I tried to wake up earlier
But they knew.
They always knew.

No

They watched.

They know
They know about us
They want us gone
we are already softer
Don't let us go
We know what's to come
We know how to save

The pills are poison.
This place is poison.

"I understand, Mother." Quietly murmuring, more breath of
air than sound.

The blue woman spoke again,

"Diane, if you don't take your meds, we'll have to do it the
harder way."

I caressed the white linen of the clothes they'd given me.
So pure,
So righteous.
I wanted to speak but they wouldn't listen,
It wasn't different here, just more of the same.

"Please, Diane."
The man in blue uncrossed his arms,

Ready.

But I was ready too.

God, may Your will be done.

ARTHUR CASLIN

The days seemed to pass unattached from each other. I drifted in and out of consciousness, waking to too much light and figures moving in and out, asking about comfort and pain. I'd fall back asleep when everyone left, and the medications eased me from this place.

I preferred waking at night.

The hospital would still be alive with movement, but it was calmer. It was also easier to adjust to the light and sounds of the night shift. The attack must have been weeks ago, but the concussion was slow to fade and seemed to ramp up any sensory input my body received. From smells to light and sounds, I was always one wrong turn from nausea, blinding headaches, or both.

Luckily when I woke this time, it was night. I took a moment, listening to the hospital's heating click off as the air around me stopped stirring. It must be further into fall than I thought; it had been hard to keep track of the days since I'd been put here. Would have been more worried about the lost time if I'd had a life to return to. At least most of my injuries seemed to be more superficial. It was just the fun of the concussion and all its side effects that seemed to be keeping me here. It was easier to stay conscious now, but I had been waking up more confused and pissed than amicable, much to the nurses' joy. I didn't like talking about it, but when I woke in these states it was like I was waking mid-fight. Ready to swing at the dumb fucks again but unable to get up or move. I'd come back pretty quickly but there'd usually be a cop or two waiting for me to wake, to ask another repetitive question. Add this to the fact that I had been forced to piss into a bag and I wasn't exactly a ray of sunshine when I woke. At least the nurses had finally removed the catheter.

Fucking cops.

They'd been back today for another interview. Even though I knew the questions were part of their training, it still pissed me off to be treated more like a criminal than the only person who had fucking helped.

They should be thanking me!

So far, they hadn't officially charged the fucks with anything other than basic drunk and disorderly bullshit. One of the cops even went on to say they were out on bail while charges were finalized. This didn't mix well with the headache their visit had brought—only fueled the rage that came next. I don't even remember much of what happened, just that I had started screaming words like *incompetence* and *disciplinary review*, and generally just shaming them for their lack of action. I probably would have remembered more if the nurses hadn't come in and pumped me full of sedatives. Not that I gave a shit about anything I said. I'd never been liked much among the cops I had to work with and it wasn't like I'd have to be working with any of them again.

I remember trying to regain some kind of composure before drifting off, but it was hard to hide my contempt from them completely. They said they would be making formal charges soon but only after they'd verified my story with other accounts from the witnesses at the scene.

But that word stuck with me.

Soon.

They said it almost like a question.

At least I was out when the nurses had come to take that damn catheter out—a silver lining to a shit day.

They damn well better do it soon for Marie's sake.

God . . . Marie.

Her condition hadn't changed much, but the doctors told us not to give up yet. Even though she was in an induced coma, she was still showing signs of brain activity. Maddie had come in later that day, when I was a bit more lucid, for company. We talked about how I was and how she'd been, and how she was happy to have the cops outside Marie's door just in case. That's when the conversation turned to Marie. I found out that the docs had decided to take her out of the coma today, but they weren't sure when or if she'd wake up.

What Maddie said next slipped through my mind again: "I just keep waiting for her to squeeze my hand or flutter her eyes like in the movies. But it's taking more time than I thought it would."

I tried not to fall asleep, but Maddie seemed glad to have an excuse to get back to Marie.

I let my eyes close against the memory of her face as my limbs grew restless under the rough hospital sheets and paper-thin gown that encased me. An uncomfortable fullness in my lower abdomen pushed me further awake. Must have been what woke me. I opened my eyes to the mostly dark room; the light seemed to slip through the blinds, a poor attempt to block out the quieter but still active hallway outside. They didn't even try to block the small thin window set within the door. The hallway's light poured in easily here, creating a spotlight between my bed and the bathroom door.

I stretched out my arms and legs a little before pushing myself into a sitting position. Even the slow movement had me wincing from the bruises on my ribs and stomach.

Not too bad, though.

I moved my neck from side to side to test soreness. Seemed fine so I took a chance and cracked my neck. Satisfying pops, mixed with more relief than pain, released the pressure that had been building since I'd woken up. Swinging my legs slowly from the covers, I started to lower myself to the ground. With only an inch or two between my toes and the floor, the brisk air caused more than my muscles to seize as it drifted up the hospital gown.

"Guess that heater setting should have been placed a little higher tonight." Mumbling to myself more for my own sake than anyone else's.

The cold settled in as my bare feet hit the chilled linoleum. I was a bit stiff and unsteady from my time in bed, but it wasn't as bad as I'd expected. Making my way to the bathroom slowly, I let my muscles stretch and warm to the movement I was asking of them. At least the bathroom wasn't too far away. I was there, drained, and ready to return in no time at all. As I turned for the trip back, a familiar scream filled my ears, guttural and terrified.

Marie!

I switched from hobbling to sprinting as adrenaline raced through my veins. I must have looked anything but graceful as I opened the door to the screaming. I got there as the police grabbed Maddie to hold her back from the nurses buzzing around Marie's bed, failing to calm her. I stared down the police, knowing they were holding the one person who could help.

"Let her go."

They turned their heads to me, replying more out of exasperation than respect, "You need to leave, sir, you are not authorized to be here."

"Authorized, my ass. I was with her when she was attacked and I'm coming to see why the fuck she's terrified." The pain sharpened and burned more than I expected. The few steps I tried to take were more limp than threat, but I didn't care.

"Maddie can help. Let her go." My voice was getting raw from trying to compete with Marie's screams, but I wasn't about to retreat, shifting my focus to Marie as I continued forward.

"Marie, it's me, you're okay. Maddie's here. You're safe. Marie?" One of the three nurses turned to me.

"Mr. Caslin, it's not the right time. We're trying to help your friend, but we can't do that if you're here, especially if we have to worry about helping you next." He made a point to stare at my legs; I was unable to hide the effort it took to stay standing.

His honesty didn't keep me from throwing back, "Then help her."

"Mr. Caslin, you need to leave. We've got this."

"I'm staying," I replied, my words holding more resolve than my body.

"Sir, if you don't leave on your own, we'll need to escort you back to bed."

"The fuck you will."

He turned, motioning for the officers. "Can you please help Mr. Caslin back to his room?"

The taller of the two dumb fucks paused before pointing at Maddie. Her eyes were wide as she tried to twist out of the other officer's hands. "What about her?"

"She'll be fine."

They didn't hide their amusement as they let go of Maddie and turned toward me like a consolation prize.

I raised my finger. "Don't you fucking touch me. I can walk on my own."

They paused a few feet away from me as I made my way out of the room. I tried to stay calm and focus on my steps, but that didn't keep me from catching my feet on the doorframe. They had to have been waiting for their chance to use force as I recoiled from the pain of their grip. I paused, tensing for the fight they wanted.

"Let me go." I refused to look into their eyes, to move—just let the threat in my voice hang in the air.

"Sir, we need to make sure you get back to the room safely."

"The fuck you do." I struggled, but it was pointless. Most of my energy had dissipated and the room had started to blur and spin from the throbbing pain creeping from behind my eyes.

They half dragged, half carried me back to the room, though not entirely free from my insults. At least they gave me the decency of letting me crawl back into the bed on my own. Though even as they exited my room, they seemed to anticipate me trying to get back up. Their shadows moved back and forth in front of the door. They were mumbling at each other.

Fuckin' pigs.

From my time in the DA's, seeing what they and others like them had done, I had little faith in their ability to protect and serve in any respect.

I tried to wait them out, even after they talked a nurse into giving me something. As the needle slid in, a familiar weight returned to my body and my eyes as I slipped back into sleep. The calm of the night returning, erasing the echoes of screams that had been there just moments before.

MARIE PERAULT

There was a light in front of me, soft, almost white as it flickered. The pitted ceiling tiles looked too heavy, too much as my eyes adjusted and my vision blurred under them. I watched them grow and shrink as I tried to focus.

Where am I?

Everything hurt, my head felt like concrete, and I wanted to lift it but even the thought made my insides swim. I took a breath, trying to steady myself as my ribs screamed, stiff, bruised, and possibly broken. I closed my eyes, trying to remember, to take inventory of my body. Small movements hurt, every part of my body pleading against me as I tried to move, especially under the heavier weight of the material scratching against my skin, wrapping me tight. And my arm . . . I couldn't move my arm. Something weighed it down. I opened my eyes and looked toward it. I'd recognize that shade of pink anywhere even with my eyes blurring across the shadows. Her head nestled just below my hand on top of her folded arm as her other arm rested on top of mine, holding me softly.

My Maddie.

A hand grabbed my other shoulder, rough, fingers wrapping around my skin tighter and tighter. I snapped my head to the man standing next to me, the motion too quick, turning my stomach as pain cracked against my eyes, searing and sharp as my pupils swam. I could see the ground rushing to meet me. A sharp smell of bleach burning.

It's him.

The scream was involuntary. I pulled away from him but my body refused to comply completely. I moved my arm to punch but delicate fingers grabbed me, just light enough to keep my arm back. I turned again, feeling the room buck beneath me as my gaze connected with Maddie's. Eyes wide with shock—the pain, the fear within them adding to my own.

"Run." I fumbled with the word, tongue thick and swollen against the roof of my mouth; she needed to get out of here before it was too late.

Others rushed through the door, metal clicking and clanging as the door was pushed open. Blurred faces, loose clothes. They joined him in holding me. Hands touching, pressing. I needed them to stop touching me. The panic itched under my skin, burning discomfort.

"Stop, stop, stop."

But they kept touching and pressing into me. I couldn't breathe, my throat closing. I tried to bring my hand to my neck to feel that I was okay, that I wasn't being choked. But their hands wouldn't let me. I screamed again.

Then I heard her whispering in my ear. "Marie, it's okay."

It was the unhurried kiss that threw me, her soft lips pressing against my temple. I calmed, trying to think. "Where are we?" I whispered, turning my head toward her. I had to close my eyes to gain control of the swimming. I opened my eyes to cold air, more people in the room now dragging her away from me.

"Don't you touch her!"

Terror electrified every fiber as I arched my back into a painful recoil, finally able to wrench an arm free.

"It's okay," said a male voice as someone grabbed for me.

CRACK.

"Shit."

Got him.

"You okay?"

A woman's voice.

Confusion overwhelmed me; *men* had attacked me. My stomach dropped as I opened my eyes to see the woman with light hair and skin standing over me but looking toward the man. I blinked hard, trying to get my eyes to focus.

That's when *his* hand grabbed me again. I didn't want to be touched; everything in the room was overwhelming, too much to take in and process.

No . . . no . . . no.

I tried to pull free, but he was ready. The pounding in my head growing, thrumming against the inside of my skull. When I opened my eyes again, black dots began to dance across my vision as a new voice joined those around me.

"Marie, it's me . . ."

Art?

Everything was too loud, too much so I screamed, wanted them to step back and give me air to breathe. A needle slid in, and I felt the liquid burn as it filled my veins. Then Maddie was there. "It's okay, you're in the hospital, you're safe."

Shame flooded me as I realized I'd been fighting the wrong people. I turned to see her face, so hard to see as the black dots grew.

My lips were thick, cracking against my words. "I'm sorry."

"It's okay." She laughed softly, the hands and the sounds disappearing as she leaned into me, hot drops splashing against my cheeks as she held my head like a cracked egg.

She's here.

Her lips against my forehead.

Safe.

I was slipping back as the pain receded.

"It's okay, everything's okay."

Those words cut across the shame. How my body, my mind, hadn't been mine.

What's wrong with me?

I was almost gone now. Had to say. Needed to say. Only got out, "Love ya."

Before the room and I faded completely.

SEPTEMBER 15, 2017
MADDIE MORI

The paint wasn't responding how I wanted. Too thick, so I'd thin it. Too thin, so I'd have to toss it. I didn't want to be here. I wanted to be with Marie, but I had to get this commission done. A perfect lighthouse in perfect weather, in a perfect life. But the rage within the brush tips wanted storm clouds, lightning, a hurricane. Anything but this scene.

So I let it go.

Throwing my brushes on the small table next to me, I squeezed black paint into a cup and thinned it. Felt it swirling within the cup as I took aim and let it fly. Blacking out the perfect, the okay, dripping dark and empty. I took reds and coppers, flashing along with everything I was feeling. Faces sliding in and out of my vision from family, to that nurse, to the doctors, to the way Marie had looked so broken from that man's hands. I spattered, brushed, used my hands to mix, smear, and stain as I drained everything I wanted to say into the canvas in front of me until I was done.

"Not your usual, but I like it."

I turned toward Deb standing just a few feet behind me, giving me a sad smile as she came closer. She rested a hand on my shoulder before asking, "Why are you here?"

I placed my hand on hers, giving it a small squeeze. "I had to finish that lighthouse commission."

"Well . . . as much as I love this, I think the client could be incredibly confused. Possibly frightened."

She's right.

The painting in front of me was the color of my worst parts. Black-soaked pain over crafted perfection, giving a perfect stage to the chaos, dripping red flashes of everything I could never voice.

"Yeah, just needed something to come out. It's been hard to focus. I'll have to start again." Today was supposed to be the day of my show but I had to cancel it. Ever since Marie got hurt, it's like everything just dried up. I couldn't see the beauty in the moments anymore, just all the parts of me that were selfish to show.

Deb gave my shoulder another squeeze before responding, "It's good to let it out."

We both stood, staring at the storm of red and copper, taking in the splatters and sweeps of the brush, of my hand. "Have you talked to Marie about what you're feeling?"

Shame twisted around my heart as the end of the paintbrush dug into the center of my thumb. "It's nothing really, just a bad day."

"Seem to be having a lot more of those lately. Is the search for your birth parents still going badly?"

This took me off guard. I let the brush relax in my hand before setting it down on the table next to me. "Honestly, I'd forgotten all about it. I haven't even thought of looking since Marie was attacked."

Deb's thumb stroked the top of my shoulder. "I know Marie has a long road ahead of her, but it isn't selfish to do things for yourself."

"I . . ." My words caught and fumbled over my tongue.

Deb's hand slipped to the back of my neck, softly squeezing. "You should at least tell her about it."

I lifted my hand and placed it just as softly on her arm. "I will."

My hand slipped from her as her hand slipped from me, patting my back before her steps announced her departure and started to fade. "I'll be in the back, if you need anything."

If I talked to anyone right now it would have been Deb, but I didn't want to feel this moment. To feel the pain of what had happened. To see my own failure in doing even the one thing I always thought I could.

Paint.

What I'd let out was something different, something wrong and angry. I didn't want to talk, to give what I'd just released a chance to come back. So I took the painting in front of me and walked it to a free stand where it could dry before I grabbed a new canvas to paint what was expected. To be what I was always expected to be: reliable . . . contained.

OCTOBER 4, 2017
MARIE PERAULT

Each time I woke, the distance between the attack and the days after was growing. Except when I was asleep, I feared the moments in between when distance was removed. When I wasn't waking up in my bed but reliving the rancid heat of his breath and how I could have done everything differently. I thought that when I got home from the hospital, things would get better—not worse. It was like there were two versions of myself: the person I'd been and the stranger I'd become in my own body. Everything was more intense. The settling of the apartment, the laugh of a voice outside, the way my skin felt when Maddie brushed a finger against me. Each a slice between ribs, a burning point of reaction, of flight. I kept the curtains closed, locked the bedroom door at night, tried to use my bed rest as a slow step back into myself, but these moments eroded even the smallest peace within me.

These moments built into anger that overwhelmed and slid too easily from myself toward those around me. I did my best to hide it. I didn't want Maddie to see me like this.

What's wrong with me?

I focused most of my energy on not reacting, not letting it show. I didn't scream anymore, but my body still betrayed me. I'd wake in starts, breathless and grabbing. That's when I'd remember my pride, the confidence in hollow threats when I'd baited him that day, how in the end I pulled an empty hand from the bag.

You did this to yourself.

This was the moment that replayed the most over and over again in my mind when I couldn't sleep. I could have faked it, used that time to plan something, anything. Now a loop ran, again and again, of his smile.

His hands all stone and muscle, forcing breath from me. As rough and scarred as pond ice.

You're in your bed.

There was a siren outside getting closer as I slid down under the blanket that held me.

I felt my arms breaking under the weight of him. I remembered the false hope in fighting back—how it just excited him more.

You're in your bed.

I pulled the blanket up to my chin, but the pressure was too much. It reminded me of the weight of his hand, so I drew it up over my head, drowning out the intensity of the siren at its worst. I couldn't breathe, so I pulled it back down. Seeing the moments before I'd passed out.

The darkness that had played in the corners of my eyes as he strangled me. His eyes had been gray, sharp. But I had refused to look away. Crafting a curse for him in every moment I had left.

He would remember me.

But he laughed

And laughed

And . . .

Stop it!

I clamped my hands to my face, willing myself back as I pushed the pain of bruises and stitches to their breaking points. It was intoxicating. The only thing that kept me from screaming. I was so ashamed of this weaker version of myself.

He barely touched you.

I took a slow breath in, trying to will my mind onto something different. But soured sweat and alcohol burned my nose. His lips, swollen and dripping, trailed thick spit across my face and chest as he marked me.

NO.

I dug my fingernails in, tripling the pain. My face was throbbing now. Softly, easing memories away.

Carving out the rot within me. The sirens had faded, the sounds of the city below humming just as loud and unpredictable.

I had to get this under control for Maddie. The doctors said it was normal, to be expected, and that there were options. But they didn't understand—I didn't need options. I just needed to accept what had happened. This was a lesson, nothing more.

"Are you trying to see if you woke up with telekinesis?"

Relaxing my hands from my face, I used them to hide the partial smile Art brought out. Couldn't let him win so easily as I glared through the bars my fingers created. It irked me he'd been able to make it into the apartment, let alone the room, without me realizing.

"Not exactly the first thing on my mind, though I should be asking for that key back."

"Maddie told me not to listen to you. And come on, you're not even a little curious? It was the first thing I tried when I woke up."

I let my hands drop with a laugh. "Of course you did. Why did you even think it was a possibility?"

Art finished walking into the room and settled on the edge of the bed with a confused look on his face. "Isn't that how everyone in the movies gets it? They hit their head and wake up with special powers?"

"Hardly. Besides, they usually wake up seeing ghosts."

Art grinned as he settled into his spot, using one arm to prop himself up. "Well then I can't rule that out since I haven't been anywhere haunted lately."

Narrowing my eyes, I cocked my head just enough to show judgment.

Art's eyes comically widened as he lifted a hand in mock shock. "What? It could happen! It's a little harder to disprove than telekinesis. Go ahead, change my mind." Art waved his hand in my general direction for emphasis.

"For that, I'd have to verify that you actually had one." I reclined back into the bed, sticking my tongue out at him like a four-year-old.

Art clutched at his chest. "Oh . . . my . . . lanta. I think the brain damage may have actually made you smarter."

"Har har har, smartass," I shot back.

"Hey, it's the truth. I'd never do anything to dampen that shining personality of yours on purpose."

"Yeah, I've been a fucking ray of sunshine since I woke up from that coma." I'd tried to make the words light and playful as they came out, but the edges sliced through my tongue as they hit the air.

Art's gaze fell and softened. "Hey, kid, you've got more than enough after what happened."

"Don't."

I didn't mean for it to sound like a warning.

I tried to move past this moment and the anger coming alive within me. "I just want to talk about something else. What's today's news?" I threw in a smile, pulling it into place with more focus than I probably needed.

This is all my fault.

Arthur paused, looking like he didn't want to follow along, but his gaze quickly shifted into something smug. "Now how do you know I even have news?"

"Well, when you don't have something exciting to share, you walk in like a storm cloud of doom and gloom saying *fuck this* and *fuck that* about pretty much everything."

Amusement twinkled just behind his eyes. "Marie, are my cursing habits finally rubbing off on you?"

I smiled. "Stop avoiding my questions. Out with it."

He leaned forward, giving my hand a small gentle pat. I froze at the unexpected touch. I thought I smelled alcohol, but it must have been in my mind. It wasn't even mid-morning yet.

Breathe.

"All right, you win, just got news from the doc. He said I'm clear and don't need any more checkups."

"Well, well, well, leaving little ol' me behind then? That sunset must be calling your name." I pretended to use my bed as a fainting couch like the ladies in those silent films. Art wasn't the only one who could add flair to a moment. "Whatever shall I do without your constant harassments?"

He laughed before replying, "Hey now, I'm not leaving immediately."

We both paused at the sharp creak of the old floorboards by the door. My heart strained before I saw who it was.

Maddie.

Relief flooded through me.

"Hey, you." The bite my words had held earlier melted into something sweeter.

Maddie smiled as she shifted a worn wicker basket on her hip. She swept her strawberry-blond bangs out of her face. She was wearing jeans and a tank top with a long sleeve blue-and-green plaid shirt open to the air around her.

"I should have known I'd find you two together."

She shifted again, moving the basket into better balance. Even with all her worries, she always had this quiet strength. It took a lot to uproot her.

"Jealous?" Art asked.

Maddie scoffed. "Hardly. How Marie ever puts up with you, I'll never understand."

Art took a moment to at least pretend to think before responding, "It's my undeniable sex appeal."

Maddie and I caught each other in an eyeroll before returning any attention to Art.

I reached out to give him an apologetic pat on the knee. "I hate to break your heart, but I'm a lesbian. Have been for quite a while now."

"You can still be a lesbian and fully committed to our relationship. We'd be like those closeted couples in the '50s, married but with our real lovers on the side. We'd always stay happy since we'd always be in someone else's life. Tell me that isn't the picture of a healthy marriage!"

I couldn't help but laugh even as my ribs protested at how hard. "Art, the last person I'm crawling back into the closet for is you. I think this is just an attempt to drag us both with you wherever you end up so you'll never be alone. That, or you're more touched in the head than the doctor realized."

Turning to Maddie, I asked, "What do you think? The doctor said he was healed but I think he may be jumping the gun."

Maddie had made it over to the other side of the bed, settling the basket to her side as she sat down.

"Well, Art, you are acting abnormal even for you."

Art laughed, jabbing his finger toward Maddie as if he was able to poke her through the air. "Marie, this is your doing, isn't it? You're turning our dear Maddie against me."

I slapped his hand from the air above me. "You got me, criminal mastermind here, has nothing to do with Maddie's own free will."

"You should know by now; nothing gets past me." Art tried to show some bravado as he leaned back with his arms folded around his chest.

I nodded toward the basket at Maddie's feet. "What's in there?"

"Oh!" Maddie picked it back up and tipped it to show the assorted yarn and knitting needles within. "I got some of the things your physical therapist suggested for hand dexterity."

"Joy, can't wait to learn something I've never been interested in." I blew out air as I fell back into the pillows around me.

Unfazed, Maddie shrugged a little before placing the basket back on the ground. "Who knows? You might end up liking it."

I heard Art's phone buzz before he pulled it out to check. "Shoot, I have to go."

"You just want an excuse to not get ganged up on again," I said.

"Not this time. I enjoy our talks." Art leaned forward, patting my arm before getting up and giving a little salute to Maddie. "See you both soon."

"Hey, Art?"

"Yeah?" He looked back at me as he tucked his phone away.

"If you decide to go, give me a heads up?" I didn't want to show any sadness, but it was hard to think he wouldn't be around soon.

"Of course. Bye, guys." And with that, he left.

I waited till I heard the front door close behind him before turning to Maddie. "I think leaving the DA's was good for him. I haven't seen him like this in a long time. Forgot how childish he was under all that bitterness. I'm going to miss having him around."

She leaned toward me, lowering her voice. "Don't tell him this, but a part of me will too."

I reached out my hand. "Come lie with me."

That's all I had to say.

Maddie slid into the bed, moving delicately as she slid between my arms; it was the best feeling in the world—her back against my chest. I tightened my hold, breathing her in. I already thought of her as summer, but I swore she always smelled of it too, floral and sweet with a touch of wind.

"How've you been, hon?" she whispered light and low into my ear.

"Better. Just wish I had more control over my body."

"You will. It's already night and day from when you first got home."

Uncomfortable feelings started to twist and build within me. I didn't want to talk about that, asking instead, "Hey, did you find what I wanted?"

"I did, but are you sure you want it now? It's nothing you haven't seen in the PT mirror."

"I just need to see up close."

She sighed, rolling over just enough to reach back into the basket.

It took a few minutes before her searching ended. She was probably hoping I'd change my mind, but I had to see. So I waited until she rolled back with a small hand mirror flashing under the lamp lights around us.

She rolled to face me, clutching the mirror almost protectively to her chest. I reached for it but stopped when her grip tightened even more, showing her hesitation. "Are you sure?"

"Yeah, I'm sure."

"Okay, but at least let me hold it." She scooted in close as I rolled to my back, making room for us to lie side by side as I watched her lift the mirror to our faces.

At first, we both reflected back, her warm skin next to the putrid colors in mine.

What a pair.

All I felt was shame as I reached up and tilted the mirror to me. I knew why she was hesitant. I'd healed quite a bit since I got home, but it still looked like the attack had been days, not weeks, ago. A nice mixture of old bruises, cuts, and lumps painted a map of every fist and pavement hit on my skin. Even my hair seemed to deflate from the damage as it lay limp and plastered to my body. Except, of course, the small section that had been shaved along my right temple; they had to crack my skull to relieve some of the pressure. I ran my fingertips along the fresh hair growth, avoiding the jagged black stiches woven in between, each follicle springing from my touch as it pricked and bounced back into place. It took a moment before I lowered the mirror to the spot I wanted to see most. Maddie must have known, trying to pull it back as she asked, "All done?"

I kept my hand strong, resisting her tug. "No, not yet."

I had to see.

Maddie paused, even let me take full control as her hand dropped to my shoulder, waiting as I tilted the mirror down.

It was weird. While most of the bruises had faded to bright colors, the ones on my neck seemed stuck in the thick of healing. They'd probably been darker, but even now the shape of his hands on my neck was still clear. I traced the outline, a morbid necklace painted in the way his fingers had splayed against my skin. There was even a rectangular "stone" at the center of one where his ring had branded me.

Maddie turned her head into my shoulder, the slow drip of hot tears against my skin making this even worse.

I wanted to look away, to look at her.

But I couldn't.

I didn't want her to see the hollow shame smothering me from the inside.

SAME DAY
RICHARD KOCH

Attempting to get ahold of Arthur after he left the hospital was next to impossible. He'd been so angry after he woke up, railing against the police and staff, especially when it came to Marie. But after, when the police left, he had seemed to drift. I had found him sleeping more often than not when I visited. Whether it was from the injuries or medicine, I wasn't sure. Even awake, he seemed more and more reluctant to see me—almost ashamed. Whatever the case, I had to get him the workers' comp documents he kept forgetting to pick up. Finally got him to meet me after work at some local coffee shop he preferred. If he showed, I'd be able to talk to him about what the outlook was with his and Marie's attackers . . . if he'd even talk about it. I didn't envy the attorney that had gotten this case, especially since they'd come from another office and didn't know what they'd be stepping into.

Stop worrying about him.

I needed to listen to myself. I had enough on my plate at work with him gone and Marie out of commission. I cared about my staff, but with him it was more akin to responsibility than friendship at this point, especially after I'd been firm in removing him from other cases. After that day, everything seemed to change between us. I just knew I wouldn't feel better till he left the state or found another job to throw himself into.

I grabbed the tarnished metal handle of the coffee shop door and pulled, my gloved grip slipping a little as the knitted fabric tried to find a hold. After the initial shock of warmth and noise, I saw him toward the back, hunched over whatever drink he'd ordered. I walked back to him, dodging a patron or two in the busy shop before I grabbed a chair next to him at the small table and sat down. Arthur jumped a little as he quickly finished screwing the thermos in front of him shut, causing a small splash of whatever he'd ordered to spill over his hands and onto the table.

"Oops, I can grab some napkins." I started to stand but Arthur pressed a hand against my arm, easing me back down. "No worries, I'll get some before I leave. Where's the documents you were talking about?"

He was acting off again. Eyes darting as he fidgeted within his seat, ready to bolt. Looked like today wasn't the day for any talk.

Good, he's not your responsibility anymore.

Swallowing, I pulled off my gloves and opened my coat just enough to grab the folder I had stuck in there before leaving the office. I handed it over but held on, resisting his tug. "Everything okay?"

Stop, he's not your responsibility anymore.

Arthur looked a little taken back, but he tugged the folder out of my hand. "Of course, just been busy with job applications and such."

The relief that washed over me was undeniable.

At least he's trying.

"That's wonderful to hear. Are you still planning on moving out of state?"

Arthur leaned back into his chair as he let out a big breath, something sharp and pungent now hanging between us.

"I've been putting out a résumé to anything that looks good. It's a mixture of out of state and in state at the moment. Can't decide, so I'm leaving it up to the best offer."

"Ahh, gotcha." I eased back.

"I hate to do this, Richard, but I actually got another call for an interview this afternoon and it's getting close." Arthur stood up, clutching his folder and coffee as he almost waited for me to give permission.

There it is—an untruth hidden in plausibility.

I might have believed him if I hadn't smelled what was on his breath, but it didn't matter at this point. "Of course, just let me know if you have any questions."

"Will do." Arthur shoved his chair a little too quickly as relief seemed to roll off him.

I reached out and touched his elbow lightly before he got too far. "Keep me updated on how the interviews go and if you need a reference, feel free to use me."

Arthur shifted the folder to the hand that held his coffee as he looked down on me and eased a free hand on top of mine. "Will do, thank you."

And just like that, he was gone. I leaned back, taking the moment in as I stared at the splash of coffee spreading across the copper tabletop, resembling an oil slick as is slid into grooves created by countless customers.

Reaching out, I let my finger slide through the mess, pulling a clean line through the middle of it before lifting it to my tongue.

Bitter, sharp, and burning.

I was right. Coffee wasn't the only thing he'd been drinking.

SAME DAY
DIANE LOUCKS

Days kept passing.
Had I gotten here yesterday?
Last week?
Last year?

It was colder now. I'd gotten into the routine of things, not that
it helped.
Time still slipped and danced around me like a thief.

I disappointed Mother,

Let slip to the doctor of my sin,
When my father had touched me, it was my fault not his.

It was hard to stay present,

But not here in my window.

Looking over the leaf-covered grounds, I watched as God painted the world around me. Fall had always been my favorite. It was when nature slowly let go, with the promise of warmer days ahead.

Of rebirth.

Of salvation.

Had Ann really been saved?

Had I helped her in time?

Nothing left to save.

You wasted it all.

No one can be saved,

Not even **you**.

Blood so much blood.

It's on you,

On your hands,

The world is red with your sin.

The devils had come back, stronger this time. Mother must have let them in when I'd disappointed her.

"I'm so sorry I told him," I whispered, hoping she'd listen this time.

Gripping my rosary as I leaned against the cold glass, I started my prayers one by one, pleading every other word.

"Please, come back.

I'll be better."

OCTOBER 9, 2017
MADDIE MORI

M arie was fuming. Only a few minutes in, and it was easy
to see she wanted to tap out. This was going to be a bad
one and from the look on Sara's—her therapist's—face, she
saw it too. Marie was stalling at her first exercise, seated in
one of those old blue plastic chairs that was more fitting for
an elementary classroom than physical therapy. I watched
as she bent and stretched in slow motion for the barely used
sneaker. Even in its less-than-pristine state, the pop of white
looked florescent against the color around her: blue medicine balls, red bands, rainbow weights and mats.

Who knew such a bright room could be the center of so much pain?

But there was joy too. It was there in the small celebrations
around us: a smile, a hug, an excited clap. I drifted off for a
second, looking at the other patients around us all focused, all
trying, before finding Marie again. She'd finally slipped on her

second shoe. The easiest part of the whole exercise. The larger motions had come back first, but it was the smaller ones, the fine motor movements, that needed work.

As I watched her now, she looked more statue than person as she stared at the laces. The anger set across her face as she silently fumed at the task ahead.

Just try.

I wanted to say it out loud, but anything mentioned during these moments only seemed to make them worse. So I swallowed each syllable, trying my best to send better thoughts her way. At least Sara was able to find a balance between motivation and criticism. Dressed in her usual scrubs, she took a moment to kneel beside Marie. "All right, let's focus on pinching the loops."

Firm but calm, always able to push her into some form of action. It made me wonder how many patients like Marie she'd had before. Couldn't imagine it was easy to have a front row seat to someone else's expectations.

I let a sigh slip as I settled further into the bean bag chair nestled in my usual corner. I didn't mind the lukewarm wall as it molded my shoulders into a soft V; it was almost comforting. I wanted to help Marie, but she'd been shutting down little by little over the last few weeks. It came out more here where even my presence seemed to throw her some days. I loved her, but I wasn't sure how to help anymore or if it was even wanted. These thoughts made me sick, like I was starting to let go and give up too early. The little lump of anxiety in my throat was back, the one I tried—and failed a few times—to hide from Marie. I didn't pity her, I just didn't want to make her sad when I cried.

My love.

At least she had Art, even with my reservations about him. They'd grown closer in the hospital, and I was grateful Marie had someone to talk to. But I didn't see the same change in him Marie had. I saw something else. He was a good guy, always had been, but he carried his sadness with him. After the accident, it changed. The sadness curdled into something else, something wrong. He let it out sometimes around her but mostly around everyone else. The closer they got, the more he hid.

I turned to watch her. She'd gotten her shoes on and was just finishing the warm-up stretches to the beat of some '90s song playing on the radio. Grungy angst dressed up in a pop beat. The name of the song and band escaped me, but it took me back to my childhood. I could still see them, the few friends I had as we put on dance parties in the living room after school. The radio would be blasting from a little blue boom box as we pumped our arms and bodies till someone's parents got home.

"Shit!"

Marie was back in the chair with a small metal foldout table in front of her. She was focused and digging through a bin filled with pom poms, small plastic toys, and oddly shaped plastic pieces. It took a minute to see what had happened. After digging through the mess in front of her, she pulled out the tweezers she must have dropped just moments before. Sara sat next to her, and I watched as she tried to get her refocused. Knowing Marie, she'd probably tried to power through it, the complete opposite of what was needed. She was supposed to take her time to sort the pieces, not rush through.

The music changed again to something more modern; I didn't even try to figure out what it was. I let myself settle into my corner again, this time reaching for my bag and pulling out my phone. The messages from friends had slowed, though a few still trickled in. I liked to check when I could.

I looked up to make sure Marie was focused back on the bin before resuming my digital escape. No messages, so I decided to scroll through my pictures for a bit. It was nice to glance through the memories, through dinner dates and photos with Marie. It was hard not to ache for her. She tried her best to put on a smile even with the growing space between us. Like she could make everything okay just because she willed it. But what happened had taken a toll and she was hiding it from me. I kept trying to bring it up or touch on something close to it, but she had the same reaction each time—nothing. She would just glaze over it and move to something else.

It was worse when the cops came, each visit identical as they asked her to walk them through what had happened again and again and again. With each retelling she seemed to lose a piece of herself, to detach from what had happened. Like it was just facts about someone else. I didn't care about the facts. I just wanted to understand what she was going through. Something we never had an issue with before. The only thing she'd let me do sometimes was hold her. She'd always feel a million miles away, but the weight of her body was a reassurance that some part of her was still there.

I stopped at the picture of us on New Years. All dressed up at a friend's party. A first for us since we usually stayed in. We both wore our favorite dresses. Mine was a slim-fitting long black dress, and Marie wore a wild, gold-sequined, long-sleeved, short-hemmed number. A friend had caught us at midnight right as the ball had dropped. I'd reached out to hold her, arms possessive yet loose around her waist. Marie had laughed as I led, in awe at my boldness, but she had closed the remaining distance between us. Guiding my mouth into a drunken kiss, wet and filled with promise. Her champagne glass was balanced in her other hand, waiting for us both to toast with a shared sip for the new year ahead.

It'll be okay, stop worrying.

"Hey, Maddie," Sara called out from across the room as Marie gathered the contents of the bin back into its container.

"Yes?"

"Could you help us with this next exercise?"

"Of course."

I took one last look at the memory before putting it away.

We were going to be okay. Marie was going to be okay.

She just had to be.

SAME DAY
DIANE LOUCKS

I pulled my feet up,
Even as my bones cried and ached against it.
I was always calmer when I curled up in his office chair like
a child.
Like someone who could be new.
The blue blanket they let me carry around fit nicely.
Even worn, it helped with the cold of the leather.

"Diane? How have the meds been helping since we last talked?"

He was older than me but not by much. His hair silver and
white reflective mirrors against the light.
Here in his office, everything was like that.
From the wooden bookshelves
Desk,

Statues.

Frames.

Everything seemed antique.

Out of place in this hospital.

Almost warm

Except for the chair.

It was always too cold.

I looked into Dr. Jacob's eyes after settling in.

A good name.

A holy name.

It was why I wouldn't see anyone else.

The rest were whores and non-believers, no matter what he said.

"I think they've been good." I picked at the blanket like a rosary.

"It's like I'm more present in my day . . . if that helps?"

Pick

Pick

Pick

I was still unsure what answer he was looking for.

"That's wonderful to hear."

It is.

I hadn't felt like this in a while.

I was lighter
Didn't feel as targeted by the devil.

"Yes, it's been nice. It's been easier to talk to Mother."

Dr. Jacob's eyebrows furrowed, and he jotted something down.

I hated when he did that.
It meant I messed up.

"But isn't your mother dead?" He looked up and waited.

"Only in body," I replied.

Enough, child.

More writing
Her wrath seared into my thinking,
I needed to make it right.

"I'm so sorry, Mother."
I'd whispered, but not soft enough, he looked up, resting the pen.

You never know when to shut up.

"Is she talking to you now?"

He didn't wait to respond as he pressed the button under his desk, calling the nurse. I knew what was coming next and there was nothing I could do to stop it.

DIANE LOUCKS
LATER THAT DAY

GOD

HELP

H. NOAH

ME

228

OCTOBER 10, 2017
ARTHUR CASLIN

The cold radiating off the metal door handle was barely muted by my kid leather gloves. We were just entering fall and the bad winter ahead was already making itself known. The warmth within the apartment building rushed to meet me. I preferred it to the hospital, was glad when Marie had left. The harsh smell of cleaning fluids and sick had creeped further and further underneath my skin each time I'd walked through those doors. That place was like a living reminder of everything I'd failed to do, especially when it came to Marie. When those assholes had attacked her, I had a chance to punish them, to finally give someone what they deserved. But I'd been too weak.

You failed her. You failed them all.

I tried to keep my mornings busy and focused on my next steps. If I did this, I didn't need to drink too early. Seeing Marie after also helped; she didn't need a day drunk at her bedside. For a while I tried visiting her, then job hunting, but it'd been useless. My thoughts would turn from my future to failures in a matter of moments. From there it was one glass, two glasses, then an empty bottle, forced to sit with my own thoughts. I didn't have a problem. I just wanted to drown out the anger long enough to get something done, even though that never happened.

I'd sent out a handful of résumés, but it had been hard trying to settle on one place. The only thing I knew for sure was that I needed to get the fuck out of Maine. I made it to Marie's door, tapping out a few soft knocks as I unlocked and opened it.

"Hey, kid."

Marie was reclined but upright in the loveseat, propped up by pillows and a soft smile. She still had bruises, but today was the first time she looked like herself. The swelling had finally faded and let her slip back into the body it had stolen. I made my way to a chair at her side, stiff and hardly cushioned. It must have been *cream* or *camel* at some point in its long life, a color softer than the chair itself. I settled in and looked toward Marie.

"I have to say, you're looking a hell of a lot better today."

"Considering how I must have looked when I first got here, anything would be an improvement."

I paused, feigning a small look of confusion, letting the moment grow just a little awkward before replying, "Huh?

No, I meant since I've known you. It's like your nose is a little straighter . . . or smaller. Did you get something done?"

The serious tone I'd been trying to hold was starting to crack, crumbling completely as she grabbed an extra pillow with more dexterity than I'd seen in a while and sent it flying toward my head. I let it hit for effect before it fell softly into my waiting hands.

"Ha. Funny, dick, it's good to see you too." She had a larger smile now, one that seemed to match my own.

"Looks like that arm of yours is still on point." She was all too ready to catch her pillow as I tossed it back. She rearranged it into the pile that was keeping her propped up.

I had to admit, it wasn't just the reduced swelling—it'd been that smile paired with it. I settled back into the chair, straightening my back. "Where's Maddie?"

"She should be getting here soon. Had to catch up on a few things at the studio. She also said she'd bring me something later to help with the boredom."

"That'll be nice. Wish I'd had something to keep me occupied when they'd tried to keep me bed bound at the hospital."

Marie laughed a little as she responded, "As I remember it, they failed spectacularly at that since you were in my room more often than Maddie."

I raised my hands to her callout. "Can't help that they underestimated how healthy I was." Leaning forward, I took her hand in mine with more pomp than sincerity and said, "I, for one, am excited for the day we can visit outside of this apartment."

"Ha! You and me both." She took her hand back as she turned to grab a clear cup from the side table next to her. It was filled with some opaque liquid she sipped from a crooked, overly used straw. "My skin is crawling from all the forced bed rest."

"I hear ya."

Marie took a moment to drain half the cup before asking, "Have you heard anything about the assholes that attacked us?" Not wanting to answer, I bought some time by stripping off the gloves, which had suddenly become too warm.

"I did hear one thing."

"What?" She paused, hesitant at the tone in my voice.

"You're not going to like it. At least, I didn't."

"Art, just tell me." She turned to put down her cup before facing me again.

"They let them out again this morning."

"What?"

The anger that had been absent for most of the visit crept back under my skin. "They made bail somehow. I thought they were fucking homeless, but even with the new charges and higher bails to match, they posted without an issue."

The news hit her harder than I thought it would. The joy, the old Marie . . . it was all slipping away again.

She looked like she had after waking up: shellshocked. I knew it was better to wait, so I did. She took a few slow breaths before raising her eyes to mine.

"So, the charges are still sticking? They're still going ahead with prosecution?"

"Yeah."

She lowered her eyes and closed them. I waited for her to speak again but the silence was starting to be too much, to itch at the places in my mind I didn't want it to. I wanted to offer some good news even if it was something she already knew. "At least the restraining orders have taken effect. They can't be within five hundred feet of you or me."

Marie's eyes hit like daggers, the wave of anger I'd caused rushing over me in her voice. "That doesn't keep me from running into them in the street. I had to put my fucking address on that order to even get it."

She lifted her hand, pointing a finger in my direction. "You know how useless they are."

I watched the anger flicker and mix with something I'd never seen on her face before: fear. She brought her hand back, using both hands to cover her face before letting a *fuck* out. Muffled, almost lost in her hands.

I wasn't sure what to do other than let the moment pass; this was new territory for us both. Didn't take long before her hands dropped, the fear fading into something softer. "I'm sorry. I didn't mean to snap, it just . . . sucks. I don't like them being out."

"You and me both." We shared a look. We didn't need to justify it to anyone, let alone ourselves. I didn't want it to stick, so I tried my luck at bringing her back. "Hey, I thought I was the one with a monopoly on doom and gloom in this friendship."

The sharpened lines across her face eased. "Oh please, you still own that title hands down."

I gave her a small shrug before settling back into the chair. "Eh, you've got a kick to you, though it's about time."

"I don't want it." The sadness I'd seen earlier weighed on her words as they hit me soft and heavy.

"It'll pass. Shit, I'm surprised I'm not worse. Guess the drugs they gave me are working on something."

Marie smiled as she seemed to come back into herself again. "Well, I admit you're less of an ass overall lately."

"Ouch!" I feigned distress as I clutched hopelessly at my chest before slumping back in defeat. "Truth hurts I guess."

"Of course it does." Marie turned again to reach for the remaining liquid in her cup. "How's the job hunt going?"

SAME DAY
MADDIE MORI

"So what did you want to talk about?" The last customer had just left and we were settled into the slower part of the day. The arms of Deb's coveralls were tied around her waist and a bright-yellow tank top clashed against its warmer brown. She lowered herself into a chair we kept for customers in the front.

I settled on the small coffee table, fingers fidgeting with my sweater's sleeve. "It's Marie. I'm not sure if I'm doing the right thing."

A flash of concern crossed Deb's face as she leaned forward. "What do you mean?"

"I just . . . I'm not sure how to make things easier for her." I brought the sleeve to my lips, chewing it as I thought for a moment before moving it away. "Do I act normal, like none of this happened? Or am I supposed to push her to talk to me? To see someone?"

"Oh, hon, I'm not really sure myself. Seems like it might be hard going back to a complete normal." Deb shifted, pulling a leg under her as she asked, "How is she doing now?"

"She seems better, but she pulls back when things having to do with what happened come up." I brought my sleeve back up, speaking through the fabric. "I don't want to push her, but I also don't want her to get too stuck in her own mind. I know how hard that can be."

I watched Deb think, rubbing her chin softly. "Has she said something you're doing is too much?"

"No, not yet."

Deb leaned forward and squeezed my knee. "Then trust her, too. I think pushing her out of her head is probably a great thing. Doing normal things is probably the best for her, especially when she can get out of that apartment for more than PT."

I was a little hesitant, still afraid it could be the wrong choice, but I wanted to feel like I was doing something—anything—to help. "You think so?"

"Of course. I can't imagine what it's like, being stuck inside for as long as she has been. What happened was horrendous but it's probably the inactivity and not seeing familiar faces that's making it worse. Just listen when she says it's too much."

"Okay, I'll start making plans. Thank you for the help." I smiled, feeling a little better, and Deb returned the smile.

"Of course. The therapist idea is a great one, but I wouldn't push it with her too much. That's the kind of choice someone has to make on their own." Deb withdrew a bandanna from her pocket, tying it to keep her hair back, preparing to work over open flame—another glazing experiment.

I nodded as another customer opened the door. We both stood and I asked, "Is it okay if I head out a little early today? I promised to get Marie something, but I have no clue what to get."

Deb nodded, saying, "Of course."

We broke apart then, me to help the customer and feeling lighter than I had in a while, and Deb going back to tend to her glazes.

OCTOBER 20, 2017
MARIE PERAULT

Placing the pile of cards decorated with "well wishes" and "thinking of you" into the plain cardboard box felt better than I thought it would. I was off bed rest completely with the pain from my injuries fading every day. It was nice to get rid of the last of the reminders.

But they're out.

My heart dropped at the thought, fluttering as I tried to run through possible exit plans if they found me again.

You fucking coward.

Anger flared white hot within me, burning the shame and frustration it had morphed from. I'd never been the one to run from a fight. Always faced everything, fearless. Now I just wanted to hide.

It's your fault this happened. Couldn't keep your fucking hand hidden you STUPID FUCKI–

"Hey, hon, need any help?"

Maddie's voice always helped ease me back, but my body wasn't as quick to follow. I was helpless, watching as my knuckles turned white, the box buckling and bending to the rush of emotions within me.

Clearing my throat, I turned to face her, hoping the smile didn't appear too forced. "No, think I got everything."

Maddie leaned in, tracing my face with her fingers before giving me a small slow kiss. "Good. Let's toss it."

I didn't tell her how that simple motion had frozen me, how her hand felt static the closer it had gotten to my neck. I needed to push past this like everything else. I needed to be okay. I handed her the box as I looked around the apartment for anything I'd missed. Everything seemed too bright with the curtains pulled back. The movements of the world outside the windows strummed my nerves. I tried not to watch the people stopping for moments that seemed too long, too suspect, putting me on edge.

Fucking coward, this is your fault.

The anger was softer this time. I tried to ignore it and the memories of that day, but I could feel myself slipping.

Stop it.

I pinched my arm hard, the pain centering me back into the present.

"Marie, what was that?" I'd forgotten Maddie was there. I thought she'd left.

What the fuck was wrong with me?

"Nothing, sorry . . . just thought a bug was on me."

She knows you're lying.

I took a slow breath before looking into Maddie's eyes. The calm I'd been waiting for started to hit.

This is all I needed.

My Maddie,

My home.

SAME DAY
MADDIE MORI

"Marie . . . hon?"

I waited for her to return from where she'd disappeared too, pretending not to notice until she'd processed whatever it was. Trying to force her back made it worse. At least her anger had lightened a bit. She seemed to be doing better, but moments like this threw me.

Marie shifted from side to side as she stood in the middle of the room, a knock from the front door finally breaking her from any thoughts as her face shifted from a blank stare to something more like herself.

This was all starting to weigh heavy, to feel like too much, but these thoughts were always quickly covered in shame and put away. I focused back on Marie, shifting the box to my hip as I reached out my hand. "Ready?"

"Always."

It had to be Richard. It was the first time he was visiting since the hospital. He'd been a huge help and far more compassionate than any boss I'd ever had.

Marie took my hand as we started toward the front door. I paused to place the box just inside the living room door as Marie continued forward. No need to dump the letters immediately.

Marie opened the front door, giving Richard as much of a hug as she was able to over the wrapped basket. Marie wasn't going to like this; her face usually fell with each *get well* present or card.

"Good to see you. This is for you, Marie. The office wanted to make sure you knew you were missed." Richard handed over the awkwardly big basket with various goodies propped up inside. He was dressed in a lovely deep-gray suit.

I was a bit taken aback by the smile that stretched across Marie's face—it was genuine. "Thank them for me. This looks lovely!"

Richard smiled back in his own way before turning toward me. "Good to see you too, Maddie. How's everything going?"

Marie took the open invitation. "Everything's been much better. Leaving the hospital has been the best thing for us both."

There was something off about this happiness, too electric and alive. Made me more on guard than relaxed as I almost waited for her mood to dive. I tried not to show concern as I asked, "You need help with that, Marie? I can carry it back."

"Oh no, I'll be fine." She had started to walk away before finishing, words slipping quickly over her shoulder as she made her way to the kitchen.

She stumbled a little under the weight of the basket, but I tried to ignore it, to slip instead into the role of host. "Come in, Richard, let's sit." I gave him my best smile as I sat on the love seat.

"Thank you." Richard shut the door behind him and made his way to the armchair next to me.

"I need coffee. Anyone else want some?" Marie had popped back into the room suddenly. Her expression looked almost normal, but there was a flicker of something else underneath— something I had seen grow each time we had gone out.

Maybe I'm reading too much into things.

I'd asked but she said it was nothing, that it was fine, every time. I shook off the feeling.

"I'd love one, with cream if you have it," Richard replied. I watched as he watched her face. He didn't seem as though he was picking up on anything.

"Sounds good to me too." I pulled my legs up, sitting on my feet as Marie shifted from side to side in the entryway.

"I'll be right back!"

The quiet that followed left me a little unsure. I'd never really been alone with Richard before, even when we socialized at office functions. I'd gotten to know him better over his hospital visits, but he was Marie's boss. I wasn't sure how to let that go enough to relax or if I should. At least I didn't have to stress too much; he broke the silence between us before I was forced to.

"How's she doing?"

I took a moment before answering. "Good overall . . . I think."

His expression softened as he settled into the chair. "Looks like she's healed from most of her injuries. Bed rest must have been rough to get through, though."

Thinking of those days was still hard to swallow—like peanut butter, thick and unyielding. It wasn't something I was ready to revisit with him.

"Oh, she was over the moon when that ended." I forced another smile, willed for it to become easier, less put-on.

Richard chuckled. "I can only imagine."

Marie moved back and forth across the kitchen tiles as she prepped the coffee. It'd be a little longer before she'd make it back. The only thing that mattered to me was that she was alive. We'd figure out the rest soon enough.

I hope.

Richard turned, following my gaze as he cleared his throat. "There's something I wanted to give you." He arched a little as he half stood, trying to find something in his back pocket.

I watched him, unsure what he meant. "You mean Marie?"

"No, for you."

He pulled out a well-loved black leather wallet, taking a moment to search before pulling out a white card with blue-and-gold metallic accents.

"I wanted you to have this. Marie has the same cards, but you should have one as well." He handed it over to me gently. Glancing at the type, I made out the words *trauma* and *counselors*.

Hide it!

I couldn't let Marie know he'd given this to me. She'd gone off on the doctors for even suggesting it the last time we visited, and even Deb had said it wasn't smart to push. Fighting against the urge to shove the card anywhere else, I tried to stay calm as he continued, "It's what we give to clients after they've been through similar things."

"Thank you, but if she has them then we're fine." A bit of panic seeped into my voice, so I changed the subject.

She is fine.

We are fine.

I tried to place it back in his hand, anxiety gnawing at the back of my throat, but he wouldn't take it. He gently closed my hand over the card. "You're probably right, but it's a good thing to have. This kind of thing is hard on everyone, even under the best circumstances, and you shouldn't have to go through it alone."

I took my hand back, loosely grasping the card in my lap, not knowing what to say as he continued, "They also have support groups for those not directly involved in the attacks. If you just need a place to go, even to just listen to others' stories. This is a good one."

I rubbed my thumb against the raised ink as I took in what he said.

He leaned in closer, resting a hand on my elbow, sensing my hesitation. "It's okay. You can keep it or toss it, it's up to you. Both are valid options."

"Thank you, I appreciate it."

"No problem. And if either of you need anything, just give me a call. You still have my number?"

"Yes."

I looked at the gold-and-blue script one last time before sliding the card into my pocket as Richard settled back into his seat.

"All right, who's ready for coffee?"

I looked up to see Marie studying each mug carefully before grabbing the first and handing it to Richard. "Here's yours . . ."

She looked back at the cups for just a second before finding mine and handing it to me. "I added some of that salted caramel creamer you like, if that's okay?"

She looked at me with too much concern, ready to take it back.

"That's perfect." I smiled, doing everything possible to erase that look from her eyes. She didn't need to worry, not about this.

Marie plopped down beside me, still buzzing from the joy she'd found. Leaning into me, taking my hand in hers, she turned to ask, "Now, Richard, I'm curious . . . how's the office been without me?"

This was good, almost normal. My tension from earlier started to loosen and melt away.

It's going to be okay.

We're going to be okay.

Maybe this was the start of what a promise looked like.

I gave her hand a small squeeze, enjoying the first sip and the moment of peace around us.

46

DIANE LOUCKS

They'd changed the meds.
Bringing nothingness and quiet.

So much quiet.

They found a way to take my grace.
My mother
The angels
Even the devils.
Then when I didn't eat or move
they changed them again.

Didn't mean to make it so strong they said,
That they didn't know that would happen.

Oh, they knew.

They wanted me to be like before
To be obedient
To look the other way

Like those nights
When Father visited my bed.
When Mother beat me for it.
When the devil took hold

It had been my fault
All of it.

I was lying across the small bed, arms reaching for help that
would never come.
Even with the last med change, my body was drenched in tar.
Slow, heavy, too tired to pray.

I got up when they said.
Ate when they said.
But there was nothing left.
But emptiness
And pain.

H. NOAH

The sky was just visible enough when I laid just so. Back against
the cold brick wall, head on the pillow.

It was here that I waited.
watched the sky turn.
Willing salvation.
For the trumpets.
And fire.

This had to end soon.
It just had to.

OCTOBER 31, 2017
MARIE PERAULT

I lost count of how many times I tried and failed to get into the apartment. The DA's words kept replaying in my head, causing my vision to blur and my hand to slip.

What did you say to him that morning?

Why did you pull a knife?

What were you wearing?

Where did he touch you?

My hand slipped again, key tearing through flesh. Red filled my vision as it opened and poured below. I tried again, able to make it in. I knew they were just trying to prepare me for what the defense attorney would do, but it felt more like they were testing if I could take it without breaking, not prepping me.

Are you sure you're not exaggerating?

Don't get mad.

Why are you reacting like that?

A juror wouldn't take that response well.

I'm not saying anything his attorney wouldn't.

It was your choice to pursue this.

But I had gotten mad, quietly, shaking, waiting for him to finish. I already knew what he believed. What everyone believed.

It was your fault.

I didn't need them to make it so blatant with their words, the way they looked at me. Every thought was jagged, slicing through me.

Stupid, weak girl.

I'd dropped my bag, my keys, everything behind me as I made it to the bathroom, holding my injured hand. The blood seeped through my fingers. I wanted to wash it all away. To scrape his words from my skin.

It would have been simpler if I'd just stuck with the physical assault.

Stupid girl.

My fingers tightened on the porcelain sink, turning bone white against cherry-red splatter. I was my own crime scene, a mockery of what remained.

When will this end?

I just wanted to be me again. Not this lesser version of myself.

The anger boiled, intoxicatingly pure. I was blood, bone, and fury. Everything they'd made me.

You are what you've always been: weak.

I tried to rip out the sink, screaming in frustration and shame. I'd make them understand what this was like. Those men would never forget me or what they'd done.

Stop lying to yourself.

I wasn't. I'd let myself burn if it meant finding peace from this.

But you already told them to drop those charges. Focus on the assault that's easier to prove.

I opened the medicine cabinet, bloody fingerprints now marking the mirror in front of me. I'd forgotten to wash first. Turning on the water, I dipped my hands in and out as the pinkish liquid swirled and disappeared. I reached for the medicine cabinet again, searching for anything that would help, pausing on the bottle of pills.

"Take as needed for the pain."

It was open and tipping into my hand, one pill . . . two pills . . .

I remembered the peace, the numbness they brought.

I wanted to put the pills back but a third, fourth, fifth . . .

What was the point?

Coward till the end.

SAME DAY
MADDIE MORI

"What are you doing?"

I found the blood first, then her things after coming home for lunch to see how the interview had gone; I didn't think I'd see her in the bathroom with those pills in her hand.

I watched as the color drained from her face. Her mouth opened and closed once, twice, before she spoke. "Nothing, just seeing if any were left. Figured I'd flush them."

I wanted to believe her, but I couldn't.

"You're not supposed to flush them. Let me take them. Why don't you treat that cut and I'll drop them off somewhere when I head back to work."

Marie paused, thinking.

I wanted to grab the pills, to shake her, to ask why. Instead, I waited, hand outstretched as she dipped them back into the bottle and handed them to me.

"Oh, and I got that reservation for our makeup anniversary tomorrow. You still want to go out?"

Marie's face fell, shame filling the vacant places behind her eyes as she tried to pretend she hadn't forgotten again. "Of course, it'll be fun."

I couldn't stop pretending this was normal. "Sounds good, I'll be home soon."

I didn't say I love you, didn't want to keep pretending this was okay. I closed the bathroom door as the pill bottle shook in my hand. A soft maraca of *what-ifs*. I grasped it tightly, willing my fear to swallow itself until it was the size of something I could handle.

What if I can't do this?

I didn't care about running as I left the apartment. I wasn't hungry anymore. The look on her face before she saw me . . . it was something I hadn't seen in a while.

Peace.

I wanted to scream, wanted to keep fighting with everything I had, but I didn't have much left.

I can't do this.

Pulling out my phone, I found the closest place to dump the pills and grabbed my bag.

This was something I could do. Something I needed to do.

It had to be a mistake.

A misunderstanding.

I needed to believe her, even if it was just for a moment.

Even if it was a lie.

I got into the car and next thing I knew I was back at the studio. Sitting in the small armchair in the front for customers. I could hear Deb in the back, but she hadn't heard me. I couldn't stop staring at the bottle of pills. I should have stopped, dumped them, anything, but this didn't feel real. But with every movement of my hand, every shift, they rattled back to me. Drowned out the world around me with

it happened

it happened

it happened

I couldn't keep the tears from splashing against the label, blurring the ink with each drop.

That's when Deb dropped to her knees in front of me, placing a hand on each knee as I looked up.

"Maddie . . . What happened?"

I took a breath in, letting it shudder and crash into me as my hand started to shake.

"I think Marie just tried to swallow these." I lifted the bottle just enough toward her that she knew to pick it up, to see what I couldn't say.

Suicide.

I watched her, tilting the bottle to read as tears blurred my vision, as she put the bottle down.

"What happened?"

I blinked, clearing my sight just enough. "She said she was going to flush them." I reached out, grabbing her hand as the numbness broke within me. "But her face, Deb . . . It looked like she was ready to . . ."

I crumpled.

Deb's arms held heavy

as the world ripped out of me

love

cruel

and too giving

every dark thought

I held against me

never someone who could fix

heal

be . . . enough.

I don't know how long we stayed there.

How long the dying light

tried to hold us

in a world colored by something warmer

something safe.

I just know the weight in my friend's arms centered, helped bring me back from the place I'd been trying to hide from. My breath slowed as I nestled my head into her shoulder, returning the strength she had let me borrow.

Deb stroked my hair and her voice vibrated from her chest through me. "Maddie, dear . . . what happened to Marie was horrible. It's the kind of thing that changes you."

Pausing her hand, she moved it to stroke the side of my face. "But it's up to her, who she chooses to become from here."

She tilted my head up to see the concern reflected within her eyes. "It's not selfish to say you're hurting too, because you are. People change, but your expectation of how someone treats you shouldn't. Your pain is valid too."

I can't leave Marie.

I opened my mouth.

What if I have to?

I wanted to say something,

Anything.

but could only fall back to her chest

pull her closer

feel the weight of someone who was there

who could make the world just safe enough

for us both.

NOVEMBER 2, 2017
ARTHUR CASLIN

The sleeves billowed as I pulled the jacket on, the fabric swaying back and forth just enough as I slid each arm into its hole. It was the first time I'd put on a suit since the day of the attack. I'd never been a big guy, but with the stress of the trial and recovery, I looked more like a kid playing pretend in someone else's clothes.

It would have to do for the meeting with the DA. I was already late. Grabbing my keys and wallet, I paused in front of the whiskey before pulling out my phone to call an Uber. Why not trade a shot for responsibilities? The doctors had given me pills to sleep, pills to get out of bed, and pills to quiet everything else, but none of them worked like whiskey. Unscrewing the bottle, I let the warm brown liquid slip easily into my mouth and stomach.

This is for their good as much as mine.

The app pinged "ride accepted" and I saw that someone named Mark in a black Nissan was about five minutes away. I made a side stop to the bathroom for a quick gargle of mouthwash before locking up, hurrying down the stairs, and hitting the street.

Mark was just pulling up as the door closed behind me. We did the usual dance of "are you so and so" before I climbed in and confirmed the address where I was headed. He had the radio station tuned to today's hits. Easy to tune out, especially since we both seemed fine with ignoring each other. The car reeked of some scent of Febreze as I took in the slowing bustle of the city around me. The morning rush had just passed, and it looked like traffic had hit a lull. We were almost to the attorney's office when I realized another tremor was starting in my hand. Same kind I'd had before the attack.

At least I'd been smart enough to pack something. Opening my jacket's inner pocket, I stuck my fingers in, grabbing a few candy-colored pills before popping them into my mouth. Following the doc's script just barely helped; it worked better popping whatever, whenever, and chasing it with booze. I was also supposed to follow it with therapy, but the scripts didn't require this for a refill so who gave a shit. I already understood what was wrong and it wouldn't be solved by a head shrink— only by someone doing their God damned job.

I noticed my mouth was more desert than oasis, so I reached for one of the bottles of water carefully placed in a small basket in front of me. It had to be one of those *free perks* drivers offered for an extra star, but I had to ask.

"Is it okay if I grab one?"

"Huh?" He looked into his rearview mirror for a quick second as I raised the bottle for him to see. "Yeah, man, go right ahead."

Giving him a nod he'd never see, I responded, "Thanks."

It took a few swigs to get them down, the dryness in my throat cracking into actual thirst as we pulled up in front of the building. So, I drained the bottle—wasn't sure the last time I'd taken in something hydrating. The lukewarm water eased the burn as it passed my lips. My driver pointed to a bin before wishing me well. Tossing the bottle in, I shot him a thanks before making my way out of the car and inside.

The glass door I'd entered through closed slowly behind me as I paused to check my watch. I was only a few minutes late, not too bad. Straightening my jacket, I looked up and across the lobby for the face of that attorney who always waited for me. It took a second before I saw him at the opposite side of the room. The fact that there was only a handful of people in the large marble-floored room helped. I hated this place. While the walls were more gray than white, they were as sterile as that hospital had been.

I took a few echoing steps toward him before lifting my hand. "Hey, Kevin."

He gave a short nod and an even shorter smile before making his way to me. He liked me just about as much as I liked him. Only difference was, I didn't hide it.

"Good to see you, Arthur. Ready to get started?"

Like I have a choice.

"Yep."

His only acknowledgment was another small nod as he walked down the hall to his left. I preferred the silence. It was better when we didn't delve into the other's business.

He paused, stretching his arm out in front of me before sweeping it to a door on our right. "We're in this conference room today." He wouldn't leave my side till I was through the door and in my place.

"There's been a little bit of a development that I wanted to talk to you about. I was able to catch up with Marie yesterday and wanted to give you both time to digest what I'm about to say."

This can't be good.

Refusing to take a seat at the long dark table, I turned to the coffee and pastries behind me. Kevin continued to a seat in the middle of the long monstrosity and sat down. This room looked more appropriate for board meetings or mergers, not a fucking one-man show. I poured a quick cup and decided to grab a spinach croissant as the pills and alcohol swirled and soured in my stomach. I took a slow breath then a bite before turning with coffee in hand and sitting across from him. The food was fighting harder than the pills had to go down, so I took a sip of the almost molten liquid and let the moisture spread a bit before swallowing. He had his hands folded and raised in front of him like he was about to pray, not wait for me to speak.

I took another sip, this time relishing in the pills' dulling effect before continuing the game. "So what's up?"

He lowered his hands to the tabletop and cleared his throat. "Well, after reviewing the evidence, the team and I concluded that we may get a better outcome if we offer a deal instead of letting it go to court."

You incompetent FUCK.

The rage that had been at bay started to wake, but everything I'd taken was helping to keep it down, keep it controlled. I continued my blank-faced stare, only pausing to bite and drink, drink and bite, here . . . there. Didn't know what I wanted to do, but enjoyed making him visibly uncomfortable as he failed to loosen his collar. He ran his finger between his starched shirt and his skin like a man trying not to be hung. "The evidence we have for any charges outside of the physical assault aren't shaping up like we'd hoped. The good news is the defense seems oblivious to this, so they'll likely jump at anything we hand them."

A mess of acid-infused caffeine and carbs roiled as it rose and burned within me.

"What do you mean, the evidence isn't shaping up? You have multiple witnesses, including the one sitting in front of you."

Out for wins, not justice . . .

I watched as he panicked, gears spinning out of control as he tried to keep me in check.

"I can't agree. It's been hard to corroborate that the attack was planned like you suggested; even Marie thinks it was chance. We have a few hearsay witnesses from the bar they visited, but there's no way to prove that they were waiting for her. Everything points to a crime of opportunity."

"Sounds like you're about to tell me the sexual assault charges are getting thrown out too."

Kevin took a moment and straightened his back even further into the soft office chair before continuing, "As things stand, the only substantial evidence we have is Marie's account and even she said it's spotty at best." He paused to clear his throat. "New evidence also suggests that the contact the main assailant made with Marie was unlikely as prolonged as first described. The doctors didn't find any torn tissue from forceful insertion of fingertips, and the only DNA in the rape kit was her own. We believe he was stopped before he penetrated her."

I let my finger trail across the top of the cheap paper cup as I chewed over what he said. "So, what you're saying is, you're not the only person incapable of doing their God damn job."

Kevin froze as a red tinge crept up his neck. "Arthur, even you couldn't confirm sexual contact. Add that to the fact that the only other witnesses there had most of their vision blocked by cars and we have nothing. You know as well as I do how these types of cases go. Do you really want Marie to go through that? To put the other charges at risk?"

"It should be Marie's choice, not yours or anyone else's."

That's when it hit me. "You don't believe her, do you? Even after everything they did to us, you can believe everything else but this—that the attack had been sexual in nature."

My words hit their mark as his tone lost its calm. He was flustered. "What I believe doesn't matter and you know that. Whether it did or didn't happen, we don't have the—"

"It happened. He assaulted her." I wasn't about to let him finish that sentence.

Kevin was doing a poor job of hiding anything at this point. "Whatever happened, we can't prove it past a reasonable doubt."

I'm done.

"Arthur. They'll get guaranteed time if we lower the degree, drop the sexual assault charge, and offer a deal. If we don't, they could get nothing. This is a win for everyone, period."

"Let's be frank then. The only person walking out of the courtroom with a win will be you and your fucking record. This is shit wrapped up in a pretty bow and you know it." I let my finger drift down as I grabbed my cup and what coffee I had left, watching with satisfaction as the red highlighted his face with the emotion he refused to voice.

"It's not about me and you're right. It's far from perfect. But it's a guarantee they'll see time. Even Marie agreed."

What did he say?

I'd hit my breaking point. Taking the cup in hand, I relished the grip, windup, and release as I threw it at him. He ducked, just barely, as it created its own Pollock-esque splatter of shit tones behind him. Finally giving me something worth looking at.

"Arthur! What—"

I didn't let him finish.

"Do whatever you like. It's not like anything I'd say would make a difference." I got up and made my way to the door, pausing before I turned the worn silver knob. "I'm done talking. Don't contact me again." I threw the door open and made it halfway down the hall before he called out behind me.

I hit the glass door with as much force as I could muster. I wanted it to shatter into a pile of broken shards, ready to slit the skin of anyone that followed.

They'd remember me then.

266

I put as much distance as I could between me and that door. I'd expected this, but it still didn't sit easy.

Same shit, different day.

I shoved a hand back into my jacket pocket, taking the rest of the pills waiting for me. Each one pulling the skin of my throat as it sank.

No job.

No love.

No fucking person to follow.

Even Marie had given in.

That's when I felt it.

The spark.

A small burn building in intensity.

I am owed.

I took out my phone and scheduled another car, watching as the small blip on the screen made its way to me.

SAME DAY
ARTHUR CASLIN

It was easy enough. All the information I needed waited for me at home. When I'd been working on Ann's case, I made extra copies of all the files so I could work on it from anywhere. Now those documents would take on a different purpose.

I need to know.

To understand.

Wasn't sure exactly what I needed but I knew where to look. I checked out on the ride home, nothing registering until my key clicked into the apartment lock. I walked into the dark hole that had been waiting for me, closing the door firmly behind me.

A lone overhead living room light sputtered, casting a yellow glow on the small messy space before me. I'd never been much for decorating, even when Kate was around. Traded her long dead house plants for casework files—both monuments to my failures.

There was nothing I needed in this room other than the bottle of Jack at the entrance. I made sure to grab it before making my way past the kitchen to the bedroom behind where Ann's story laid outstretched across my small desk. It was cluttered with empty glasses and crumpled takeout napkins. I hadn't been able to put her case up—didn't want to just add it to another pile. So I left it sprawled across my desk. A mixture of her face and police reports. I had let things clutter and obscure the rest. It was the first time I'd sat here since it all ended, the worn office chair catching on the carpet as it creaked under my weight. I grabbed a glass that was mostly empty, swigging back the stale watery whiskey before pouring a fresh double.

Ready to begin.

But a picture of her house caught me. While my place wasn't exactly the homiest, it was at least filled and comfortable. Ann's house had been empty, stark-white walls that seemed to exist only to hold the huge collection of Bibles. I remember the rest had been filled with errant crosses and cheap furniture as hard and unyielding as her life had been.

I took a swig, and the comforting burn started to spread and warm within me. I broke my gaze from the house and picked up the autopsy report.

"Shows signs of emaciation."

Shows?

Ann's sharp and hollowed features seemed to scream through the autopsy photos. *Show* was such a small word for what one small meal a day had done to her.

Fasting, the Bitch called it.

"multiple bruises and contusions in various stages of healing. Strong evidence toward a long history of abuse."

The heat of the whiskey twisted and fueled the rage within me. At least I could revel in it here. I flipped through the report to the rest of the pictures, letting the pinky that had been supporting my drink fall and trace the lines across Ann's back. The rod the Bitch had used had left crisscrossing scars both new and old along her spine.

Stop wasting time on what you've already seen.

I set the drink down and the glass magnified the images below it, forcing the slashes into deeper focus. I rested my head in my hands. The frustration was overwhelming as my fingers traced a path across my forehead then slid through the dark oiled mess of my hair. I paused, my face just above the cool surface of the desk.

Sleep was calling to me, but I wasn't ready yet.

It never helped anyway. I usually felt worse when I woke up. So, I fought against it as it tried to pull me in, aching for just a few hours. I almost caved, but Ann's words pulled at me from the corner of my eye. I took one of her many journal pages out and started to read. My eyes landing on a recap of another beating.

I'm so sorry. You were clear, but I'd drifted off into another foolish daydream and missed most of what you'd said. Please forgive me for that and for asking you to repeat yourself. It was selfish. The rod reminded me of that.

I admit it's hard not thinking of Father and where he might be. He shouldn't have taken my failures so close to heart. His misguided mercy twists inside of me undeserved. He and I both know this is the only way I'll ever learn . . .

Her soft words blurred and disappeared as blistering white heat rushed through me, igniting a second wind.

I knew where to go next.

I rustled through the papers until his name pulsed, almost dancing before me. I grabbed the police report for Walter Loucks, flipping through the pages until I saw it.

Current address.

SAME DAY
RICHARD KOCH

I was sitting on the couch when he came in. Riley was a moving storm of emotion that was hard to miss. He probably thought the speed he entered the house at would be enough to mask the tears shining against his light ocher-brown cheeks.

"Son?"

He didn't stop but I saw the hesitation in his movements as he continued his path up the stairs to his room, the door shutting with just enough force to sound like a warning. Standing, I took a second to stretch the stiffness from my body before following behind.

I made my way slowly from the cold wooden floors of the living room to the carpeted stairs. I wasn't in a hurry, hoping my pace would help Riley collect himself before I made it to his door. I waited a few moments, listening to him shift and settle before knocking lightly on the door.

"Everything okay?"

I waited, but the room had become silent. I slowly opened the door just enough to see that he was lying on his bed with eyes closed and his puffy sound-canceling headphones on as tears streamed down his face. It looked like he had shoved the headphones on roughly; they dug into the soft curls of his high fade. His hair had never been as dark as his sister's or mine—more of a rich brown with hints of his mother's warmer hues reflected in the light. It wasn't hard to pick out Dani's delicate features within his own. Even his sister had started to catch up to his height and would likely be towering over him soon.

I moved to his bed, sitting down at the edge on top of the dark-blue comforter, taking in the superhero posters wallpapering his room. Many I still wasn't sure I could recognize as I rested a hand softly on top of his ankle. Riley opened his eyes. They always reminded me of sunset, shades of flaxen sunlight golden and warm. The tears had lined his eyelids in soft pink, bringing out a hint of green I'd never noticed before. He'd known I was there, I could see it on his face—must have been hoping I'd leave him alone instead of coming in.

"What's wrong?"

He pushed up on his elbows before sitting up, pulling down his headphones with one hand to rest around his neck.

"Nothing, just had a bad day."

I tilted my head just enough and waited, knowing he could see I didn't buy it.

He let out a long breath. "Adley broke up with me." The emotions within his words were not hard to miss, especially as he bit down on his lips, pressing them into a thin line as he tried to keep them locked in place.

Ahh there it is. First love.

"I'm sorry, Riley. I know it's rough." I squeezed his ankle as he looked down, trying to fight back more tears. My heart broke with his. I could already see he was a kid that loved hard. I never worried much with his sister; she was as fierce and strong as her mother. It was Riley I worried about. He was the heart of this family, more altruistic than I thought possible. Too much like myself at his age.

The world isn't kind, but at least this can be fixed.

"Do you have anything due tomorrow? Any tests?"

Riley looked up, confused, his mouth dropping open a little. "No, nothing I can think of."

"Well, how about you play hooky?"

"Really?" His eyes lit up at the idea as he leaned forward.

Smiling, I replied, "Really. We all need a mental health day once in a while. I'll need to check in with your mom, but if she's okay with it we can call you out sick. I can also get out of work a little early and we can see that new movie you've been talking about."

"Really? That would be amazing. Thank you, Dad!"

He sprang forward unexpectedly. The shock of it threw me for a moment before I wrapped my arms around him, holding a little tighter than was needed. He hadn't hugged me like this since he was much smaller. Something told me it was okay to continue as I held on just a little longer, smelling the rich musk of his spray deodorant and the slightly sour scent of hormones every teen room always seemed to hold.

We both need this.

The sound of my cell broke us apart. A shadow of hurt moved over his face as I slid the phone out of my pocket. Work calling.

I saw it then: the space my job had created even though I'd tried to prevent it. The pain from his earlier heartache dropped and curdled within my stomach. I silenced the call before sliding the phone back into my pocket. If it was important enough, they'd leave a message. This was where I was needed most.

Riley's face lifted as I patted his arm before standing up. "I'll check with mom when she gets home, but you should make sure you don't have anything important tomorrow."

He grabbed for his backpack. "I will."

I leaned down as he looked up. I kissed the top of his head. "Love you, son. It'll get better. Just something that needs time."

SAME DAY
MARIE PERAULT

couldn't stop looking. The bruises had faded, the stitches were out, the swelling gone, but the person I saw reflected was alien . . . wrong. I'd opened the sliver of a window in the small bathroom, relishing the chill that caressed my shoulders and legs in the thin tank top and shorts. I'd been wearing some version of this since getting home. Switching them out for different pairs or tops when needed . . . or forced.

This is me.

I gagged on the truth, wanted to see the marks.

When they were worse, I didn't have to explain staying inside or not wanting company. That version of me could justify what I was asking. But now I was left with someone who looked like me but wasn't. Someone riddled with fear.

Coward.

It hadn't been this bad until the walk last night with Maddie.

Until I saw him.

We'd stopped to bicker about which shop to visit. I didn't care; I was just happy to be out and to give Maddie a reason to forget what had happened earlier. But Maddie had stopped at each window, unable to decide.

That's when I saw him, just a few feet ahead.

I couldn't see his face, but I knew.

The man surrounded by men in front of Bull Feeny's—of course he would be near a bar. Same height, same build. My veins iced, freezing me into place. I couldn't move or breathe. Just felt my muscles lock as I stared at the back of his head.

Why wasn't I breathing? I wanted to but the air stayed trapped, burning within me. Everything he'd done on replay. He wasn't wearing a tracksuit. He was in jeans and a coat instead, but it had to be him. There were too many people behind me, and I'd have to run toward him and down a side street to flee.

Same shape, same hair.

Then he'd turned, proving I'd been wrong. I could breathe again. Inhaling the bitter aftertaste of shame as it festered within me. I had made plans for this moment. It was supposed to be different.

Coward.

I gazed in the mirror a few minutes longer, wishing my skin had scarred, had altered with me. But it was unbroken, pale as fresh cream.

Another lie.

I pressed fingertips to the dark circles and deepened lines now under my eyes.

Will this be enough?

Slowly taking a breath, I let the cool air settle within my lungs. We were going out, no way past this. So, I opened the mirror to the old 1950s' style medicine cabinet in front of me and grabbed my makeup.

This is what the old me would do,

What Maddie expected.

Coward.

I started the routine, trying to think of something to wear. Maddie wanted to get fancy drinks and eat at a nice restaurant. That meant sweats were out even though I wanted to wear them, to be background noise wherever we went.

If I'm unremarkable, I'm safe.

That's why I'd tried to cut my hair when I found out they had gotten out, but Maddie had stopped me. She set up an appointment with a hairdresser, but I made the mistake of trying. Thought I could convince myself I was safe in my car, that it would make me less visible, but I saw him everywhere. Only made it a few blocks before turning home.

I could cut it now, there was still time. Women with short hair were less likely to be attacked. Long hair made it easier to . . .

Someone outside the window screamed in laughter. I froze as terror scraped within me. I felt his hand, so tight. The roots of my hair ripping out. His fist only tightening its hold. A crack in my neck

As he pulled it to the point of breaking. How his breath hot, thick, and . . .

ENOUGH

My hands dug into my arms as I crumpled on the floor. Pain was the only thing that brought me back. I didn't want to cry, didn't want to hide anything else. It was getting harder to keep this from Maddie. I wanted to stay safe, to stay in this apartment, in our bed. I just needed a little more time and it'd be okay. But I didn't have more time; my medical leave was almost up. I wanted to ask for more, but *mentally fucked* wasn't covered under my plan.

Yesterday had been bad, but I'd come back from it, realized that a guaranteed deal where they'd be locked up was better than taking a chance. I would know where they were, which— after my almost-encounter—was better than nothing.

Fucking coward.

I pulled myself up, finished the makeup that was missing, and went to the closet, grabbing a long tunic-like shirt with a dark floral pattern and slight fit. I decided to pair it with black leggings, a deep-red cardigan, and tall brown boots. This seemed okay. Nice enough to go out, but not showy. There was safety within the layers and folds of extra fabric.

Then we left.

I didn't mean to do it, but somewhere in between getting dressed and walking into the restaurant I'd switched to auto pilot as I tried to take in every noise, every movement, every shift in voice. It wasn't until we were seated and a few glasses of prosecco in, that anything changed. It was probably the alcohol, but I didn't care. The shadows and sounds dulled as the faces around us receded and disappeared.

The world was easy again. Maddie and I were easy again.

I didn't want it to end. So, after paying the bill we decided to go to The Bar of Chocolate for dessert and martinis. It was later than I would have liked, but my anxiety with crowds had lifted after the first bottle. In this moment with Maddie, I was okay and I wanted to ride it out for as long as I could. As we walked out of the restaurant, a hint of winter brushed against our skin. It felt good, like I was alive.

Maddie had taken out her phone to get a ride, but I reached out and tipped it down.

"How about we walk?"

Maddie's forehead crinkled just a little in confusion as she asked, "You sure? It's a bit of a distance."

"I'd like to try. If I get tired, we can still call a ride." I reached out to grab her hand as she smiled.

"Okay."

Holding her hand wasn't enough so I raised it to my lips, softly kissing each of her fingers. Maddie was the only stable presence during all of this. She deserved more and I wouldn't blame her for leaving, but I was glad she stayed.

Turning downtown, we started to make our way to the bar. The main shops had closed but the night scene was just coming to life. The energy around us intensified with dancing and laughter.

This was the city I knew, the city I'd fallen in love with.

As we hit the cobbled streets of Old Port, the crowds picked up. The worst would hit a few hours later but the narrow street was already starting to choke up with groups of college kids and greased-up professionals, all celebrating the end of the week. Maddie squeezed my hand as we made it to the small entrance of the bar. It's what I loved about this place. Almost like a secret, off to the side and hidden between the two larger bars beside it. I looked to Maddie. The sun was almost down but the fading reds and oranges painted her face. Her smile came easy, her hair teasing back and forth across her nose in the breeze.

I smiled back. "Hey, you." I raised my free hand, wanting to brush hair behind her ear, but Maddie intercepted it, pressing her cheek into my palm. I tilted her head just enough for me to lean in, the warmth within my chest building. She tasted like honey, soft and sweet as she opened to me. The bubbles from earlier still lingering on her tongue, pulling me in deeper. I'd have stayed like that forever if she'd let me.

"Now touch her boobs!"

A voice, too close, shattered the silence between us.

I turned, raising my eyes to the bar on our right. A group of preppy jocks flocked around its entrance, watching, waiting for a reaction. That's when I saw him. Standing in the center of the group, smug and preening. Bolstered by the drinks he'd already consumed.

Intoxicated children.

Another smaller and more giggly mess shouted, "Give us a show, take it off!"

I was frozen again but with the feeling that usually tore through after the shame:

Anger.

I hid myself, but never who I loved. I would never let anyone take that away.

My teeth gritted, enamel cracking into gravel as my vision narrowed. "The fuck did you say?"

My words seemed to bolster the group, drawing them closer, a circling pack, focused on amusement.

The leader, the one who smiled first, stood in front of me now. Tall, lanky, dressed up in clothes only his parents could afford. His face glinted with ignorance and amusement, ready to play this game of his own making.

"Oh, come on. It was just a joke. Lighten up, sugar."

He was right in front of me, breath as sour as *his* had been.

Another faceless boy leaned into his ear. "Pay her. Whores don't do shit till they get paid."

This cued the one who laughed to empty his pockets. Coins flashing and falling down on me and Maddie.

When this started, we'd been holding hands, but Maddie had shifted, grasping at my arm, trying to pull me away.

No, love. You don't turn your back on animals.

I planted my feet, ready. Watching for weakness. "Leave, now."

I zeroed on the first, the leader. He would be the one to bend if he bent at all.

His smile only stretched, more hyena than human as he leaned in even closer. "Or what? Guess dykes can't take a joke." He laughed as he threw his words back to the boys, strengthened by the chorus that echoed back.

His breath was embers on my face, burning the air with liquor. It grew stagnant and thick, filling my lungs.

"C'mon now, what are you going to do?" he asked, face stretched in amusement, a wolf in clown's clothing.

That's when I felt it.

His hand, pushing my shoulder back. I flashed to a memory of pavement. How my skin had scraped raw under *his* weight.

I snapped.

I'm not sure how he ended up on the ground. With me on top of him. Or how my hands rose and fell so quickly, hitting again and again. But here I was, and God it felt good.

SAME DAY
MADDIE MORI

Marie ripped from me. She'd been there one moment, flying the next. I looked at my hands as the screaming started. I don't know how she did it—how she'd taken that guy, at least a head taller than her, down so quickly or with such force. A part of me relished watching his smile crack into something painful. Retribution in a matter of moments, but it should have stopped there.

"Marie . . . hon, stop! Please stop!"

Marie was dropping her fists into him as if he were bread, or thin ice on a frozen pond. Deliberately and with more force than was necessary. I crouched beside her, catching a fist, but when she turned she turned to me as an inconvenience, eyes empty. She'd disappeared again.

"Marie, honey, plea—" I made the mistake of trying to pull her off him. The flash of pain came hot and searing as she ripped her hand back. Each nail scraped across the skin of my face. I couldn't help but stumble back, cupping my cheek in my hands as blood dripped through my fingers and down my arms.

I can't help her.

I can't even stop her.

I fell to the ground as panic shot through me. A crowd had grown, so I turned my eyes to them.

"Someone, please help us!"

But no one would acknowledge me. They just kept their phones turned to the action as I bled and pleaded. I dropped my hand, pushing myself to stand. The kid's friends had booked it as soon as Marie had taken him down, little boys filled with more air than follow-through. A small blessing in this case.

It's bad, but it could have been worse.

"Someone, please!" I cried out again, even though no one would come. I had to try.

Positioning myself behind Marie, I locked my arms under hers, hooking her from behind. I tried pulling her off, but she was too strong. Her legs kicked as she tried to break free from my grasp, both of us in a temporary stalemate. But it was enough. As soon as her fists stopped hitting, he looked up. His eyes were swelling and filling with blood, but he was alert enough to see his chance, wiggling from beneath her to freedom.

Marie wouldn't stop even as he ran, feral in her pursuit. She'd managed to free her arms, but I kept a tight grip on her waist, holding just enough of her back so he could slip through the crowd.

The terror on his face . . .

"Marie, what did you do?"

Marie switched her focus to my hands, struggling as she twisted and pulled in earnest.

Why is she fighting me?

Another burst of pain, this time from a crack of her elbow to my side. I let go, gasping from the shock of it, and watched. She paced back and forth as the crowd finally backed up, afraid. That's when I saw the cop pushing through, focused solely on Marie.

"Ma'am, are you okay? We had a report of a fight."

He was nothing to her, background noise to wherever she'd gone. Still pacing back and forth like a caged animal, ready to attack. I stepped forward, raising my hand. "We're okay, officer. We just had a run in with some college kids. I think she's still upset from that."

He nodded as he turned to me, eyes widening in disbelief.

I must look worse than I feel.

I watched him catch sight of her hands, how the blood that covered them was still wet enough to smear across her face when she raised them in frustration.

He looked back at me. "Looks like she may have done the running into."

He took a step toward her with his hand on his baton. "Ma'am, I'm going to need you to sit down."

She couldn't, just paced and paced and paced.

I have to do something.

I started to rush to her side.

"*Stop* right there. I need you to back up!" His voice came hard and fast, stopping me mid-stride.

"Please, she was attacked and almost died a month ago. I think this brought it back for her."

But he wouldn't listen.

Marie had stopped pacing just long enough to turn to him and reach out her hands as she started to take a step toward him. I knew that look. She wanted help.

He took her down.

He must have been saying something to her, but it was hard to hear over the screaming.

I'd never heard that sound come out of her before. It was heartbreaking and there was nothing I could do as my screams joined hers.

I asked him to stop, pleaded, but the words just repeated, and he kept holding her down, grinding her into the stone. I pleaded again and again, even as my arms were pulled behind me, as I was pushed to the ground and locked into place.

54

ARTHUR CASLIN

The streets were quiet and dark as I made my way across the uneven bricks to my car. It was the kind of cold that made you want to turn back, but this was too important. My black, slightly rusted out 2002 CRV was just a few feet away. The winters had been rough, but this car had got me through. I'd likely ride this thing into the ground but not tonight. I slipped behind the wheel and started to drive. I remembered this city, even without GPS. Made it halfway to his house before losing my nerve. I wanted to talk, to understand, but I found myself driving around and around, unable to stop. Not until I saw the lights drifting out of a random dive bar. Who knows, maybe I'd find my resolve at the bottom of a glass?

Luckily, it was still fairly early for the party crowds. I was able to pull into a spot up front before walking inside and finding a seat next to the bartender. I made sure to keep my distance from what must have been the regulars. I didn't want small talk, just to fade into the barely lit shithole around me. The only person I wanted to talk to was already making his way toward me.

"Can I get you something?"

The bartender paused, looking up from the glass he was drying with a look that said, "It better be simple." He was a portly fellow, tattoos covering his body like clothing. The years he had on me spoke more of experience, not weakness.

"I'll take a double of whatever liquor you grab first."

"Coming right up."

He turned, walking to the shelves behind him while I pulled out a twenty for when he returned. There was a bowl of peanuts in front of me. I cracked one after another, piles of shells and nuts steadily growing. I wasn't hungry, I just needed something to do with my hands.

What the hell are you thinking?

It was a valid question. I'd already talked to him several times, sifting through his statements and the things the Bitch had done. But there were things I couldn't ask, things I'd wanted to. Like how was he able to just stand there and watch what had happened? Why'd he leave her behind? But Marie had been with me every time, stopping me before I could ask. Kept reminding me he wasn't the one on trial. It wasn't my choice not to prosecute. At the time, I had a much bigger Bitch to fry. It was true he never joined the abuse.

No.

In the end he did nothing, just watched Ann go through it all, letting her believe it was her fault.

Some father.

I took a long, slow drink, disappointed in how dull the burn of hard alcohol had become overall. Breathing out gave an extra kick to the gin, and its usual bite at the end helped remind me of the actual alcohol in the drink.

My knuckles turned white as I gripped the glass too tight. The tremors were back so I dug my hand into my pocket, grabbing more pills and chasing them with my drink, almost emptying the glass. I tried to massage some of the tension out of my hands, rubbing, bending, and stretching them as my mind wandered through the mess of it all.

I have to know.

Why did he let it happen?

I took out my phone, running my fingers along the darkened screen. I'd leave it to fate. If he picked up, I'd go ask. If he didn't, I'd turn around and think of something else in the morning.

I dug out the piece of paper I'd copied all his information to and propped it on the empty pile of shells. The cracked and worn wooden surface gave an eerie glow from the reflection of the dim light above. I typed his number one by one by one . . .

Ring.

Ring.

Ring.

He must be out.

Ring . . .

Ring . . .

"Hello . . . ?"

I drained the rest of my drink and made my way to the door.

55

SAME DAY
RICHARD KOCH

After I got the call, I reached out to Carter immediately. He wasn't there to help but he got one of his officers working on both of their releases. I got there just as they released Maddie, and I almost didn't recognize her as they brought her out. So much blood had dried across her face, most of her features had been obscured. Her usually straight hair a tangle of knots and dried clumps of dark red. When she got closer, she looked down as the blood cracked and fell onto her clothes. It was like she was ashamed, but there was nothing for her to be ashamed of.

She looked back up as soon as she had made her way in front of me; the only clear spots on her face seemed to be where the tears had washed away. I could see the small cuts and scrapes across her face and hands, the small tears in her clothing. It looked worse than the wounds seemed, but it was still terrifying to take in.

"Maddie . . . what happened?"

"Some kids down in the Old Port started harassing us, and Marie . . ." Her voice choked on the words. "Marie just lost it. I've never seen her like that."

"No, Maddie, what happened to you?"

She looked down again, tears threatening to spill as she raised her hand and traced the lines across her face. "I tried to pull Marie off one of the guys . . . but it's like she didn't see me and just reacted. I don't think she realized what she did."

My heart hurt for Maddie. I could see the love for Marie, the worry and shame. But she was missing the worry for herself. I took her hands in mine. Seeing the fresh bruising still red and angry around her wrists with darker shades of black forming. Other abrasions ran up her arms and across her face, separate from what Marie had done. I had a feeling what the answer was going to be but needed to hear it from her first. "And these?"

A few tears fell on my hand, throwing a translucent ruby light before hitting. "From the arrest."

Anger writhed within me but I swallowed it for now; she didn't need to see it. I gave her hands a small squeeze as she looked up. "How about you go to the bathroom and clean up a bit? I want to take you to the hospital to get your cuts cleaned properly."

It was easy to hear the panic take hold within her voice. "Marie didn't mean it. I'm okay. They aren't that bad."

I moved my hands to her shoulders and looked straight into her eyes. "I know she didn't, but I want to make sure you're taken care of first. They're having issues with her release paperwork, so we should have enough time to go and make it back in time to get her. I'll make sure of it." I smiled a little, waiting until she nodded. "What you both do from there is in your hands, though talking about what happened would be good for you both."

She nodded. "I'll be right back."

I waited for her to disappear completely before heading to the front desk. I was ready to let go of what I'd swallowed earlier. This time I wasn't going to edit myself to make my anger into something more palatable.

I was furious.

I didn't recognize the cop at the desk: pressed uniform, short-cropped light-brown hair, pale skin, and green eyes. Old enough to have been out of college for a few years, if he'd gone. He picked up a mug for a drink, calm and relaxed until he caught the look on my face and the tone in my voice.

"Can you explain to me why the young lady you just released, Maddie Mori, was covered in blood and bruises?"

He choked a little as he swallowed. "Uh, sir, I think it was from the altercation she was a part of."

"Funny. That doesn't exactly line up with what she said or the fact that she didn't even get basic attention to her injuries while she was detained."

"I, uh . . ."

Leaning toward him, I lowered my voice. "I suppose there is a reason why excessive force was used in her arrest as well."

He looked around for a way out, likely for someone else to pass me on to, but seeing no one he turned back to me with a spark of anger licking off his words. "Now, sir, I was not a part of the arrest and am not familiar with . . ."

I was done listening, so I took out a small notebook and pen along with my card. I pushed the latter toward him on the counter as I flipped the notebook to a blank page. "You should notify whoever you report to that I'll be speaking with them in the morning and that they should have the report ready for me with every detail of the incident, arrest, and detainment ready to go."

The cop glanced at the card, the red tinge of anger that had started to grow dissapearing as I continued, "I am taking Maddie to get medical attention and when I get back, I expect my employee—Marie—will be ready to be released and in better shape than I saw her partner in."

"Yes, sir."

"Now before I leave, I'll need your name and badge number."

I saw movement from the corner of my eye where Maddie had

disappeared. Looking up, I could see Maddie walking toward me in the distance, looking a little better. Turning back to the cop in front of me, I let my words sharpen as I released them.

"Quickly now."

SAME DAY
MARIE PERAULT

was in the shower.

How'd I get here?

I remembered the fight, the cop. How Maddie had talked and talked to me during it, but all I heard was static.

As soon as hands had touched me, all that anger burned, turned resolve into ash . . . into nothing at all.

When Maddie got me home, she couldn't look at me. I couldn't look at me. So I told her I needed a shower. Not that I needed to feel.

Coward.

The water fell, relentless rain in a thick mist. Steam easing across the floor. I'd turned it as far as it would go.

Pain was good.

Prosecco had numbed. Made the shadows recede. But pain helped me feel or something close to it. I relished the burn against the raw skin on my face. The cop had pressed just enough of me into the ground to send me back to that moment with *him* and how *his* excitement hardened and pulsed eagerly in beat with my head hitting the pavement.

Coward

I wanted to scream, to smash through the glass and open myself to the wreckage inside of me, but Maddie would hear. Come too quickly. What was wrong with me?

Coward

The water was cooling but wasn't cold enough to numb.

Sitting in the center of the shower, I pressed my head against my knees, squeezing my arms harder into my body.

My God, I'd hurt Maddie.

Shame rippled through me as I dug my nails into the skin of my arms.

It wasn't enough, made it harder to breathe but wasn't painful. So I grabbed my hair next. Thick ropes tangling between fingers as I pulled.

Pain followed but threw me with a snap back to *his* hands.

I didn't want that. I didn't want to remember. I wanted to feel. The tears came, thick streams as unremarkable as their maker.

If only I could disappear as quickly and suddenly down the drain.

57

SAME DAY
MADDIE MORI

The bathroom door was too solid and straight against my back. I tried not to think of all the ways to break it, splinter it to its core if Marie grew too quiet, refused to get out, if it was locked. I didn't want to think she was capable of it, but tonight she seemed capable of anything. I'd loved this old door when we'd gotten the place, but now I wished for something made of plywood and air, something easier to break. I'd been here sitting on the floor since Marie had gone in, heard the shower turn on but nothing else. The steam seeped beneath the door slowly, causing droplets of water to form on the wood where it touched.

They'd taken us in together but in separate cars, and I didn't blame them. Marie needed three or four officers just to keep her from hurting herself or others.

God, her eyes.

I'd never seen that look before. The cop had knocked the emptiness out and replaced it with terror. It's why I'd called Richard. I didn't know what to do, and Deb wouldn't have known either. He'd been so kind and understanding, just as worried as I was.

I couldn't stop the tears as my breath hitched; they burned as they hit the raw skin underneath. I covered my mouth, trying to stay hidden. I didn't want her to think I was keeping watch, even though that's all I'd been doing since the attack. Watched and pretended, watched, and kept silent. But she kept disappearing more and more into herself. So, I swallowed it all: the pain, my expectations. Tried to exist without existing. I was angry for giving up so much of myself again.

In exchange for focusing on my art, I'd started to live for the handful of things she said about the weather, a show, or some other distraction. Each word was nectar, sustaining in its own way. But then I'd say something, ask the wrong question, or move too quietly. She'd stop and snap, swallowing herself back up again with an almost apology, disappearing until it was time to sleep. This was the only time of day she'd let me close, walking barefoot, feet sticking lightly to the wood floors. She'd crawl into bed and wrap my arms around her. The nightmares were the only thing that broke these moments. They're why I stayed awake, waiting for them until sleep won. I wanted to be ready for the first whimper or jerk of her body. I'd hold her tighter, whispering sweet things, or sing our favorite song until whatever it was passed, and her breath calmed back into sleep. I was past sleep deprived—hadn't been as hard as I expected to get used to less. Just hadn't expected to lose so much of myself to her. I didn't realize how much until her fingers had raked across my cheek. She hadn't meant it, but it had been enough to jolt me back into myself.

My muscles were starting to tighten from the lack of movement. I should have paid attention to the time. Had it been too long? The steam, which had been thick and heated, was thinning.

I have to see.

Leaning forward, I pushed myself into a standing position. Stretching and bending side to side as I rose, pulling for comfort in my own movement. I lifted my arms, arching backward as the knots that had just been made loosened before I turned to the door.

"Hey, hon, you okay?"

I waited but all I could hear was the steady fall of water. Fear now replaced the space tears had taken. I knocked slowly but firmly.

"Marie, do you need anything?"

Nothing.

I reached for the knob, silently pleading.

"I'm coming in."

The doorknob twisted and clicked. It wasn't locked.

The door creaked as I pushed against it, light steam rolling around its edges, clinging to my hair and filling my chest as I breathed.

The mirror dully reflected the muted light behind me. Marie would be to my right so I took a few steps in, closing the door just enough so I could see.

"Marie?"

No answer. I closed the distance a little too quickly and my feet slipped on the wet tiles beneath. I paused, finding balance using the towel rack beside me before opening the frosted glass door. She was sitting in the middle of the shower, fully dressed, holding herself as the water fell across her back. I didn't need to touch her to realize she'd used up all the hot water. The air was already taking on a chill as the thick steam dissipated.

"Marie?"

I reached out and brushed her shoulder, barely touching a fingertip. Might as well have been a backhand as she scrambled to the farthest corner with her hands raised, trying to fill the smallest part of the shower as bottles and scrubs rained like casualties behind her.

"No, no, no, no, please no." When she couldn't move any farther, she looked up, arms raised, ready.

I watched as she slipped from fear to rage, her voice changing to something more guttural and injured. "Why'd you sneak up on me like that?"

I can't do it anymore.

I can't pretend.

This hurts and I'm scared too.

I let the tears fall unchecked as I sank to the floor across from her, letting the water soak through. I watched her change again from rage to sadness just as quickly as before.

Where has my Marie gone?

"I'm so sorry, Maddie." She started to move toward me, reaching out. "I . . . I don't . . . I didn't mean to."

I raised my hand for her to stop. "Marie, what am I supposed to do?"

I brought my knees up to my chest, loosely hugging my hands around my ankles as I tried to stay out of reach.

She'd stopped moving toward me. Now leaning farther into the water behind her, she closed her eyes. I wasn't sure if she was going to talk or stay in this new pose, water flowing over her head and down her back. Then she opened her eyes, searching for mine.

"Maddie, something's wrong with me."

"What do you mean?" I watched her face crumble with the question.

"It's like my body, my emotions aren't mine. I don't feel in control." I watched her wring her hands just a little too hard.

I raised my shirt to my mouth, chewing it in comfort before asking, "Is that what happened tonight?"

"Maybe? I think so. It was good for a while, but then everything changed, and I got so angry." She moved her legs into a kneeling position, sitting on her heels, her hands now clenched against her black leggings. "It felt good, like I was in control, but I hurt someone . . . I hurt you."

Marie took in a slow jagged breath before asking, "Why did it feel good to hurt him?"

I moved in closer.

"Nothing's wrong with you, but I—"

"What, want to leave?"

"No, God no, Marie. I just . . . I don't know what to do, or how to fix this. It shouldn't even be on me to do it."

She looked down, ashamed. "I didn't mean for that to happen, to put that pressure on you. What if this can't be fixed?" Her body seemed to fall in on itself again, this time in defeat.

"I don't believe that." I wanted to be near her, but I didn't want to push too hard. "Is it okay if I hold you?"

I watched her body grow rigid for a moment as she thought it over. "Yeah, it's okay."

I crawled over, unable to hide a gasp as icy water hit me. I positioned myself behind her before shutting the water off and wrapping her in my arms.

I took a moment to breathe her in before kissing the side of her head gently. "I don't believe this can't be fixed."

I squeezed her just enough that her body responded by relaxing into me. I let my head fall, finding refuge on her shoulder.

"Maddie, it's all my fault."

I was surprised but fit my hands into hers. "What do you mean?"

Her body tensed up, her voice sharp and bitter. "They attacked me because I messed up."

What?

"Hon, that wasn't on you."

Her voice shook as she spoke. "How could it not be? They thought I had a knife until I showed them I didn't. I could have bluffed, done so much more."

"Marie, you did everything possible. If you hadn't, I . . . I don't think you'd be here." I raised her hands, entwined with mine, as I hugged her against me. She was more doll than participant and tried to slip away, but I wouldn't let her.

She turned her face against my chest and whispered, "I'm not me anymore."

"Of course you are." I moved my chin down, softly kissing her neck for a few moments before lifting it again. "What happened doesn't make you less."

We both sat in silence, the dripping of the shower head tapping against our bodies. We held on to each other, to the warmth in our skin. In this moment, it was almost enough.

"Marie, I think you need help. What you're going through is more than I can handle."

Her body tightened against me. "Are you leaving?"

"Honestly, if this doesn't change, I'll need to. But right now, I just need you to fight. I need you to want a healthier normal. It shouldn't be on me to save you . . ." She squeezed my hand harder than I expected, leaning her head against mine.

I tilted my face up just enough to whisper in her ear, "Marie, honey . . . This is a have to."

"I know."

I'm not sure how long we sat there leaning against each other.

We didn't feel the cold, the water dripping slowly from our hair and clothes.

Only listened to the other's heartbeat as we held on to the peace of the night and something we hadn't felt in a while . . .

Okay.

SAME DAY
ARTHUR CASLIN

pulled up to a small house at the end of the road. Dark, almost-living shadows seemed to sway back and forth from the bare trees surrounding it as they gave way to the soft wind. The shafts of moonlight made it easy to see that the property was well taken care of.

32 Terrigan Ave. This is the place.

I parked across the street, sitting for a moment as I looked out the window. The house, if you could even call it that, was a simple structure annexed by the surrounding homes. Bland and easy to forget, just like the man inside.

As I got out of the car, I was hit with another wave of hesitation.

Call Marie.

I didn't want to. She'd talk me out of this, say it wasn't right.

Maybe this is my last sign?

I took out my phone, dialed, and waited.

She didn't pick up.

This is meant to happen.

I walked to the front door, sticking to the paved path that wound its way through the perfectly manicured lawn. I only had the warm low lights within the house to guide me, but the stark-white stones beneath my feet seemed to soak every soft ray and radiate it back. Beckoning pure as it called me forward.

I have to know.

Have to ask.

Then I'll leave.

I knocked a couple of times and waited. After one minute, then two, and almost three passed I found myself catching my breath.

What if I had called a cell and he's not here?

I raised my hand, about to knock again, as a muffled shuffling started to make itself known from behind the door. I waited for the bright light of a porch light that never came. Instead, one by one, the locks started sliding free—a fourth now, fifth, and sixth.

Damn, how many does he need?

"Yes?"

There he was, just as I remembered: shorter than myself by at least a head, with the same graying hair that easily spoke of his fifty-plus years. The light washing out behind him seemed to silhouette and amplify his slight, almost-petite frame.

"Walter Loucks? It's me, Arthur Caslin. I led the prosecution on your wife's case. Do you remember me?" I extended my hand, and it was quickly met with his own.

"Of course I do, Arthur! I've wanted to thank you for the work you did on her case but was told you'd left the DA's." His hand tightened around mine as he brought his other one up to join. "God's grace really shined within the courtroom when she finally got the help she needed." He squeezed my now-limp hand one more time before letting go. "Has something new happened?"

I shifted my weight, taking my hand back and massaging it as I tried to ignore his usage of *God's grace* and *help* in relation to her.

"No, sir, I just had a few more personal questions I wanted to ask you. Something for my own peace of mind if it isn't too much trouble."

"Come in and ask away. It's the least I can do." Walter stepped back with an arm outstretched, faltering just for a moment. "Oh, and careful on your way in. There's a step. My outside light burned out a few days ago and I keep forgetting to pull out the step ladder to fix it."

As I stepped in, I got a clearer look. His thick gray sweater was more knotted than cable knit and almost blended perfectly with his paper-white skin. Still dressed in the clothes he'd likely worn earlier that day. The only sign of him turning in was the blue fleece house slippers on his feet.

My smile was as empty as the words that wouldn't come out. Not that Walter noticed; he just stood to the side chatting happily as he let me in—a welcome that was less of a jolt than what was waiting for me inside.

All the books, paintings, and plush seating hit me like a slap across the face. It was everything Ann's house hadn't been. Warm, friendly, almost picturesque. All that was missing was an old fat cat and something freshly baked to make this some fairy tale welcome.

Walter led me through a small entrance to the hardly bigger living room and kitchen area.

"Sit! I insist." He pointed to a large overstuffed couch in the center of the room. "I don't get many guests so there isn't much, but would you like some water, or a nightcap?"

"A drink sounds good to me." I couldn't bring myself to use the same word. There was something about the joy in his voice that grated against my every nerve.

I sat down on the couch, watching him flutter here and there, looking in different cabinets and shelves within the kitchen. He was moving so rapidly, I was getting motion sick at the sight.

"Honestly, I don't want to be too much trouble. I'm good with just sitting and talking."

"Nonsense! Ahh, here we go. A nice bottle of red." He raised it over his head like a prize before placing it on the counter and continuing, "I also have some bread and cheese in the fridge."

My mouth dropped open.

Where was this father when she needed him?

The quiet, withdrawn man I'd known now radiated life in a manner more irritating than joyful to behold. I stayed fixated on him as his hands fluttered across the small platter, cutting, placing, preparing everything just so before presenting it to me with the wine and glasses intertwined under his arm and through the fingers of his other hand. Pouring himself and me an overflowing glass of wine, he took a seat in the even more impossibly stuffed chair to my right.

"Now, what was it you wanted to speak to me about?" he eagerly asked as he cut a shaving of what looked like cheddar before shoving it whole into his mouth, chasing it with the wine.

"Just a few things." I wanted to bite the calm and kindness out of my voice, but getting nasty would only shut the fool up. "They may be a bit out of line, but I just . . . I'm trying to understand."

His face lost a little shine. The smile that had been its centerpiece just a moment before fell in its own kind of surrender. "Go ahead. It's probably nothing I haven't asked myself before."

I took the knife from the plate in front of me, small, flat, but surprisingly weighted in my hand as I cut a few slices of the same cheese Walter had eaten just moments before. I wasn't hungry, I just needed to do something with my hands. "Why'd you never step in?"

I looked up to see what little color he had left drain from his face. This was the man I knew: flaccid and weak with shame flickering behind his eyes.

"Oh." He placed the glass he'd been clutching down on the table before retreating into the chair that held him. "I guess . . ."

Spit it out, Walter.

"I . . . I thought it would just make it worse if I stepped in. That if I did something, anything really, that me and Ann would both pay for it."

This is new.

I sank back into the cushions, tracing the edge of the silver in my hand with my thumb. "Both? You've never mentioned this before."

"I didn't think what she did to me was important. Diane and I'd been so happy in the beginning, both lost and in search of a home. Something we thought we'd found in each other, especially when we found out we were expecting. But something happened after Ann was born."

Walter shifted in his seat, grabbing his glass to take another sip before beginning again. "Ann was safe for a time. She was the only one who was able to make Diane smile . . . to bring her back when she drifted too far. But that changed when Ann got older."

My knuckles turned white against the unforgiving metal of the knife. I tried to stay calm as I asked, "What kept you from taking Ann?"

"I'm ashamed to admit this, but a part of me was relieved when Diane left me alone. Another part of me believed we deserved it, that we'd be turning from God if we turned from her too. When I failed, I didn't want to damn my daughter as well." His thin, wasted hands rubbed his face, a desperate plea to a false God, before looking to me.

His eyes had changed.

They were empty now,

just like the Bitch's.

The anger was thick and dense as it overwhelmed me. "No, you just left her when you'd had enough, only for her to be drowned days after."

Rage took hold.

Encasing.

Erasing.

I was standing in front of him, but it wasn't me.

That me had wanted to talk, wanted to understand,

but IT had had enough.

IT couldn't believe the words coming out of his mouth.

The words he refused to change even with a knife to his face.

He was in tears now, sobbing, shaking. Fully resembling the shell of a man I'd met as he pleaded.

"I didn't realize—I would have taken her if I had . . . Please . . ."

Please?

I lunged
hands grasping
forgetting the knife.
As I knocked him over in the chair

I made a path with his body.

As something foreign took hold
And I watched,

Not that I cared.

IT hit him.
Over
And over
Again.
With fists,
With feet.
throwing him here,
There,

painting him across
The floor.

Ann never had a chance. Why should he?
He managed to ram an elbow into IT's face, but IT didn't feel
anything but surprise.
He took that moment to go for the door.
Can't have that.

IT shoved a foot in front of him and pushed.
he flew a guided path, to the left.
Straight into the wall.
Falling hard,
Face smashing to the floor,
As pools of red grew reflective.

IT started toward him again but stopped at the sight of the
walking stick leaning near the front door.

Images of Ann's scars
Flashing
Throbbing
Through IT's head.

The stick was thicker than the rod,
but would do.

IT walked, almost skipped as IT retrieved it.

There was no escaping, even though the bastard tried

Crawling,

Moaning,

Growing weaker and quieter.

Just an animal seeing its time had come.

The smooth knotted wood was cold but eagerly warmed to IT's touch.

IT listened with a smile as the crawling took on a more frantic nature.

"Was it like this, Walter? When Ann was limp on the floor, the Bitch still ready to continue?"

IT's voice was so detached, I almost didn't recognize it as my own.

I turned to face him. He wasn't moving anymore.

Eyes wide, staring back.

I started toward him, stick twirling like a baton,

getting closer and closer.

"No, I don't imagine it was. I mean, Ann never fought back, just took it over and over again. Not like you."

I was next to him now.

H. NOAH

I pointed the stick down, tracing its knotted handle across the side of his face.

He turned his head away in fear, silently screaming.

I lowered myself to him, sliding my hand down the stick as I went, grabbing his chin with the other. I brought his head back with a snap. He didn't get to look away. Gazing into his empty terror, I couldn't keep my head from slowly cocking to the side in amusement.

"What's this feel like?" My voice calm and tepid.

I didn't expect him to have anything left.
He ripped his head from my hand
Sunk teeth into flesh,
grinding them across bone.
He even tried for the stick.
That's when IT came again,
The rage.

The emotion.

It rang through my ears.
sharpening my vision.

It was the only thing I noticed as I smashed his face in with the head of the walking stick.

As I turned him over,
Gifting him
with the same markings
Ann had held.

Unable to stop till the rage receded,
And the shaking took its place,
The stick now falling,
Clattering,
from my hand.

Sinking to the floor beside the body. I grabbed for the knife that
lay only a foot away.
There was gurgling.

"Still breathing?" I murmured.
Unable to decide whether I was disappointed or not.
In the end it didn't matter
Slicing across his throat
As soft and giving as brie.

Time to go.
Couldn't leave fate to his God. Mine knew what had to be done.

ARTHUR CASLIN

H ollow.

In the air around me.

In the people I passed.

As I walked

And walked.

And.

Went down streets,
alleys,
over lawns.
any direction.

320

Everything a blur,
As I continued.
Every answer
just out of reach.

Why,
Why,
Why?

I was leaning against some stone wall in a park.

Had to be back in the city
but wasn't sure where.

I stared at the light-polluted sky above me.
Weight of nothing dragging me down
Slowly under its weight
to the pavement.
As the skin of my back
Dug and
Broke,
To the stone against it.

And there he was.

H. NOAH

Giftwrapped and waiting as he jogged down the dirt path,
feet digging soundly into the earth.

The Tall Fuck.

He recognized me.
I could see it in the way he slowed,
Stopping just close enough.

He was smiling.

My hand already caressed the blade in my pocket

While he smiled.

I stood as shadows danced across his face

whispering to me.

He must have noticed something was wrong . . .
whether it was the blood,
the bruises,

Or the knife resting in his side.

I held on to the handle as gravity did the rest,
the blade slipping out as easily as it'd gone in.

And walked away.

This was enough.
It felt right,

I was finally doing something right.

NOVEMBER 3, 2017
MARIE PERAULT

I woke up with Maddie, got dressed, and pushed myself into something like a morning routine. Work wasn't waiting for me, but today was going to be better. It had to be.

As the coffee brewed, I pulled out the card Maddie had given me the night before and stared at its familiar surface. I must have handed out hundreds of these to clients—never thought I'd be calling them myself. I had to call, but how? I was a fraud for even holding it. I remembered each of their faces, their stories. They'd survived worse than me. Deserved help more than me.

Coward

No.

I promised Maddie. Last night would never happen again.

No harm in pouring a cup of coffee first. So, I pushed back from the small round laminate table and mismatched chair to grab my old touristy mug with lobsters and lighthouses. I poured just enough so I had room for some of the peppermint mocha creamer I loved. Each year it came out sooner and sooner, but I didn't mind. I sat back down, taking in the kitchen around me. Like the apartment, the appliances were dated and worn, but that's what we loved about this place. We even added our own retro finds when we could, resulting in a collection of every decade. Colorful yet somehow cohesive.

But the card kept calling.

I looked down as the cream danced softly, mixing in the mug as it rested against my lips.

Coward

I bit back the flash of anger within me.

I didn't want to do this.

I'd make Maddie understand

Why this wasn't the answer

Then last night started to play back

The anger fleeting.

As it gave way to shame.

Maddie breaking in front of me.

I'd done that.

I watched the swirls in front of me as a tear broke the surface

A burst of cream

Pausing the torrent

Breaking its cycle.

Finally taking a sip, I let the soothing warmth fill my mouth before swallowing. Whoever I became, it wouldn't be the person I was last night. I lowered the coffee and grabbed the card, bending its thick paper stock between my fingers, once, twice, before grabbing my phone and dialing.

"Trauma services, this is Melanie, how can I help you?" The voice on the other end seemed soft but distracted.

"Uh . . . hi, I was wondering if you had counseling services available?"

Her voice changed like she knew. "Yes, we have several options. Were you looking for more of a group setting or more one-on-one support?"

"I'm not sure, I've never done this before." Pure shame started to rise and heat my face.

Why am I doing this?

"No problem at all. I'd suggest one-on-one to start. A counselor can help you decide if that's the best or if a group session may be more helpful. Does that sound okay?" She paused.

I want to stop.

But I pushed. "Yes, I'm good with that."

Her voice seemed lighter now, less cautious. "All right, let me see which counselors are available."

It was easy to hear the quick tapping of keys across the line as I took another sip from the coffee in front of me. Wasn't what I expected—guess they don't ask too much over the phone.

"Looks like we have several options. Would you prefer a male or female counselor?"

"Um . . ." This took me by surprise. I hadn't really thought about that.

She seemed to sense the hesitation. "It's okay if you don't have a preference. For some, it can be hard to be in a room alone with someone who's the same gender as their abuser."

That word turned over hard and bitter in my mouth. This word didn't fit.

What did?

I'd been the stupid one.

Coward

"Everything okay?"

"Yeah, sorry." My voice came out a little choked. "I think I might prefer a woman. At least to start."

"No problem at all, any specific time or day work best?"

"I'm out on medical leave, so I'm pretty free. Soonest appointment would work best."

She paused again, silent except for the keys click-clacking back. "There's one appointment today at 11:00 a.m. if that works. It was a last-minute cancelation but if it's too soon I can keep looking."

I looked across to the microwave clock and saw that it was about fifteen minutes past eight now.

No turning back.

"That should be fine, I can make it."

"Wonderful! I know Doctor McKinnon will be happy to meet with you."

It took a few more minutes of me reciting my name and contact information before she dove into the "first-time spiel."

Then it was done.

I was surprised by how good it felt.

I hung up and looked for Maddie's name, and that's when I noticed the missed call. Clicking it, I saw that Art had tried to reach me . . . must have been during the fight. I hit "call back" and waited for him to pick up, but it went straight to voice mail. He must have forgotten to charge his phone before going to sleep.

"Hey, Art, it's me, Marie. Sorry I missed your call last night. Call back when you can." I started to hang up but had an overwhelming urge to say more. I'd probably hurt him just as much as Maddie.

"I miss you, Art. Hope you're doing well."

Hanging up, I backed out to Maddie's name in my texts. I sent her an update on the appointment and what I might do after.

Even if this turned out to be the wrong step, it was still a step in any direction.

ARTHUR CASLIN

The sun was rising too quickly.
Made it to the door before the light illuminated my victories

Splattered across clothing.

Flaking from skin.

I watched, dark-brown flakes, crackling with any movement.
As I sat behind my door, waiting.

For police,
For anyone,
To trace the blood here.

But no one came.
No one.

So I stripped and showered.
Was going to check the news on my phone
But I must have lost it somewhere.
This would have worried me if I had planned ahead.

I didn't need a plan.
Everything was clicking into place
Especially when paired with more whiskey
And pills.

No need to sleep.

I knew what was next.

So, I grabbed a microwave dinner
And drank.

Waiting,
For the clock to hit ten.

Visiting hours.

SAME DAY
DIANE LOUCKS

Lifting the blue blanket, I shook it against the morning rays, making my bed. They'd changed the meds again. It was easier now to wake up and make time for myself.

Before they came.

Before I had to start their day.

It was nice to actually sleep.

The voices were back but they'd quieted and thinned.

Mother's had stayed but there wasn't any light left in it.

It turned vile,

Rotten.

Easy to push aside.

But now there was too much quiet
Too much space
For Ann's face.

I didn't want to remember.

I thought she'd been lost.
That I was doing God's work
But it didn't feel like that anymore.
I saw my mother's hands tearing at sheets, whispering.

"Shhhhhhhhhhhhhhh."

Kneeling, I used the wooden frame to support my body to the
floor. The doctor said to put something soft down.
But the hard floor called to me. Kept me grounded within my
body.
Reminded me of my sins.
Of Ann.

She'd been a lovely child.

When she was small.
When God's light still shone in her eyes.

The shadow of wings fluttered across the bed, filtering light.

It was here, Ann's devil.

Mother's voice screamed

Look what you did
You called it
Run
Run
Run

I didn't want to look.
The light was gone.
I screamed,

And
Screamed,

And
Screamed,

Until a soft jab pricked my arm.

H. NOAH

The warmth came

Then quiet.
It was warm
So warm.

SAME DAY
RICHARD KOCH

I looked up as a couple passed my booth, holding hands and buzzing about something I couldn't make out. The diner was fairly empty as it hit mid-morning, but this was my favorite time to come. No matter where I sat, counter, stool, or booth, the quiet hum of regulars easing in and out was a nice lull to settle into.

This had always been my favorite place to go. From undergrad to law school, my life may have changed but this train-cart-turned-diner had been a constant for me. Same coffee, same people, same atmosphere. Not that I minded change; I loved watching the city breathe with more life than I'd witnessed in the last forty-odd years. Portland was a city finally finding itself and what it stood for.

"Would you like some coffee while you wait?"

I looked up to the waitress dressed in khaki pants and a diner T-shirt. An outfit meant for conformity, turned on its head. From long dangling earrings to the collection of loose metal bracelets on each arm, she brought music to every movement and step. She held the menus out, waiting for my reply.

I tilted my watch; I was early, but Carter wouldn't mind.

"Yes, that would be wonderful." I took the menus and set them aside until needed.

I usually didn't make any appointments early. I tended to show up just in time. But the office had been quiet this morning. The chaos after Marie and Arthur's attack had calmed once we'd figured out how to cover the extra cases. Today was unusually slow. No need to appear busy at an empty desk.

"Here you go. I brought the cream and sugar just in case but I'm more than happy to take it back if it isn't needed."

"You read my mind, thank you."

"No problem. I'll keep an eye out for when your friend gets here, but if you need anything just let me know."

"Sounds good."

Looking down, I tipped in the sugar, then cream, as the sound of her exit faded. The mug was aged enamel with the glazing slightly cracked but still sound. I took a spoon and mixed, adding the clink of metal to the light bustle around me.

It was hard to think of last night, to see the pain in Maddie's face and the fear in Marie's. At least it was fixed, as well as it could be. I thought when it came to Marie and Arthur that Marie was better off, but I'd been wrong, or maybe I just hadn't seen Arthur fully crack under the weight of everything yet. I let the spoon clink a few more times as it slowed. I'd call him after. Enough time had passed that he shouldn't take it as the check-in it was.

"Something on your mind, Richard? You're looking a little more serious than usual." Carter shared a half smile as he sat. I'd expected to see him dressed down in something more civilian, but he had his uniform on. Something big must have happened.

"Nothing at all. I thought this was your day off?" I took out the spoon, lazily pointing it in his general direction before setting it on the napkin next to the mug.

"Supposed to be, but last night was a shit show in the city." He leaned into the highbacked wooden booth as it creaked against his shifting weight. It was easy to see he wasn't exaggerating as he rubbed his eyes and face in an attempt to stay awake.

"Did you need to head out early?"

"No, should be able to stay for a bit. Only need to leave quickly if I'm called back in. Didn't have time to eat this morning and I'm starving."

"So, what happened?"

Carter leaned forward, smirking. No matter what happened or what he knew, he enjoyed building up to it.

"In due time. I need a coffee, food, and a little break in conversation from the mess I've been trudging through this morning."

Chuckling, I lifted the mug to my lips. "Uh-huh, sure you do."

He laughed as he turned to find our server. Almost on cue, the musical percussion that preceded her made its way closer.

"Can I get you anything, officer?"

"A coffee would be great, and—" Carter glanced quickly at the menu, even though we both knew what he was going to order. "Could I also get a corned beef hash omelet?"

"Of course. Anything for you, sir?" She turned to look at me, waiting.

I swallowed the coffee quickly as I shook my head. "No, I'm all set for now."

"No problem, I'll be back shortly."

After she made her retreat, Carter settled back in, turning to me. "So how's Dani doing?"

I took another drink of coffee before setting the mug down. "Dani's great. She still loves teaching art to the kids. Only complaint is the school budget, but that's not new."

"How long has she been at Portland High now?"

I took a minute to think as I shifted the worn mug between my hands. "God, she left Westbrook High back in 2001, I think? So about seventeen years now . . . if I have the date right."

Carter let a low whistle fly. "Seems like yesterday she even made the switch. Not like you and I; we started together and will probably leave together. Something I've been leaning toward sooner than later."

"You and me both."

"Oh really? I thought it would be hard to get you to leave?" Carter waved his hand in disbelief.

At least the jingle of incoming coffee was enough to change the topic before we got into it further.

"Here you are." The waitress placed a matching mug in front of Carter, taking a second to pour before raising the almost brimming carafe toward me. "Would you like yours topped off?"

"Yes, please."

Echoing thanks in turn before she walked away, we settled back into conversation.

"So how about you, Carter? How's Lynn?"

"Probably not doing as well as Dani." Amusement etched into his voice as he lifted his mug, ready to take a sip. "With Britney heading off to college next year, she's been anxious about how she'll fill time without her. I suggested volunteering, but she wants to pick up a hobby." Forgetting to drink, he set the mug back down before leaning into the booth again.

"A hobby? I didn't think she had any outside of keeping track of Britney."

Carter laughed. "That's the catch: she's not too sure either. Which will likely lead to a mess of things, truth be told."

I chuckled, glad that was still a bit in the future for my own family. "Well, at least she'll have the time to figure it out. Riley still has a year before he heads out with Miranda shortly behind him. Don't even want to imagine what it'll be like without them just yet."

"I still don't." Carter paused and grabbed his mug, gulping from it a little too eagerly, almost draining it before setting it back down. The melancholy of the moment seemed to snap him back into the morning's events as he drifted somewhere in thought.

"Man, must have been a bad night."

"That's one word for it."

A college-aged kid suddenly appeared next to us, same uniform—khaki pants and shirt—small and mousy, the exact opposite of our waitress. Notably quieter as well.

"Hash omelet?"

Carter lifted his hand. "Right here."

The kid put down the food and disappeared off to the side. Carter wasted no time as he inhaled the food in front of him. Only after he'd eaten about half did he take a break to drain the rest of his coffee and remember the topic at hand.

"I think I made it to the first scene about three or four this morning. Hard to remember exactly."

"First scene?"

This is bad.

"Yup and it gets better. Remember that guy who testified at his wife's trial? She'd killed their kid 'cause God told her to or some shit?"

"Of course, that was the biggest case we had this year."

"Well, some of my boys got called to the father's house for a noise complaint. Only, what they found wasn't a dying animal. We think it's him, but there's nothing identifiable left."

I took a sharp inhale, unable to place the feeling filling my chest. Walter had been a kind man caught between his own failings and what had happened. It was easy to see each time he'd made his way into the office, bent and shuffling more from guilt than age. "That's horrible. The only person in his life I'd heard was capable was his wife, but she should still be in the hospital. She didn't get out, did she?"

"No, no, she's still there. That was the first thing we checked. Doesn't end there, though. I went to make sure the scene was secure and while I was finishing up, another call came in."

"Was it connected to Walter?"

"Not that we can tell so far. Some kid got attacked in East End Park, still alive but just barely. You might need to prepare Dani if she hasn't already heard. It was a senior from Portland High—looks like they might have been fitting in a run before school. His parents should have been informed and it's only a matter of time before the school gets notified if it hasn't happened already."

I pulled out my phone to see if I had any missed messages. "Nothing from Dani yet, but I'll check in with her on her break. Probably too early to tell, but do they have an idea what happened?"

"No clue. Both scenes are still being processed and homicide is usually tight lipped until an arrest needs to be made." Carter finished off the rest of his breakfast as I grabbed my mug, letting myself settle into the wood behind me as I took a moment to enjoy the warmth of the mug in my hand.

"I'm surprised. Usually the office is buzzing when something like this happens, but it was the opposite when I got there this morning. Guess I may have left too early."

Carter let his fork drop after taking in the last bite. He reached for his mug, lifting it halfway before realizing it was empty. "I'd doubt anyone knows outside of people who've seen the police tape. The press hasn't even gotten wind of it yet, though I doubt it'll stay that way for long."

"I do too, probably already running with something."

Carter's phone went off.

"Hello? Yup, no problem, I'll be right in." Shoving his phone back into the pocket he had just retrieved it from, he looked across the table to me. "Looks like I'm going to have to take a raincheck on the rest of this conversation."

"It's all right. Glad you were able to step away at all."

Carter pulled out his wallet, counting a few bills and placing them under his mug. "I'll shoot you a message once I get some time. Send Dani my best. Hope she didn't know the kid too well."

"Sounds good, and I hope so too. Tell Lynn hello for me when you see her."

"Will do, talk to you soon." And just like that, he was gone.

I raised my mug, sipping as I glanced at the overcast sky outside the window next to me. The clouds hung thick and full, turning a color that threatened snow.

"Are you ready for the check?"

I looked away from the window, surprised the waitress had been able to get so close unnoticed. "My friend's all set on his end, but I could use another refill and something sweet. Any muffins with chocolate today?"

"We've got a double chocolate muffin, would that be okay?"

"It's perfect, thank you."

Gathering up the evidence of Carter's presence, she took a moment to make sure she'd grabbed it all before disappearing back into the kitchen. I looked back out the window, trying to drain the last of the coffee as I watched people walking past. I didn't want to think of the lives that had been impacted today, especially if one of those lives was Dani's. She loved those kids like her own. Losing that one kid last year to suicide almost wrecked her. If she knew whoever this kid was . . .

God . . . he better make it if she does.

I placed my empty mug toward the edge of the table, ready for the refill as I pulled out my phone. A part of me wanted to call Arthur first, but this was more important. Besides, one call and another coffee between now and then wouldn't make much of a difference.

DIANE LOUCKS

They kept putting me in this cell.
Torn padded walls.
With the light off.
Steel door.

There was a window where light shined through.
But I didn't want to look.
To see it.

They'd taken everything again.

I tried trading hymns,
Prayers,
to the silence within me.
but Mother was gone

H. NOAH

I didn't mean to ignore her.

They said I was a danger to myself.
To others.
But I had nothing
The meds had taken it all.

I didn't want to be alone.
So I beat the walls
And cursed their names
Only to fall.
To plead,
to anyone.

I didn't want to feel anymore.
Didn't want to think of Ann.

So I thought of Walter.
Remembered the summer days after we had first met.
I ran when I was sixteen, to the shelter where he had run too.
Where we fell in love.

Will that be my heaven?

346

We used to lie in the fields outside of church

The scent of wildflowers,

Of heat,

Of cool breezes.

We used to lie there and dream of all the places we would go.

In those moments . . . there had been hope.

Happiness.

Even without the grace.

I wasn't alone when I was with him.

But he'd left me.

Everyone had.

ARTHUR CASLIN

I t was almost too easy to get in.

Just opened the door and walked to the waiting room.

Shit,

Probably even looked like I belonged.

Suit,

Tie,

Respectable

safe.

The florescent room was overwhelming both in order and color. The white blinded, from walls to floors and everywhere in between. There was something shining beneath the paint. I tried to shield myself as I slumped into one of the many chairs that lined the room, hands covering my face. But I couldn't escape it.

The Bitch had to come through here,

Eventually.

There were already nurses,
patients,
doctors,
visitors,
aimlessly wandering the space
Between me and her,
Unaware.

The minutes merged into hours
But it didn't matter.
This was the day the Bitch learned what suffering was.
The day she met the real me
and her maker

I shifted to my other side, looking at the magazines laid out next
to me, untouched.

I let my eyes wander across the shiny smiling faces
Both drawn in and repulsed.
False caricatures.

The room was empty now.
The ward's door swinging open.
The stench of bleached corridors behind me was over-
whelming
Unable to clean or fully mask
The disease within.

I peeked through my fingers. An older woman was being led
through the entrance. It was hard to see her from the way she
hunched and dragged her feet behind her. The layers of winter
clothes adding to the distortion, more hermit than human with
only a pale braid of rotted corn silk peeking out.

She must be getting admitted.

The nurse had her sit in the row across from mine.
Her scrubs childlike
filled with cartoon animals
All looking
All laughing.

The nurse's voice wasn't much better
Singing a mockery of kindness.

"Mel, hon, your daughter will be here in a minute. Do you promise to stay here until she comes?"

The woman sat peering out from her layers
at nothing.
swaying slightly,

back and forth,
back and forth.

My fists started to clench on their own.

The nurse crouched in front of her then,
forcing connection.

"Mel? Do you promise?"

The nurse waited again.

The swaying stalled long enough for the woman to nod slightly before she sank back into whatever world held her.

"That's my girl!" the nurse mused with a smile even bigger than the cartoons that clung to her.

She rose. "I need to fill out some paperwork at the front, so
if you need me before your daughter comes I'll be right there."

The nurse pointed her gaze and finger at reception, but I turned
back to the magazines
I massaged my hands
Sore and bruised
Avoiding the bite.
Now red,
Angry,
And oozing.

The woman across from me still had a daughter.
I wasn't looking for her.

I traced the edges of the pictures with a mottled hand,
the remnants of blood around the bite
were dried filth
clinging to skin.
That's why I fit in here,
Camouflaged in my surroundings.

It was easy to see now
The white of the walls cracking and flaking to gray
The chairs worn to yellow pus

Lights dulled,
reflecting the rot within

The woman's swaying picked up speed,
The motion catching at the corner of my eye.

Her movements now frantic.
Hit
Like a pebble on water,
Waves
crashing repeatedly
Against me.

What brought her here?

The door opened again.
An airy figure wrapped in a heavy coat
With a bright-blue dress
Flowing beneath her
Came toward us.

This must be the daughter.

She was young,
about twenty,

with long golden hair that haloed
even tied back with a thin white ribbon.

At least she'd escaped her mother's cancer.

"Hey, Mom, how are you?"

Her voice eased softly into the air between them as she sat down
next to the woman.
Reaching toward her with a smile,
pausing at the last moment
Before bringing her hands back
Restrained to her lap.

At least the swaying slowed.

"Sorry for being late, I ran into Johnny on my way here."
She paused as she looked at the woman listening for a response
But all she did was sway

back and forth
back and forth.

"He's doing good, real good. Asked about you."

I turned to look directly at the woman
 she was holding something in the folds
clutching
A shine of metal
straight with right angles.

A fucking cross

I should have known.

She'd been sitting across from me
taunting.
Just like the Bitch.

There only to
Remind me
that my job was undone.

"I told him of your progress. How you're walking and eating
on your own now."

I didn't want to hear the girl's misguided pride
Not for that creature

H. NOAH

"He was so happy!"
She smiled till sadness took hold,

"Well, the last time he saw you was after the accident, after
Dad . . ."

The sorrow called to me
Eased under skin
but she didn't reach for me
she placed her hand
on that woman's chair.

That simple need
agitated the woman
No longer swaying
but rocking.

Back and forth,
back and forth.

It wasn't the Bitch
But her presence dug raw.
Hot irons
pushing me to my limit.

I clenched my teeth.
grinding tiny pieces of bone
with rage.

The knife
resting ready
In my pocket.

I'm not here for her.

"You'll be home soon, Mom."
lifting her hand
to caress the creature's arm.

The Bitch recoiled, lashed out
decorating the dear girl's face in red
A mark
I knew too well.

The girl lifted her hands to her face
With tears that begged to spill,

"I'm sorry, I forgot."

H. NOAH

The rage was boiling,
burning.

The thing looking at me now.
Laughing,
proud of her jest.

It was the Bitch herself
sitting only feet away.
Always taunting.

I didn't fight against the numbing haze
As it took me;
I was at home.
In nothing.

Standing in front of the Bitch.
Everything else faded
but the knife
as it plunged
into her twisting form.

Again
and again

and again

and again.

Bucking and catching

On bone

And cloth.

Something

clung to my back,

grabbed for the knife.

Easy enough to throw off,

To forget.

There was a cry.

A chorus of praise

ringing out.

I brought my hand back

continued,

but the knife wasn't there.

No matter.

H. NOAH

It was a sign;
even her God needed me
to finish it right.

I pulled the thing to the floor
caressingly,
gently,
wrapping hands around her neck
a most blessed ornament;
grasping
until her eyes reflected her soul.

Cold.

Empty.

The flash of blue caught my eye.
looking up
I could see the dear girl.

But why is she in the corner?

Holding her arm up as she pressed against the wall,
Blood dripping

no longer giving voice to the scream her lips had formed.
The knife glinting
From where it had plunged

That's where it'd gone.

The girl watched now
Doe eyes shattered
staring into me,
like Ann's.

What had I done?

I looked to the face beneath me
Doll's eyes
Bleeding red
reflecting my face.

NOVEMBER 15, 2018
MARIE PERAULT

The bouquet of sunflowers was far too heavy. I shifted them back and forth, up and down, from one hand to the other for the entire ride. Don't know why I even got them—I knew he hated them. Just seemed like something I was supposed to do. I let them hang awkward and limp in my right hand as I walked, ready to drop or give. Maddie wanted to help, but she knew this was something I had to do on my own. *Needed* to do on my own. Even a year later, it was hard for me to understand.

Staring at the little mass-produced map they'd given me at the office, I tried to retrace my steps to where I was, where he would be just up ahead, circled in blue. Even with the map, I was lost within the sea of granite rising endlessly around me. Only up close did the gray waves break into something familiar. Each stone unique in name, date, a mixture of phrases and psalms. Labeled how they'd left, son, wife, grandparent. I already knew his wouldn't. Art was lost in a maze of families, lovers, and semi-someones, but it was hard even now to think of him as what he'd been: a friend.

A grouping of stones seemed to read similar to the map just a short distance ahead. If I was right, he wasn't too far now. I took a moment to shove the map back into my coat before switching the flowers to my other hand and moving forward. I kept thinking of what he'd say. Probably some joke, a bad one since his exit had lacked the usual punchline.

If Art was still here, you wouldn't be doing this.

This year snow came early, though it hadn't been much. I still loved the satisfying crunch it gave underneath my boots. It was nice to focus on the little things, how each exhale would cloud and brush my face as I walked through it, the thick air disappearing just as it iced over my eyelashes.

If he was alive, I wouldn't have visited, not after what he did.

No one could understand why he'd done it. Other than Walter, he didn't have a connection with any of the others. Police didn't care. The person who'd done it was dead, case closed. I think it had to do with Ann. Not sure why he went for the kid, but he'd gone to the same hospital her mother had first been held in before she'd been transferred.

Staff had said in the witness statements that something had been off with him but that they thought he was waiting for someone. That he was harmless, until he wasn't. Worst part was, no one could get him off her. He just sat and stared into her eyes.

They said he only moved when the police arrived,

And only then it was for the officer's gun.

But that wasn't my Art,

Not the one I'd known.

I looked around as the shapes and small hills finally gave me some bearings. I'd been here for his funeral, if you could call it that. The few of us who showed felt the same mixture of shame, anger, and loss. I didn't want to give eulogies. I wanted to scream. Maybe it would have been more cathartic if we had.

I stopped a few paces away, his name etched in plain stone. There were no flowers, no rocks or coins of remembrance above. No one mourned for him but me. I closed the distance between us as I kneeled to set the flowers over his head, but I couldn't let go.

"Hey."

I waited, silence surrounding me.

"It's been a while. I'm sure you'd have something to say about that, or not . . . maybe you'd understand."

The weight of the sunflowers dipped to the ground beneath me, taking some of the burden.

"I tried to come sooner, but this was the first day I didn't feel like telling you to fuck off."

I let the laughter hang from the corners of my lips, soft and sad.

"Guess I still can't."

He would have said something funnier. He always did.

"I fucking miss you."

The tears were building thick and hot. "And I'm still so mad at you. Both for what you did and for leaving me . . . Art, you were the only one who understood what we'd gone through, and you took that from me."

The tears that had been falling steady pattered against the plastic of the bouquet. I placed them down gently before sitting to the side of them, leaning against the stone. The snow melted into my jeans, but I didn't care.

"That day didn't make me stronger. I think that's a lie we tell ourselves. That we don't lose anything when shit like this happens. But we do . . . I did. I think that's why I got so angry, even started seeing someone for it. Her name's Rachel. She believed me when I said I didn't feel stronger for it, didn't try to change my mind. Only said, 'Nothing's taken without something else being left in its place.' I just have to figure out what it is."

I started to trace the letters of his name, even as my gloves made it harder. I outlined a few more lines before letting a sigh escape.

"I don't think I'll ever be able to forgive you for what you did. I'm not even close to it. But we're gonna talk . . . or better put, you're going to listen. If you're here somehow, it'll annoy the shit out of you and even if you're not, it'll still be good for me."

A laugh left easily, lighter than the last.

"Who knew this was all it took for you to finally listen."

I saw Maddie's outline in the distance. I must have taken longer to find him than I realized. "Well, looks like our time's up for now."

I leaned into the stone, letting its ridge cut into my shoulder as I bent my head into what I pretended was the crook of Art's neck for a hug that wouldn't come.

If he were here, he'd have it ready.

I took a slow and steady breath, making sure to wipe the tears away as I let one last thing slip. "You fucking dumbass."

I turned, stood, and brushed off as much snow as I could before Maddie got to me.

"Ready?" she asked. The cold painting a red blush across her cheeks. The summer tan she'd built had faded just enough so it was easier to see.

"I am. Feel silly about sitting on the ground, though."

Her laugh sounded more like bells than a jab. "I was wondering about that."

I smiled, reaching out to grab her hand, doing my best to hold on through both our gloves. "Well, if you're going to call someone a fucking dumbass, it's good to do it to their face."

"I guess so." She squeezed my hand, a sadness creeping into her voice. "You ready to go? I can make another lap around if you want more time."

I pulled her in a little closer, breathing in the scent of summer, a hint of bluebells this time.

Then it clicked.

I placed my hands on her face, tickling her cheeks and lips with my thumbs until the sadness receded and I kissed her.

Without her, I would have ended up here too. And for that, for everything she gave me . . .

I was ready.

SAME DAY
MADDIE MORI

I watched her for a while, red coat and yellow flowers against pure white. It was hard not to see her, not to follow, but she needed this more than I needed to experience it with her. I turned away so I wouldn't watch her disappear completely as I decided to make my way toward the older part of the cemetery. I hadn't really enjoyed walks like this until I got to the East Coast. Someone had suggested walking through the old graves of Boston. I'd dragged my feet, thinking of the gawdy polished stones of the south, but that changed quickly. The cemeteries here were windows to the places and people I'd only read about in history books.

I was starting to hit the older stones now, something that would have been easy to see even without looking at the dates as each marker grew thinner and more ornate with ferns, cherubs, and skulls. I'd been so taken with the stark depictions of death that I found a book on the iconography. Morbid but fascinating to see how comfortable they'd been with death, so much so that each image had its own time period when it had been in vogue.

I wonder what changed.

Perhaps when kids stopped dying and people started to live longer, ignoring death became a luxury. For me it had felt like a death when I'd left the south. Never realized how much of myself I'd cut to fit into each expectation. Didn't expect to do it again with Marie. But this felt different, like a start. Like I was finally finding myself. It had taken a while, but I had a lead on the agency that might have done my adoption. It had been almost impossible without access to the paperwork that had burned, but I'd done it.

As I walked to the next row of stones, one in particular caught my eye. This one had an urn surrounded by weeping willow leaves above a delicate script. Most of the stone had worn smooth as it fell sharply into the earth, tilted and threatening to fall to the left. But I could still make out the name *Constance*, a mother who'd died in 1830. I stopped for a moment before moving on.

I'm glad Marie came.

Since Art had passed, she'd been avoiding everything about him. In truth, so had I. He'd been important to us both. For Marie it'd been his friendship, but I owed him much more for saving her life. Though a part of me was glad he was gone and that he'd left before taking Marie with him.

Marie had been going to therapy for a year now. I'd even started to go to that group Richard had mentioned, then started one-on-one sessions of my own. I hadn't realized until I went how much I was still hurting from what had happened when I was younger. How I'd been searching for comfort, for stability, in everyone but myself.

Marie had been having so many good days. It felt like she was finding peace and if this was a part of that, I'd support her. I wished I could ease the guilt Marie had for missing him. But love isn't conditional; you can't revoke it even when you want to.

My Marie.

I walked along the rest of the stones, slowly tracing a way around the outside of the cemetery. I turned to find Marie every so often, but at this distance even her colors were muted and hidden. I wasn't too worried about losing her. I'd helped find his grave the day he was buried. Not many had been there besides us other than Richard and Art's ex.

Kate.

That day had been hard, mostly because a part of me had been glad. He'd changed so much in the end, even if Marie hadn't seen it. I'd been worried. I didn't like to think about the *what-ifs* like Marie did.

I turned my head to the gray sky above and wished for more snow. Marie may have loved summer, but winter was the season that held me. Closing my eyes and wishing just enough, I took a few breaths of the cold metallic air around me before pulling out my phone. Half an hour had passed.

Is it enough, or too much?

I hoped she wasn't waiting for me. Turning, I traced my way back through the graves, both old and new, until I made it to the crossroads we had left together, following her shallow footsteps through the snow.

It took a minute to find her, resting next to the gravestone, legs kicked out, her body leaning against his stone.

Am I too early?

I was about to turn back when she stood up, brushing off the snow as she came toward me, grabbing my hand and pulling me into an embrace as she pushed my worries aside, trading them for a laugh instead.

My Marie.

This was how we held each other on the nights she woke up screaming, after I found her collapsed on the floor. When we laughed and loved.

I was happy for this moment; she was here in my arms. She was okay.

When she pulled me into a kiss, my world was the extent of hers: warm breath, vanilla, and laughter. This is where I wanted to stay, with the crisp air and candy-coated lip balm.

She was my winter. The rush of chilled snowflakes melting on my tongue, the breathless adrenaline behind every sled ride. Most of all, she was the warmth of warm cider, spreading across frozen fingertips and lips.

What it meant to be home.

Marie pulled away, smiling, but I wanted more. I tugged her back for one more kiss, not as deep or long but just as satisfying.

She pushed back again more playfully this time, holding my chin between forefinger and thumb as she ran the latter over my lips, smiling again as if biting back a secret.

I rested my hand on her arm, drawing it down a little. "What are you up to?"

"Marry me."

It took a moment for what she'd said to sink in. "What?" I pulled back a little, narrowing my eyes and waiting for the punchline.

"This isn't the most romantic place, or time, or even the best words. But being here made me realize something."

A small snowflake fell to rest on her cheek, a promise fulfilled. I raised my other hand to wipe it away as I asked, "What's that?"

She shifted a little before responding, holding me tighter with every word. "When I look ahead, I see you in every moment I have left. Good or bad, you're the only part of my future that makes sense."

I'd started to cry without meaning to as the joy became overwhelming. She used her glove to wipe the tears away, a hint of worry on her face.

"I love you, Maddie."

"I love you too."

The worry eased into something softer as she gave me a squeeze. "So what do you say?"

"I thought you'd never ask." I pulled her in as the snow fell soft and heavy.

SAME DAY
RICHARD KOCH

It was 4:30 on a Friday. During slower times like this I'd usually be home, but with Marie coming back on Monday I wanted to make sure everything was ready. I'd probably be leaving late but today had been peaceful, almost light. I hadn't had one of these days in a while. The busy work that usually got pushed aside became an escape behind closed doors. Especially when the office had started emptying to the snowstorm outside. My muted world became even more insulated as the inches of snow fell.

I could leave now. I'd made it through the worst of the work, but this was the first real snow of the year. The idea of entering the small twisting streets at rush hour was not in the least appealing. Besides, if I focused now I could finish the rest—something that appealed more than watching people relearn how to drive in the snow.

Grabbing my phone from its charger, I shot Dani a quick message.

Richard: Going to stay a bit later to avoid crowded roads. How about I pick up dinner?

Dani: That would be a lifesaver, sounds like the kids decided on pizza.

Richard: Why am I not surprised. Pick up the usual?

Dani: Yes, though cheesy bread sounds good too.

Richard: I can do that. I'll text you when I'm about to leave.

Dani: Don't stay too late, love you.

Richard: I promise, love you too.

I pulled up the site to order, placing an order for pickup around six before putting down my phone. I looked at the photos lining my desk. My favorite was an old picture of Dani in the studio, before the kids. She was at a potter's wheel, hunched and practicing her throws. I'd gotten a break between classes and couldn't resist snapping a picture while she'd been working. Even then we both understood the path I'd taken wouldn't be an easy one, but it had been fun to find the things that helped us both through it together.

We'd been together almost thirty-four years now, once February came around. Thirty-four years I wouldn't have wanted to spend with anyone else. I moved to another photo, the one of us at our first place. I could still smell the mildew and cheap scented candles we used to light when we'd hole up in our one-bedroom apartment, the books and papers of whatever our current studies were nestled in some kind of order between us. We built the world we wanted from that starting place: the jobs we'd get, the home we'd buy, the kids we'd have. They were my lifeline through the world around me, especially after that day.

It had been a year, but I remembered everything so clearly.

I'd been worried about Dani and the death of that student; I didn't know I'd be the one leaving it shaken.

He was your responsibility. You should have known. Why didn't you catch it?

All I could think was, *If only I'd called, if only I'd tried more.* Even though it was ridiculous to feel like I needed to hold that much of the responsibility. After that day, I realized I wasn't the only one asking those questions about myself. They never said it exactly—it was hidden in looks and softened questions, but a part of me still broke. Even with all I'd done and accomplished, it was still easier for them to find fault in my character. And worse, I'd started to think that was about myself too.

I knew being Black and working in the criminal justice system would be hard, but I thought I'd proven myself, made it past that point, only to realize I hadn't left it, that I'd only made myself smaller over the years by bending to others' expectations. I'd done everything possible, but I couldn't keep myself from looking at his case files. The more I looked, the more I saw that no one had anticipated this. Arthur had made his own choices in the end.

As I looked at the pile of paperwork in front of me, it was hard not to feel the absolute exhaustion of it all. Retirement was something I couldn't get out of my head. Maybe it was time. Riley was already in college but I could spend more time with Miranda, take time to visit Riley. Once Miranda left, there'd be nothing tying us here other than Dani's work. She might be ready too.

We could look for that house in the woods we'd always talked about. She could finally have her studio and I could find peace between the pages of the books I never had time to read. I still believed in this city and the world around it, but it was time to carve out something that was ours. There'd been no sense in Arthur's death, no letter or manifesto, just notes on case files that painted a picture of someone I'd never known.

I'd done my best to heal the office after. Brought in counselors, said yes to Marie's sabbatical, did everything possible to prevent it from happening again. Yet I was still falling short of everyone else's expectations. I didn't want that anymore. I'd done good, even if others refused to remember it.

Glancing back toward the paperwork, I grabbed the next packet in the stack and started. I'd bring it up tonight, ask Dani what she thought. All I knew was I wanted to start making choices for myself, decisions that kept my happiness and the happiness of those I loved at the forefront. I was done hiding parts of myself for others' comfort. It only hurt me and my family in the end.

I turned a page, listening to the music in this moment as the snow tapped against the glass, slow, steady, and new.

SAME DAY
DIANE LOUCKS

The little blue devil had found me.
  Since they'd let me leave the padded room
it had come back each morning to mock me.
To remind me of my sin.

I tried to pray
but it kept me from it.

They said it was too cold,
That birds had flown south.
But devils didn't need warmth.

I watched it each day until they called for meds.
I wanted to scream again
But that would lead me back to the room.

H. NOAH

I was tired of the shots
Of meds changing.

So, I watched.

What does it want?

It always came to the window.

Hopped,
Then pecked.
Hopped,
Then pecked.

Until it gave up and groomed itself.

I tried to listen,
To hear what it said,
But it stayed silent.

Like Mother.

If this was its plan, it needed a new one.
I'd gotten use to its movements and routines,

It seemed predictable,
Almost harmless now.

Almost.

I kept watching.

The doctor had asked about the light in Ann's eyes.
How it had faded over the years.
How I'd been the one to see it.

He said it must have been lonely for her,
Why she had started to talk to the "bird."
Tried to compare what she felt to me missing my grace.

I told him no
she had me.
She had God.
She didn't need the devil.

He asked if Ann had gotten all of me.
All my kindness.
My love.

His words had hit hard.

Tried to tell him how being soft had welcomed the sin within her.

Made it feel welcome.

But a part of me had twisted at what I'd said

Continued to fester within me

I laid outstretched over my freshly made bed.

What if I was wrong?

I'd been thinking of Ann more, of when I saw her light and when I'd noticed it fade.

It was there that day when the devil had come.

No, it was there because you weren't.

Tap

Tap

Tap

The bird was back. Hopping up and down on the windowsill.

Maybe the doctor is right.

I watched as it fluffed itself into twice its size, as scripture ran through my head and out of my lips. "So God created the great creatures . . . and every winged bird according to its kind. And God saw that it was good."

Does that mean this bird is good?
That my dear Ann was good?

The devil had chosen a snake, after all. And his servants usually chose black cats, rats, and toads.
If you thought about it, a bird touched the heavens. So how could something evil do the same?

I watched with renewed interest as it hopped and danced.
A light within it started to glow as it paused and tapped against the glass. It was familiar light,

Ann's light.

Overwhelmed, I stood clutching my chest
as it cocked its head in return and nestled into the windowsill.

Could it be?
A messenger,
My messenger.

H. NOAH

My baby girl.

I must have saved her
I wouldn't have harmed her
Not my baby

I cried out this time as a feeling overtook me.

Regret.

Love.

I reached out to her,

tears streaming,

"Ann? Please forgive me."

ACKNOWLEDGMENTS

I never thought I'd get to this point. When I put my writing on the backburner, I thought it wouldn't get any further than a hobby I picked up from time to time for fun.

I'd like to thank my advanced fiction class and professor back in 2011 who made the impression that this story mattered even when it was just about Arthur.

Thank you to my family, friends, and beta readers who all encouraged me to take it further than I could ever manage. Especially my brother Alec, who helped give incredible direction on the story's overall development, even though it wasn't his kind of fiction.

A huge thank you to my sensitivity readers and editors. Specifically to Iori Kusano, who not only gave incredible insight into Maddie but the overall story itself. And especially Brenna Bailey-Davies, who helped not only clean up my writing and make it shine but also helped me see the value within my own work.

My last thank you is for everyone I've connected with and met through my social platforms. Y'all got more excited for my work than I thought possible, and your kindness and encouragement helped me get through every moment when I thought of putting the story down again.

WORKS CITED

(Listed in order of appearance)

THE POEMS OF EMILY DICKINSON, edited by Thomas H. Johnson, Cambridge, Mass.: The Belknap Press of Harvard University Press, Copyright © 1951, 1955, 1979, 1983 by the President and Fellows of Harvard College.

I will sprinkle clean water on you, and you shall be clean from all your uncleanness, and from your idols I will cleanse you.
BibleRef.com. (n.d.). Retrieved October 16, 2021, from https://www.bibleref.com/Ezekiel/36/Ezekiel-36-25.html.

In Him we have redemption through His blood, the forgiveness of our trespasses.
BibleRef.com. (n.d.). Retrieved October 16, 2021, from https://www.bibleref.com/Ephesians/1/Ephesians-1-7.html.

So God created the great creatures of the sea and every living thing with which the water teems and that moves about in it, according to their kinds, and every winged bird according to its kind. And God saw that it was good.
BibleRef.com. (n.d.). Retrieved October 16, 2021, from https://www.bibleref.com/Genesis/1/Genesis-1-21.html.

ABOUT THE AUTHOR

They've been a massage therapist, social worker, poet, teacher, and more. Picking up a B.A. in Criminology and an M.S. in I-O Psychology. They've also lived in Alaska, Maine and many places in-between. They are currently still trying to find a forever place as they travel the US.

Website: www.thehnoah.com
Links to Socials: beacons.ai/thehnoah

CPSIA information can be obtained
at www.ICGtesting.com
Printed in the USA
FSHW011531010222
88046FS